Falconer's Quest

HEIRS OF ACADIA

-FIVE-

Falconer's Quest

T. DAVIS BUNN
ISABELLA BUNN

BETHANYHOUSE
Minneapolis, Minnesota

Falconer's Quest
Copyright © 2007
T. Davis Bunn and Isabella Bunn

Cover design by UDG DesignWorks
Cover photographer: Steve Gardner, Pixel Works Studio, Inc.

Scripture quotations are from the King James Version of the Bible.

Published by Bethany House Publishers
11400 Hampshire Avenue South
Bloomington, Minnesota 55438

Bethany House Publishers is a division of
Baker Publishing Group, Grand Rapids, Michigan.

Printed in the United States of America

Paperback: ISBN-13: 978-0-7642-0358-9 ISBN-10: 0-7642-0358-4
Hardcover: ISBN-13: 978-0-7642-0359-6 ISBN-10: 0-7642-0359-2
Large Print: ISBN-13: 978-0-7642-0360-2 ISBN-10: 0-7642-0360-6

Library of Congress Cataloging-in-Publication Data

Bunn, T. Davis, 1952-
  Falconer's quest / T. Davis Bunn, Isabella Bunn.
      p. cm. — (Heirs of Acadia ; 5)
   ISBN 978-0-7642-0359-6 (hardcover : alk. paper) —ISBN 978-0-7642-0358-9
(pbk.) —ISBN 978-0-7642-0360-2 (large-print pbk.)
      1. Acadians—Fiction. 2. North Carolina—Fiction. I. Bunn, Isabella. II. Title.
   PS3552.U4718F35   2007
   813'.54—dc22   2006038409

T. DAVIS BUNN is an award-winning author whose growing list of novels demonstrates the scope and diversity of his writing talent.

ISABELLA BUNN has been a vital part of his writing success; her research and attention to detail have left their imprint on nearly every story. Their life abroad has provided much inspiration for plots and settings. They live near Oxford, England.

By T. Davis Bunn

The Gift
The Book of Hours
One Shenandoah Winter
The Quilt
Tidings of Comfort & Joy

The Great Divide
The Presence
Winner Take All
Elixir
The Lazarus Trap
Heartland

SONG OF ACADIA*

The Meeting Place   The Birthright
The Sacred Shore   The Distant Beacon
The Beloved Land

HEIRS OF ACADIA†

The Solitary Envoy
The Innocent Libertine
The Noble Fugitive
The Night Angel
Falconer's Quest

*with Janette Oke   †with Isabella Bunn

Chapter 1

February 1836

John Falconer made it through the days in very small steps.

Ada's illness had come with the first winter storm, which gripped the Carolinas for eleven days with fierce winds and hard-slung ice. Falconer had sat at her bedside, hands knotted on the coverlet, and stared at the beloved face. Ada looked as white as the snow now gathering on the window ledge. His lips felt stiff as he whispered first her name, then prayers he scarcely heard himself utter. He bowed low over his clenched fists, finally breaking the room's tense silence with a groan.

In just a year and a half, Falconer's heart had been so altered he could scarcely recall a time before Ada's love filled his days and warmed his nights. Eighteen months earlier, he and Ada had stood before the bishop in their Moravian church and said their vows. Young Matt had stood proudly at Falconer's side, delighted in his new father and overjoyed by his widowed mother's newfound happiness. Falconer touched Ada's face, with its sheen of perspiration, and wished his physical strength truly counted for something. If only he could wrest back the days now gone,

9

peel back time, and have her smile at him once more.

And then Ada had passed with the storm. Everything had been so impossibly swift. The illness, the decline, the passage, all in less than two weeks. No one knew precisely the cause. She had slipped away from them, gentled into a slumber that did not end. The elders gathered, called it a tragic wonder, and murmured to each other how she had been so softly called home. Why was it that one so crushed, but still so strengthened, by the ferocious winds of life was now gone from them?

Telling young Matt was the most wrenching task Falconer had ever set for himself. The two clung to each other, rocking slowly back and forth. Though Matt's grief drenched Falconer's shirt, Falconer found himself unable to weep. Perhaps it was the exhaustion, for he had scarcely eaten or slept since Ada's illness had begun. He had known men who were hard stricken in the heat of battle and felt nothing until the dire threat was gone. But for him, even after it was over, the only thing that touched him at all was his son, not of his flesh but certainly of his heart. Falconer spent uncounted hours holding Matt and letting the boy weep for the both of them.

They buried Ada on a wet Tuesday morn, a fiercely cold day in February so dark the chapel bell's tolled regrets were echoed by the sky and the wind. The community of Moravians, who had known Ada all her life, shared the ceremony and the profound sorrow with stoic but no less genuine understanding, watching Falconer and Matt with eyes full of sympathy and questions. What would happen to them now?

The day after the funeral, Falconer shuttered the inn he and Ada had run and accepted the invitation of her uncle and his family. Together with Paul and Sarah Brune and their children, the two mourners might slowly find comfort in the sharing of an impossible burden.

Impossible that a woman so full of life, love, and goodness could be stricken and lost so swiftly. Impossible that Falconer could know the blessing of home and family for scarcely a year and a half. Impossible that he was expected to nurture a boy who had lost both blood parents and now had only a wounded sailor for a guardian.

The spring was slow in coming. He and Matt worked the Brune farm and prepared the land and tended the animals. Falconer, dressed in the simple homespun of the Moravian community, did the work of three men. He allowed his beard to grow in dark and rich. The good North Carolina earth worked into his hands, and the physical labor toughened him in ways the sea never had. The work and the good people proved a strong and healing balm. But what saved Falconer, what kept him rooted to the world and the day at hand, was his son.

The dogwoods finally bloomed a month and more late. The pear and apple orchards added their own white fragrance to the hills and the softening breeze. And suddenly the winter was gone. The entire world leapt into rebirth. The farming valleys were alive with the bleating of newborn lambs and the mothers' chucklings. New shoots rose from what had been empty furrows. The sun rose higher and stronger, and the men shucked their coats and worked in shirtsleeves. The entire community reveled in the hope of spring.

Evenings, when the sun dipped and the Brune family gathered upon the porch to watch the westering sun and the daily promise of glory to come, Matt nestled next to Falconer on the porch swing. It was an uncommonly wet summer, and the day's rain clouds dispersed in bands of copper and gold spread across the Salem valleys. Eventually Matt would sing, his voice at first small and fragile, but as

11

the summer progressed, stronger, more confident.

Sometimes Sarah Brune joined in, her alto adding a lovely harmony to Matt's pure, bell-like melody. The young lad sang his favorite Moravian hymns, many of them in their original German. That did not matter in the least to Falconer, who spent the evening hours thus, his earth-stained fingers stroking the boy's fine blond head, listening to the promise of peace cloaked in sunset and song.

In July, the church elders came and spoke with him about the Moravian community's only inn, still in disuse after all these months. They carefully talked of widows in Salem who needed a good man. They gently challenged him toward finding hope in spite of the world's woes. Falconer stood with them, nodding and accepting their words, trusting their wisdom. But in truth, what occupied his mind was the sudden realization that he had never wept. As he watched their horse-drawn rigs return to the village, he wondered if he would ever feel anything else besides this pervasive numbness.

That night as they sat on the porch, Falconer, his voice low, asked Matt if he wanted to return and reopen the inn. Matt buried his head in Falconer's chest. Falconer did not raise the subject again.

Two days later Falconer went alone into Salem. He met with the elders and arranged for a young couple who had helped with the inn's chores to take over as innkeepers for him. While he discussed the list of duties with them, townspeople approached Falconer, appearing as though drawn from the sunlight and the summer heat. Although they saw him and Matt every Sabbath, they took his visit with the elders as a sign. Even without Ada's sanctioning presence, they quietly welcomed him fully into their fold.

August arrived with a blistering heat, and the rains subsided. The deep-blue dome of the sky presided over an increasingly parched land. Falconer shared the community's fear of a lost harvest. They all began stocking what they could for a long winter of grumbling bellies. Breakfasts were reduced to grits and fatback, noon fare became biscuits and whatever fruit they found lying upon the ground, and the evening repast might be a simple stew from a farm animal no longer able to feed. The Brune house garden was harvested and replanted, and every dawn Matt joined the other children drawing buckets from the well to water the vegetables by hand. Falconer ate his simple breakfast to the dry squeaking of the well handle, paired with his silent entreaties for intervention from the Almighty.

Falconer found the Sabbath worship a time of both peace and confusion. He was glad he had never felt a need to become angry with God. Why this had not happened, he could not say. As he sat and listened to the community choirs join in song, or bowed his head in prayer, he felt the faintest glimmers of divine peace enter his wounded breast. On the homeward journey, though, Falconer stroked his beard and wondered if he would ever waken from his largely empty inner state.

The first week of September, after six scorching weeks without rain, the skies darkened. The wind whipped up clouds of precious earth and flung them in billowing waves across the valley. The dry leaves of corn and wheat and tobacco rattled in thirsty anticipation. Shriveled apples and pears dropped like nature's drumbeats upon the parched earth. And then the rain came.

The entire Brune family raced about the muddy front yard. Falconer stepped off the front porch and tilted his head to the sky. He felt a hand slip into his and looked down at Matt. The boy's hair was matted to his forehead and turned so pale it looked silver. Falconer felt his face stretch in unaccustomed lines, the action so foreign it took him a long moment to even recognize it as a smile. The rain had washed away the impossible distance, and Ada appeared once again to Falconer in the clear eyes, in the upturned face, in the rain that poured in pewter rivulets over his head. Ada was still there. She had not completely left him.

Falconer swept the boy into his arms. Matt's own arms came up and around Falconer's neck. The two stood in the rain without speaking. The boy's cheek rested upon Falconer's beard as they watched the Brune family dance and laugh and frolic in the wet joy and the new hope.

Two weeks later a stranger arrived, asking about Falconer. The Salem community counted Falconer as one of their own. None would give up information about a fellow Moravian without first making sure the attention was welcome. These were, after all, evil times.

Some time earlier, the North Carolina capital had moved from the coastal community of New Bern to Raleigh. The stated purpose was to extend the government's reach further inland. Even so, much of the state had fallen into administrative chaos. Brigands ruled many of the smaller Carolina roads. The Moravians were called enemies by the newly elected state administration, which disliked how the Salem community took in escaped slaves and formed a vital link in the Underground Railroad. And Falconer had done more than most to further this work. All the proceeds from his share in a Carolina gold mine had gone to purchasing slaves and spiriting them away. A plantation he had acquired in Virginia became yet another stop on the Freedom Train line northward. No, this was not a time to be open with an outsider—not until they had taken his measure.

When word finally came to Falconer that a well-dressed stranger was asking for him, he saddled his horse and rode into Salem town to his own inn. As he approached it, he saw the man, who turned out to be no stranger, seated on the very same bench Falconer had used for his own morning devotions when he and Ada ran the establishment.

"Hello, Reginald," he called as soon as he recognized his visitor.

The owner of Langston's Emporium, along with any number of other business ventures, squinted against the morning sun.

"Falconer?" The man closed the Bible in his lap and stood.

Falconer slipped from the saddle and roped the horse to the railing. Reginald Langston lost his footing as he stepped off the front stoop, his eyes round as he approached the taller man. "Is that really you?" he asked, his voice sounding shocked.

"Have I changed so much?"

"Have you . . . Don't you see yourself in the mirror?"

"The Brunes don't own a looking glass."

Reginald stepped in close enough to grip Falconer's wrist. His fingers did not come close to connecting. "As I live and breathe. It is indeed you."

Falconer accepted the other man's handshake, realizing he was not the only one that had changed. Reginald Langston had always been ready with a smile and a laugh, large in girth and trusting in nature. Instead of the dark broadcloth suits preferred by most Washington men of stature, Reginald wore doeskin trousers tucked into boots of fine English leather, a soft brown traveling coat, and a waistcoat with gold buttons. But not even these fine clothes could mask the weariness and the worry in his gaze, or his features sagging with far more than the months since their last meeting. Falconer took note of the two armed men who shadowed Reginald, far enough away not to intrude, yet there and ready just the same.

Reginald took a step back and said, "I can't tell you how sorry I am about Ada. I only heard over breakfast."

Falconer directed a nod toward the packed earth. "I am sorry I did not write."

Reginald waved that away. "How long has it been?"

"She left us in February."

"How are you, my man?"

Falconer looked up. "Coping. Sometimes more than that."

"And the boy?"

"He's just gone ten. A strong, fine lad. He no doubt has kept me as sound as you find me."

"Might I pay my respects to your wife?"

"Of course."

Reginald ordered his men to stay behind. The two obviously were not pleased, but did as they were told. The day was harvest fair, a faint hint of breeze out of the north, not cool so much as comfortable. The village was empty of men and many women, as almost everyone used the good weather to bring in the crops. Even so, Falconer felt unseen eyes upon them as they proceeded through the village's heart.

At the gravesite Reginald said a silent prayer. Then, "She was an extraordinarily fine woman."

Falconer nodded and pointed at the weather-beaten cross beside her own. "I had her put to rest beside her first husband. I felt it was important for our boy."

"You amaze me," Reginald said quietly. "Can we sit here for a moment?"

The bench they selected was the same one where Ada

16

had spent long, lonely days, staring at the cemetery and her first husband's grave, before meeting Falconer. Ada had brought him here twice. The first visit had been upon the day of his return from jail, where he had been incarcerated for buying, then freeing, a group of slaves. She had told him of her own lonely struggle and the multitude of hours she had sat and yearned for what her heart could not even name. The second time was the evening before they were to wed. They had sat in this very spot for almost an hour. Then she had risen and smiled and embraced him. Falconer's heart lurched as he remembered her arms around his neck, his whispered words in her ear. He sighed and almost imperceptibly shook his head.

When Reginald finally spoke, it appeared to Falconer as a response to an unspoken question. "Were it not for my own dire need, I would not dream of asking anything of you now. One look is enough to know of your woes, my dear friend. But ask I must."

"Is it something to do with . . . with Serafina?" Falconer found it uncommon strange that he now had to search to recall the name of a woman whom he had dearly loved, though never claimed as his own.

"My dear friend, not at all. Perish the thought. No, the lovely lady is fairly trembling with joy. She and her husband both. Though I must say the two of them are more than upset with your lack of communication."

"I'm sorry, but I could not bring myself to answer her letters."

"And now I see the reason why. She will be very sad to learn the reason for your silence." Reginald fumbled with a button to his waistcoat. "She should be delivering their first child any day now."

"Please tell them I wish them every joy." Falconer waited a moment, and when Reginald did not speak, he pressed gently, "So it is not Serafina."

"No. It is myself. And my dear wife, Lillian. We are at our wit's end, I tell you. Our wit's end." Reginald Langston became agitated, and he rose and began pacing before the bench. "Lillian had a son by her first marriage. You knew she was widowed, of course."

"Yes." Falconer remembered Reginald's wife had previously been married to an earl, rather a scoundrel of English society who had squandered his money on ill-fated ventures.

"Byron was to succeed to his late father's titles, but Lillian had sold them," Reginald went on. "She was penniless and heavily in debt and had no choice. Byron, however, failed to understand either the need or the deed. He was always a difficult son, impetuous and rather a snob. Very much like his late father, so Lillian tells me. The boy ran through his inheritance in a few short years. Also Lillian had left him quite a nice London town house, which he mortgaged. Without telling his mother, I hasten to add. And he spent all that as well."

"Gambling?" Falconer wondered. Another wayward son of wealthy parents.

Reginald clearly was reluctant to speak ill of the lad. "Does it matter?"

"I really cannot say until I know the problem."

"Then, yes. Gambling and vile women, by all accounts. He loved the trappings of power and accepted none of the responsibilities. He went before the magistrates once too often. A duel over a married woman, though married to neither of the men dueling, as it happened. Lillian begged for my help, which of course I gave. Our London partner, as you know, is Samuel Aldridge, a former diplomatic agent and a man of considerable influence. And of course you know Gareth and Erica Powers. Through their intervention, we managed to have the lad released. On one condition. Byron was to leave his past, his ways, and his London life behind. Samuel arranged for him to take a position of assistant manager at a new trading outpost."

Falconer realized he was already caught in the hunt. Not by the story. But by Reginald's need. For this was what Falconer knew he could never refuse. He could not say no to a friend. Falconer asked, "Where?"

"Marseilles. Do you know it?"

"The harbor. The port. I've not been further inland than the seaman's market fronting the quayside." He could smell the place now.

"Never been there myself. But our office is on the main avenue leading up from the port." Reginald had not stopped his pacing before Falconer's bench. "Byron arrived as scheduled. He worked there for six months. That is, he came in occasionally, mostly to collect his wages."

"He kept to his past ways," Falconer surmised. When Reginald continued to pace in silence, Falconer picked up the story for him. "He did no work. He lived for the night and dark deeds. He again got into debt."

Reginald stopped pacing and stared at the nearest gravestone.

Falconer said quietly, "He owed money to the wrong man."

"So we have been informed," Reginald agreed, his voice low.

"Is Byron alive?"

"We were desperately afraid that he was not. We heard conflicting rumors. He had taken up with vile merchants, he had been found in an alley—nothing that could be confirmed even by our own agents."

Falconer waited for a time, then asked more softly still, "What have you learned?"

"A letter arrived from Samuel. He was approached by a missionary's wife, that is, his widow. She appeared in London. Traveling from Algiers. She claims to have seen Byron. Not merely seen him. Been shown him, like . . . like a prize heifer."

"Or a slave."

Reginald stared at him, his gaze hollow. "According to this woman, he had been sold to a North African brigand by the name of Ali Saleem." Though Falconer's intake of breath was very soft, Reginald caught it nonetheless. "You know him?"

"The name. Every seaman who traverses the southern Mediterranean has heard of Ali Saleem. He is the last of the Barbary pirates."

"So I have been informed. This Ali Saleem let the poor woman go, even arranged transport back to civilization, upon receipt of her oath to pass on this information. The brigand has offered to release Byron for gold. Quite a large amount of gold."

Falconer rose to his feet. "I must speak with my son."

Reginald's face was grim with old woes. "I will not have you doing this out of any sense of indebtedness. You owe me nothing. No matter what we might have said in the past. We are friends. I release you from any promise you might have made to me. Do you hear what I am saying?"

Falconer gripped the other man's arm. He turned Reginald around and guided him through the cemetery gates. "You are a friend, Reginald."

The man said miserably, "I wish I had not come." Falconer's squeeze on his arm was the only answer.

Falconer left Reginald at the inn's front entrance and rode his horse back out to the farm. Keeping his horse to an easy pace, he lifted his hat to a pair of women returning from the fields, his thoughts all the while racing far and wide. He tried to rein in the blood surging through his veins. He tried to pray.

But all the while, his mind turned over and again to a single reality.

Though they were six days' hard ride inland, his nostrils were filled with the scent of the sea.

Chapter 2

The Moravian elders had interacted with Falconer on a fairly regular basis, but this night was different, according to Sarah Brune. She insisted upon Falconer dressing in a clean, starched shirt and fresh trousers. The shirt's buttons were cloth and the trousers scarcely met Falconer's ankles, but with a new black long coat, also of homespun, his appearance matched the serious nature of his meeting.

He had asked to talk with the elders at their weekly meeting in the community hall, one door down from the church. His earth-stained and battle-scarred hands fiddled with his wide-brimmed dark hat as he waited, feeling like a schoolboy called to the headmaster's office. The hall was not full, nor was it empty. Any member of the community could attend, and many did, especially during the winter months, when work was light and the evening hours long. But this was September harvest, and most folk were far too busy to take part in the regular event. Even so, with Falconer being one of them now, with the inn an important element in the community, and with news of the stranger's visit having traveled quickly, most families sent a grandmother or an older gentleman whose limbs no longer could work the fields. One person per clan, to pass along the news and speak for kinfolk if required. It was the Moravian way.

The community's normal business was done, and the elders were in a good frame of mind with news of a bumper harvest and barns packed to overflowing in spite of those weeks of drought. The prayers were mostly of praise and thanksgiving, the discussions easy, the arguments absent. No village woman was brought up for the sin of gossip, no wayward youth had required punishment, nor was there news of further dissent with the powers that be in Raleigh.

But as soon as Falconer arose to recount his conversation with Reginald, the elders' demeanor turned serious, if not dour. He recounted the Langstons' problem with their son, the personal debts and their outcome. He did not embellish. He answered the questions as best he could.

He waited.

The chief elder was none other than Paul Grobbe, one of the first men Falconer had met upon his arrival in Salem a couple of years before with a band of exhausted former slaves. "What of the inn, Brother John?" he now asked.

"I stand ready to do as you advise." Falconer motioned to where the nervous young innkeeper sat with his wife. "Brother Karl is here as well."

Grobbe motioned for the young man to rise. "Do you wish to continue with this work?"

The young man's stammer was as obvious as his nerves. "I-If the elders will it, g-good sir."

Grobbe looked to either side. None objected. "You have seen to your duties well. There have been no complaints from visitors. Your wife provides an excellent table."

"Th-thank you, Elder Grobbe."

Falconer said, "I am willing to sign over the running of the inn until Matt comes of age."

"What say you, Brother Karl?"

Karl glanced at his wife, who used the corner of her apron to dab at her eyes. "Th-that has been our h-hope,

Brother J-John," he managed to say.

The elder Grobbe paused a moment. Long before his gaze shifted, Falconer knew the time had finally come for the question he had pondered ever since speaking with Reginald three days earlier.

Grobbe asked, "What about the boy?"

"I would rather Matt be allowed to speak for himself," Falconer replied. He looked at the boy beside him and sat down.

"Very well." Grobbe motioned to Matt. "Young Matt Hart, what say you?"

The boy's fingers trembled slightly as he held his hat in the same manner as Falconer. But his voice was steady. "I have nothing left for me here, sir."

One of the elders stiffened in protest. "Salem is your home and your family's heritage!"

Grobbe silenced his colleague with a single glance. He turned back to the boy and said gently, "I pray in time this will change for you, lad."

"I pray I can say the same, sir. But right now . . ."

"Yes? Please continue, lad."

"The only thing that makes me happy is singing at sunset with Father John."

The previous elder could be held back no longer by merely a piercing look. "Your family helped establish this community! How could you possibly *think* of walking away from your heritage?"

Matt did not look at the speaker but kept his eyes on the elder Grobbe, a man he had known all his life. "A frau stopped me on the street today, sir. She choked up as she hugged me. I continually see sorrow in all the faces I meet. The boys don't treat me the same—the same as before. They mostly ignore me, and some call me names."

"We can soon put a stop to that," the second elder forcefully chimed in.

"It won't matter, sir," Matt responded, turning now to look at him. "I don't want to be the lonely orphan boy. I want to go someplace where people don't think about or talk about my missing mama every time they see me."

Falconer studied the lad standing beside him. Matt had sprouted a full eight inches in the past year. There was a mature leanness to his features, a steady calmness to both his gaze and his words.

"You have been through far too much for a child of your years," Grobbe murmured.

Matt might have shrugged. "When Father John spoke to me of Master Reginald and his difficulty, I found myself wanting something for the first time since Mama passed."

Grobbe gave him a moment, then gently urged, "What was it you wanted?"

Matt spoke in the same calm voice. "To leave. To be where I am not known."

This time Grobbe cut off the elder's protest before it was fully formed. "What of your place here among us?"

"I may return, sir. I do not see that day now. But I shall pray on this as hard as I am able. For my mother and my father both lie here in peace, and I think they would want this, though right now I cannot say for sure."

Falconer edged back a trace in his seat. Until that moment, he had not clearly seen how the boy had been changed by the tragedy. Or how he had grown.

As was their habit, they sat together upon the porch, this time with coats about them against the fall chill. The next day would be anything but normal, what with a dawn rise and their final breakfast with the Salem folk, and this last evening of song and contemplation held a bittersweet air. Sarah had protested at the news of their swift departure, although not overmuch. For any who looked carefully could see that, since the elders' meeting, Matt carried a notable difference about him. There was a wind in his sails now, a new spark to his eyes. Though he said nothing, even Aunt Sarah, who loved him as dearly as she did her own bairns, saw that this change was for the better.

It was Sarah who now turned and spoke, not to Falconer or the lad she loved but rather to her husband. "Have you asked him?"

"Not yet."

"If not, when?" But her husband was clearly loath to speak. She harrumphed something that might have been *Men*. Then Sarah leaned forward so she could look around her husband and asked, "Are you angry with God, Brother John?"

"No, Sister."

"I ask you this because I will not have you leave this home with wrath in your heart, especially not for your Maker. There is a difference between sorrow and burning rage."

"Sarah."

"No, husband. If you will not speak, then I will have my say."

Falconer stood and moved to the rail so he could see all six faces. Paul and Sarah Brune, their seamed features glowing with harvest tans. The three children, two boys in their late teens on the swing and a younger girl by her father's chair petting the cat. All holding the same hearty farmland vigor. And Matt. "You are right to speak as you do, Sister."

"Am I, then." She settled back in the rocker and did as many of the Moravian women when talking among themselves, slipping her hands beneath her apron and folding them together. Beneath the curve of her small starched cap, her eyes glowed strong in the dimming daylight. "Tell me why."

"Because I must care for the boy. And he will judge the world through what he sees in me."

"Do you speak these words because you know I wish to hear them or because you know them to be true?"

"I promised Ada I would do right by the lad. I said I would love him as our son and raise him into the man she knew he would be. I can only do this with God's help." He saw Matt wipe at his eyes and forced himself to focus upon the couple. "I could not make it through each day without Him. Even when He is distant, even when I question His ways, even when I am . . ."

Sarah rocked softly, giving Falconer time to find his strength. "You are a good man, Brother John. You will become whole again."

"I scarcely know what that means."

"You will be healed," she said. "And you will be the father Matt needs you to be."

Falconer saw a bit of Ada in the woman, which was hardly a surprise. Ada had been raised in this very household after losing her own parents to an influenza that had devastated the Moravian ranks. "How can you be so certain?"

"Because I hear God speak in time to your own words, Brother John. Even when you cannot hear Him, even while your heart remains wounded by your loss. Still and now, He is with you." The rocker creaked softly in cadence. "You may not go in peace, Brother John. But you will go with God. And you mark my words. He will use this road to draw you near once more."

Chapter 3

Before the sun had risen, Falconer and Matt took the northwest trail out of Salem, riding a pair of fine horses and leading a pack mule. At midday they halted by a swift-flowing creek and ate provisions from their bulging saddlebags. Sarah Brune was determined they would arrive at their destination with food to spare. The day was fair, and they made good time.

At sunset they found an empty meadow by a deserted cabin and camped under the eaves. In spite of brisk temperatures, Falconer slept deeply and did not dream. He awoke to swallows chasing the first rays of daylight, the horses cropping grass, and the soft breath of his son, whose bedroll was beside his. He lay there for a time, feeling the faint stirring of something deep in his bones. He found himself wondering if there was more to this quest than simply coming to the aid of some dear friends.

Late in the second afternoon, they arrived at what once had been the Moss plantation and now belonged to Falconer. The new overseer had hung a sign by the post road announcing *Little Salem*. The overseer was Moravian, the youngest of nine brothers and thus destined to receive almost none of the family land. Though he and his wife missed their kin and the Salem community, they reveled in farming a spread of this size. The house had been divided into four segments. Two families had matching apartments, a pair of rooms had been set aside for Falconer, and a portion of the cellar was rebuilt as a Freedom Train hideaway.

After dinner Falconer took Matt down the side lane to where the orchard formed a live border between the main house and the rebuilt cabins, now housing six other landless Salem families. Each had been deeded a portion of fertile bottomland. Falconer could hear children playing in the last throes of daylight. He liked the fragrance of the few apples left to rot into the earth. He liked the sound of bees humming. He liked most of all how his heart responded to these things.

Falconer now said to Matt, "I've had the impression something's bothering you."

The boy jumped and touched a low-hanging limb.

"It's all right if you don't want to talk about it. I'm not one for pressing you to speak. But if you wish to talk, I am ready to listen."

Matt took so long in responding, Falconer almost suggested they return to the house and bed.

But Matt then said, "I feel like I'm doing something wrong."

"Why is that?"

Matt shrugged.

"It is hard for me to communicate with a motion of your shoulders, son."

Matt said in a small voice, "Is it wrong to be happy?"

"Ah." Falconer resisted the urge to take hold of the boy. "Let me see if I can add some meat to that bit of a question. You feel that you are being disloyal to your mother by enjoying our time on the road?"

The voice grew smaller still. "Yes."

"I confess to feeling the very same thing."

Matt halted in his tracks and looked up at Falconer.

"I cannot deny the sensation. It seems improper some-how, looking forward to a tomorrow that does not hold her."

"I do miss her so much."

"As do I." Falconer crouched down beside him. "Were she here, do you know what I think she might say?"

"What?"

"I believe she would tell us to make this our quest. We have one quest already, of course. We shall try and rescue our friend's son. But Ada would say we should have another quest, one that may well prove equally important to us in the seasons to come. Do you know what that second one might be?"

Matt swiped one cuff across his cheek. "To be happy again."

"To be certain that is part of it. Another part would be to find our way into a new future. It may not be the one we would have asked for. But it is ours. And we should come to a point where we can claim it."

Matt used both hands this time, smearing the wet across his cheeks. "Will I forget her?"

"Not ever. Not in a hundred thousand days." This time Falconer did not resist the urge to embrace him. "I am very blessed. All I need do is look at you and I see her looking back at me. Since you cannot share this same blessing, I must try very hard to be strong. I must make a safe harbor in my heart for the love she taught me to hold. And I must have it there for you to find whenever you look at me."

They did not take the main road to Richmond and then on to Georgetown. Instead they held to smaller routes. The horses were as amiable as they were strong. He and Matt covered close on twenty-five miles a day, as near as Falconer could reckon.

They traveled with a distinct ease between them. Matt did not return to his previous high cheer and joyful chatter. Nor did Falconer expect it. But the boy did talk, inquiring about what he saw, for he had never been farther afield than the valley beyond Salem's southern border. Twice he smiled—once in a moment of awestruck abandon when they emerged from three days of dank forest ways and found themselves upon an eastern ridge. All the world seemed stretched out before them, and at its very border lay the great inland sea known as Chesapeake Bay. The second time was the next morning, when Falconer described the town of Portsmouth and the sailors' inn where they would berth that night. Matt had never seen a city before, never viewed a ship, never heard the call of gulls or the music of crashing waves. Falconer spoke of them all, and a bit about his former life.

They crested a final rise, and there before them were the rooftops of Portsmouth town. And beyond them, clustered like a wintry forest, were the bare watery beacons of the only place Falconer had ever known as home.

"Father John?"

"Yes, son."

Matt pointed to the east, beyond the smoke rising in the still clear air. "What are those?"

"They're called masts. They're the main poles for holding a ship's sails aloft."

"Masts."

"Most oceangoing vessels have three of them. Except for the square-riggers used by fishermen and coastal shippers. Those have two. One of which is called a lateen. The crossbeams you see there are called booms." Falconer grinned. "I suspect that is far more information than you wanted."

Matt seemed to be chewing upon the strange words. "Have you ever met a pirate?"

"Aye, son. That I have."

"Was he as fierce as they say?"

"Fierce as thunder at midnight. I once heard tales of a pirate who wove burning candles into his beard before attacking. The pirates I knew did not need to be afire to scare me."

"You were frightened?"

"Right out of my tiny little boots."

Matt smiled then. And the sun seemed to dip down closer to earth than was customary, for the light shone from his face. "Your boots are big as boats, Father John."

"Maybe so. But the rest of what I said is the bare truth. I was so scared I couldn't swallow."

"I shouldn't like to meet anyone who frightened *you,* sir."

"May God keep you safe from ever doing so. I hope and pray this voyage is a good one for you, son."

Portsmouth was as fine a harbor as any Falconer had known, with room for steerage and a good sandy bottom. The water was brackish, only a third as salty as the ocean. The inland bay was protected from hard blows by a long string of barrier islands some eighteen miles to the east. Portsmouth was the favored calling point for much of the East Coast traffic, and the city bustled with equal measures of pride and good fortune.

Falconer left their horses at a stable near the inn Reginald had told them to use. Reginald Langston was a man of his word, for the stable hands were ready to meet them. Reginald had agreed to acquire the horses and send the money back to Paul Brune. As soon as the innkeeper

saw them enter his front portal, he bustled about, refusing
to let Falconer carry his own saddlebags, and ushered them
personally into the finest rooms the inn had on offer. After
the modest Moravian farmhouse, the rooms were very fine
indeed.

Falconer took Matt to what the innkeeper claimed was
the best bathhouse in Virginia, a place of stone flooring
and brass fixtures and even a stained-glass portal. They
were led to a private chamber with two steaming baths.
Matt was wide-eyed over the luxury of not sharing his
bathwater with the three Brune children, particularly after
the long summer drought. Falconer eased his way gradually into the hot water, then rang the bell and summoned
the house barber.

He asked the boy, "Would you mind if I cut off my
beard?"

Matt had already worked up a full head of lather and
had to swipe his eyes clear. "What, Father John?"

"My beard. I was always clean-shaven at sea. Most sailors are. But if you wish I will keep it on."

Matt looked askance. "The barber will shave you here
in the bath?"

"It's the practice. Might be a good idea if he trimmed
your hair as well."

Matt ducked his head under the water and came up
blowing.

"Is that a yes?"

"Mama liked you without a beard. I heard her say
that."

"Aye." As a matter of fact, Ada would not let him grow
one, for she claimed it scratched her face. Falconer had
taken to shaving before bed, a practice he had kept as long
as she had been with him. He tugged at his damp locks
and wondered if he would ever know a day where her

absence did not sigh from every crevice. "That she did."

"Do you think I shall ever grow a beard?"

"Sooner than you think."

"But it will never be as dark as yours."

"There are many who say fair hair is handsome on a lad."

Matt submerged himself again. "How do sailors wear their hair?"

"Many grow it long, and tar the ends. Mine was long enough, but I held it fast in a ribbon. Sometimes a leather thong."

"You wore a blue ribbon in your hair when I first met you," the boy recalled. "Did you cut your hair for Mama?"

"No, lad. So I would fit in with the brethren, much as a seafaring dog ever could." Falconer reached across the distance. "There's a mirror on the side table. Reach over and hand it to me, please."

Matt did as he was told. "The scar on your face has gone bright red."

"It's the heat." Falconer doused the mirror to clear away the steam, then found himself tensing as he wiped the surface and took aim.

A stranger stared back at him. A wild dark beard laced with silver. Thirty-two years of age and already time's wintry hand was etched into his beard, though not his hair, which hung lank and unkempt about his face. His scar, the one that narrowly missed his left eye, could be seen above the beard and was indeed a fiery red. Like most seamen, Falconer had always been fanatical about keeping his hair well tended and his face clean-shaven. But it was not his hair which made him look unfamiliar.

His features had always been sharply defined. More than one person had called them carved from flesh-colored stone. Now they looked cavernous. His skin, leathery from decades of salt and wind and sun, was dark brown after the summer spent farming. He touched his cheekbone, as though testing his own identity. He looked like some fierce hunter of old, a craven beast scarcely removed from the forest and the glen.

When Falconer set the mirror aside, Matt said, "You can shave off your beard if you wish, Father John."

Chapter 4

Langston's Ship Chandlery was precisely as Reginald had described, fronting the harbormaster's office and built with the same stout colonial brick. The shop was jammed, but the moment Falconer entered, a stocky man with a heavy limp stumped toward them. "Master Falconer?"

"Aye. The same."

"Master Langston's compliments, sir. The owner's tied up with other business what should have been finished two days back, but wasn't. On 'count of certain other gentlemen what were late in arriving. He's sent me in his stead. Soap is the name, sir, which is good for a chuckle given the wares you'll find here. Richard Soap." He knuckled his forelock at Matt. "A grand good day to you, young sir."

Falconer asked, "You're British?"

"American, sir. American as they come, and proud of the fact." When the merchant moved toward them, Soap waved him away toward the other customers. "But I was born in Blighty, I was. Righted that mistake soon as I was able. I've served fifteen years on a Langston vessel. The skipper made me his steward when my knee gave out. Master Langston offered me a landside berth in this very shop, that he did. But I've salt in my bones now."

"I worked as a chandler myself. Four years. In the Carib."

"Did you now. Did you. And today we serve the same master, as it were."

Falconer caught the tone. "Do we speak of Reginald Langston?"

The steward grinned, revealing a gap where his two front teeth should have been. "Master Reginald, he said you was a member of the holy flock. But when I saw this ruddy great giant with a fighter's scar come through the door, I thought, here now, the skipper could well have taken a false measure of this one."

"He was not wrong."

Matt piped up, "Folks of Salem town say when Father John prays, the strongest tree bends its knee."

"Do they now." Richard Soap tousled the boy's blond locks. "Why is it you call your father by such a name?"

"Because he is my second father. My first died when I was five. My ma said I could honor my papa and Father John both with the different name."

"What a wise woman she must be." Soap struggled to keep hold of his good humor. "So now you're off on your adventures while your poor old mam sits alone by the hearth?"

"No, sir. We lost my mother too in the winter just gone."

Faces turned their way all through the store. Falconer looked at his son standing there, his fresh-washed hair shining and his face so earnest. He felt his heart swell with pain and pride both.

"Now there's a sad tale if ever I heard one." Soap looked from one to the other. "I've stepped right into the thick of things, and I'm right sorry, I am."

"No offense meant or taken," Falconer replied.

"Come with me, young master." Soap draped an arm around Matt's shoulders. "We had a shipment arrive this very morning from the Spice Islands. I believe I spied a quarry of cinnamon sticks in one of them chests."

Matt looked at Falconer, who gave him a nod of assent. As the pair of them moved toward the rear storerooms, he heard the boy ask, "Are the Spice Islands very far away?"

"Far as the moon, or so it feels in the midst of a calm. And never have you seen a calm like the tropics, lad. Weeks with the sails hanging limp as your dear old mam's laundry, may the good Lord hold her close." A door creaked open, then shut upon the words, "Why, my little man, there was once a time . . ."

Falconer stepped toward the rear of the store, where tables were piled with seamen's garb. He found what he was looking for straight off—shirts which tied at wrist and neck, high-waisted pants with legs that could be buttoned tight to slip into sailors' boots, even a tricorn hat with stiff curved brims to shield his vision in foul weather. Falconer selected an empty seaman's chest and began loading his new gear. He tried on a navy greatcoat that looked as though it might have been sewn for him. Then he spied the cutlasses.

The curved blades were stacked behind a locked cabinet with stout iron bars. Beside them were every manner of pistol, gun, and weapon. Falconer knew them all.

Falconer caught sight of his reflection. Beneath the greatcoat he still wore his Moravian homespun, yet already the clothes seemed the barest fable. As though the previous two years had not existed. As though he had shaved off not only his beard but all the months he had spent away from the sea. For standing before him was the man he had once been. Strong and steady and stalwart. A face burned and blasted by far more than sun. Features that shouted danger, lean and fierce. And that scar.

"Father John?"

Falconer drew around. "What do you have there?"

Matt clasped a bundle of twisted golden-brown sticks to his chest. "Master Soap said I should take a double handful, sir. For the journey."

"Only if he will let us pay for them."

Soap replied, "It's Master Langston what's paying, good sir. And I warrant he'd be right pleased for my pressing them on the lad."

There in Matt's young face he saw the only answer the day required. Falconer asked, "Did you thank the gentleman?"

"Yes, Father John."

"Let him wrap them for you, then wipe your hands clean and come back here."

Soap jerked his chin toward the locked cabinet. "Master Reginald said to tell you, whatever you need, it's already aboard the vessel."

Falconer nodded and did his best to block the boy's view of the weaponry. "Son, do you wish to wear those clothes on board?"

Matt looked down at himself. "It's all I've ever owned, sir."

"I know that, lad. I want you to understand, if you'd be more comfortable staying as you are, why—"

"None will object, lad." Soap listed heavy to port as he walked toward them. "Especially not after one glimpse of your father there."

Falconer kept his gaze upon the boy. "There are many changes to come. You will be permitted to pick and choose, if I have anything to say about them. Starting with what you wear."

"Will there be other boys on the ship, sir?"

"Aye. At least a couple of middies."

"Four," Soap corrected. "Youngest is but a nob of ten."

"Middies are midshipmen," Falconer explained. "They are sent to learn the ways of the sea and ships. There may also be other young passengers."

Matt pointed at the clothes Falconer had dumped in the seaman's chest. "Will they be dressed in such as these?"

"Aye, they will. And shall I."

"Then I wish to have the same, Father John."

"And a right proper seaman you'll make," the steward declared, "or Soap is not my father's blessed name I wear with pride."

Reginald Langston met them upon the clipper's aft deck. A young midshipman, still several years from needing a razor, had piped them aboard. Falconer raised his hat to the middy's salute and a second time to the captain on the quarterdeck. The captain frowned and turned his back upon Falconer.

Reginald dredged up a smile for Matt, then pulled Falconer to one side. "There are problems."

"The steward told me of business matters."

"Oh, piffle. There are always problems with business. No. I was referring to the ship. Captain Harkness does not . . . well, he does not approve of you."

Falconer glanced over. The skipper still resolutely ignored them. "He knows of me?"

"No. And that is the problem. He finds it uncommon strange that with a ship full of trusted men, I find it necessary to go outside the company for an ally on this mission."

The captain turned, but only to scowl fiercely at Falconer. Harkness wore his landfall uniform, which was no surprise given the fact that the company's owner was aboard.

"It is of little import."

"On the contrary. I dislike the idea of starting a voyage with hostility in the dining cabin." Reginald fiddled with his vest's middle button. "Harkness is an ambitious man. I have chosen to give him a ship regardless, for he is a good skipper, fair in his dealings with the sailors, and scrupulously honest."

Falconer interpreted, "He sees this mission as a missed opportunity for his own advancement."

"I fear so," Reginald agreed. "It is the first time I have ever had occasion to set a company's ship upon such a course, where we sail at my timing and refuse goods for any port beyond London. While Harkness does not know the mission, he does know it is important to me, and he sees you as occupying a trusted position he would like to claim for himself."

Falconer studied the captain. A few years older than Falconer, of stern bearing and features to match. A nubby nose, tight green gaze, forward-thrusting chin, hair cropped so close to his skull Falconer could see the scalp from where he stood. "What do you know of him?"

"Born in Charleston, lost his mother at birth, father an itinerant preacher who carted him all over the former colonies. The man has never known a proper home, save the aft cabin he now occupies."

"When you have opportunity," Falconer said, "tell the gentleman I shall not seat myself at the captain's table unless he himself requests it."

"I shall do no such thing," Reginald declared hotly.

"The success of our mission may depend upon working well with him, Reginald. We need him as a willing partner in this venture."

"My dear friend, I cannot relegate you to eating belowdecks."

"I have grown to the man you see now on burgoo and hardtack," Falconer replied, referring to a shipboard breakfast for all but the wealthy passengers, a mixture of oat gruel and beef grease, stewed all night long. Once the ship's fresh produce was consumed, everyone on board ate hardtack, the dry unleavened bread that was served with salt beef pickled in barrels of brine along with salted peas. Falconer said, "Shipboard fare will serve us both well enough."

Reginald sighed noisily and changed the subject. "Lillian was not pleased with your instructions that she remain in Washington."

"She might have proved a peril to us all, had she insisted upon making this voyage," Falconer explained once more.

"Yes, perhaps. Though I must tell you it was a most difficult decision for her to take. She has sent you a letter. I have it somewhere. She assures me she has held to a pleasant tone. I also carry letters and best wishes from Serafina, three of those, and her parents, one from each. And her husband, Nathan Baring, has written several introductions to people he assures us will be of considerable help along the way. He agrees with your decision not to visit Washington, by the way. He says it was most sensible, and sends you his sincerest regrets over your loss. As do the others." Reginald pondered the deck by his polished boots. "There. I believe that is everything. Yes."

"We shall have ample time to discuss such matters."

"Indeed so." Reginald opened his coat and withdrew his pocket watch. He flipped open the cover, then smiled at Matt's round-cyed surprise. "Have you never seen such a timepiece before, lad?"

"No, sir. How does the cover spring so?"

"I shall show you. And more besides, because the back opens to reveal the most remarkable instrument you shall ever lay eyes upon. But all that must wait a bit." Reginald nodded approval as the steward directed two seamen to carry Falconer's chests into the aft cabins. He then called to the quarterdeck, "We are ready to depart, Captain."

The captain, clean-shaven save for long sideburns that ended in dagger points, bellowed, "Officer of the watch, prepare to make way!"

"Aye, sir." The lieutenant stood by the portal leading belowdecks. He raised his own voice and called, "Cast off there! Bosun, pipe the mainsail!"

Reginald watched the sailors leap to do the skipper's bidding. He lowered his voice so that Matt would not hear. "I fear this mission shall prove mortally dangerous."

Falconer tasted several replies before settling upon, "Your visit to Salem has already proved a healing balm. I can only hope that I shall be able to return the favor."

Chapter 5

Two days after clearing the barrier islands and entering deep ocean waters, they met with a blow straight from the southwest, the driest of Atlantic winds except when escorting a hurricane. Captain Harkness spent the better part of a day searching the far reaches with glass to his eye and conferring with his chief lieutenant, a studious young man by the name of Rupert Bivens. The captain eventually decided they were in no immediate danger, and Falconer agreed. They held steady to their course and did not turn north.

The ship was a clipper, as were half of the Langston fleet. A newfangled design, these clippers were distrusted by many sailors. They were narrow at the beam and handled like a racing horse, quick off the mark and very sensitive to any alteration of course or wind. But they flew. Falconer had traveled twice before upon them and remained fascinated at the way they sliced through even the roughest of seas.

The waves crested as high as the ship's foredeck, and beneath the blue-black sky the waves marched into the horizon like silver mountains. Their course held them to an angle, so they met the waves just ahead of the starboard beam. The ship did not bob nor sway, as Falconer would have expected. Instead, the vessel gripped the wind in teeth of canvas and cleaved straight through the incoming crests. He spent hours by the wheel, observing how the steersman turned it ever so slightly, such that the ship met the wave's crest almost head on, and then allowed the departing swell to guide it back on course. Even in these great seas, a light hand was required for such maneuvers.

Many of the passengers were rendered helpless by the heavy seas. The ship rolled and at times took water over both gunnels. The rigging creaked and the wind sang in the rigging. From his place beside the steersman, Falconer could hear any number of belowdecks passengers moaning in agony. Thankfully, Matt remained untouched by seasickness. He spent hours at Falconer's side, adopting the wide-leg stance to absorb the motion and viewing the majesty of this new world in wide-eyed silence. From time to time he would ask a question, and Falconer would respond at length, introducing him to the sailor's lore as he would any new midshipman.

The crew took an instant liking to the boy, vying for his attention and opportunity to teach him something new about ships and sailing. In the hours when Matt busied himself with shipboard activities, Falconer read and reread the many letters brought from Washington, and even smiled a time or two over the words. Serafina had used Lillian's most recent portrait of her son Byron to sketch an excellent likeness. Byron was twenty-six now. His upraised chin, narrow nose, and arrogant expression revealed a man who felt born to privilege and power.

Falconer spent a goodly amount of time with Reginald. But in truth he preferred nothing more than the company of his boy, and Reginald Langston did not press himself very often upon the pair. They spent many hours in quiet companionship. When one of them spoke, it was often to reminisce. Neither of them talked overmuch about the precious days with Ada. The crisp sea air and the growing distance to anything they had shared with the much-loved woman granted them space, and now the space was lit by the spark of recollection.

Over tin bowls of burgoo one morning, Matt upturned his spoon so that the sloppy mess dripped back into his bowl and asked, "What do you think Mama would have said about this?"

"Nothing good."

The mixture was colored a treacly brown and to Falconer's mind tasted of tar. Matt continued, "I wonder what her guests would say if she'd served up such a bowl at breakfast."

Falconer ate with a seaman's ingrained habit, spooning the burgoo so fast he tasted little. He set his empty bowl aside. "There are many things in this world that are open to mystery. But one thing I can say for certain. Even if the inn's very existence hung in the balance, Ada would not have served her guests burgoo."

"Mama was a good cook."

"She was that."

"And you ate a lot, Father John. She loved watching you."

Falconer smiled into the wind. "It was not a hard task, doing justice to your mother's cooking."

"Mama used to say if ever you lay abed, you would grow big as a brown bear in a week's time."

"Aye. I remember that as well. Eat your food, son. It's important to keep up your strength on such a voyage as this."

Matt did as he was told. "It's awful stuff, this burgoo. Do you ever grow used to it?"

"Aye. But not such that it ever tastes good. At least not

to me. Though I've met sailors who claim they relish nothing better."

Matt scraped his bowl clean. Falconer took it and stacked it upon his own. "I believe you've as much on your face as you put inside your belly, lad."

Matt used a corner of his shirttail to wipe his mouth. "What was the most favorite meal Mama made for you?"

Any breakfast, Falconer started to say, but the sudden lump in his throat kept him from responding. In those early days of their marriage, Falconer had taken to sitting in the kitchen, drinking his first mug of sailor's tea and watching the strengthening light play upon her. His wife. Bustling about their kitchen. She often sang to herself as she worked, and the light caressed her face and illuminated her hair. And the light in her eyes when she glanced his way. . . .

"Father John?"

Falconer cleared his throat. "Her apple flapjacks."

"I liked them as well. So much."

Falconer saw the lancing pain flicker across Matt's features, a mirror of what he knew his own face showed. Falconer ruffled his son's hair. "I spy the middies gathering for their morning lesson. Why don't you join them?"

Falconer sat alone, his face into the wind, and waited for the sea to work its magic and continue the healing of the rift in the flesh where his heart was.

Six days out was the first shipboard Sabbath. The morning watch set sails over the foredeck. Those passengers who felt well enough gathered for a service, capes and coats gathered tightly about them in the wind. The captain spoke about Isaiah, quoting the prophet at length and not once glancing at the text. As they sang the closing hymn, an albatross took up station by the lee stern. The great wings remained motionless in spackled-gray splendor. A number of the passengers, including Matt, were delighted with the appearance. Falconer, however, had never known the bird to fly this far north. When one of the ladies declared it to be a good omen, Falconer felt a steel edge of fear, as though he knew the words to be wrong, but he had no conscious reason for his certainty.

Around midnight he came awake with a ragged start. Falconer had spent years enduring nights cut short by nightmares. He swung his feet to the floor and paused to taste the cabin's air. There was no lingering hint of an already forgotten dream. He dressed swiftly, reaching with a sailor's ease for clothes he could not see. He checked on Matt, who slept easy in the aft cabin's other bed, then slipped out.

The wealthier passengers occupied six cabins arrayed along the rear of the ship. The uppermost chambers were traditionally known as the captain's and owner's cabins. Reginald Langston occupied one, and the captain remained in his traditional berth only because Falconer refused to usurp the ship's commander. He and Matt berthed one deck below. The outer walls to both their cabin and the corridor were angled slightly by the ship's narrowing girth. From below he heard the rough rumble of the ropes connecting the ship's rudder to the wheel. From above came the quiet slap of a sailor's bare feet. Falconer leaned against the wall, slipped on his boots, and climbed aloft.

The night was clear, the wind steady. The stars thick as froth. The waves shone silver-black and marched in somber majesty beneath a quarter moon. The wind blew from the same quarter, not having shifted a notch, not rising or falling, as stable as any seaman could ever wish for. Falconer spied the lieutenant, who leaned against the foremast where it rose from the foredeck, whistling an idle tune. The steersman continued to meet each incoming wave with handy ease. The watch stood at their stations. All was well.

Falconer was about to put his sudden concern down to an overabundance of dried peas at supper when the door leading from the poop cabins slammed back. Captain Harkness appeared, his feet jammed into sea boots and his greatcoat flapping over his nightshirt.

The lieutenant stiffened to a semblance of attention. "Evening, sir."

"What's your report, Bivens?"

"Wind steady at south by southwest, Skipper. Ship's making good time."

"Is she." Harkness stumped up the narrow stairs leading to the quarterdeck. "Any sign of storm?"

"Sky's been clear all night, sir."

"No thunder off the horizon?"

"Not that I've heard."

Harkness jammed his fists deep into his greatcoat pockets. He gave the ship a careful study. Only then did he notice Falconer, who stood behind crates of chickens lashed to the main mast. Harkness might have nodded at him, but in the darkness Falconer could not be certain. "Do a sounding."

"Aye, sir." The lieutenant motioned to an able seaman, who took up the coiled slender rope with a heavy brass weight tied to one end. He slung the weight off the lee railing and allowed the ship's motion to carry it down and back.

The seaman called softly, "No bottom, sir."

"Cast again."

When the answer came back the same, the captain grunted and once more inspected the sails. "Have the men go aloft and check the rigging."

"Aye, sir."

But there was nothing amiss topside. Even so, Harkness remained on the quarterdeck through the dawn. Several times he glanced down to where Falconer stood by the main mast, but Harkness did not address him.

The seamen had caught their master's concern. The next day's watches held to a sense of tight alert. The crew bounded at the first call to whatever duty arose. The passengers who were not prostrate with seasickness went about their business, and clearly the skipper saw no need to voice his concerns to Reginald Langston. The day came and went with the active regularity of a long sea voyage.

The sunset was another splendid affair. Gradually the sea turned to great copper mountains and deep bronze valleys. The sky, clear as glass, glowed momentarily and then relinquished itself over to the vast field of stars and the same quarter moon. Falconer, exhausted by a day of tension without reason, retired immediately after dinner. His last glimpse abovedecks was of the captain by the quarterdeck railing, strained and fatigued by a day far worse than his own, staring out at the empty southern reaches.

Falconer awoke again in the middle of the third watch. He lay in bed trying to tell himself that it was nothing. But he had long lived by trusting his gut, and just then, his gut churned with genuine fear.

He dressed, checked on Matt, slipped down the hall, and climbed the stairs to come out on deck.

The lieutenant nodded to him and spoke with the respect due a guest of the owner. "All is quiet, Mr. Falconer."

"Aye." But he was not so certain. "Permission to climb aloft."

"Of course, sir." Clearly the young officer had been informed that the stranger had served shipboard.

"Thank you." He clambered swiftly up the ropes with the ease of a man whose hands had long been molded to the tarred hemp. He pulled himself into the crow's nest, nodding to the middy wrapped in his greatcoat. "All's well, midshipman?"

"Aye, sir. Thought I saw a whale off the starboard side, but it didn't sound a second time so I can't be sure."

"Not so close as to be a threat."

"No, sir. Not that it seemed to me."

Falconer nodded. The most important thing to come from the exchange was the fact that the middy was both awake and alert. "Do you have a glass on you?"

"Aye, sir." The midshipman reached into his pocket and handed over his telescope.

"Thank you." Falconer extended the spyglass and turned to the southwest. Directly into the wind.

Then he saw it.

It came and went in such a glimmering flash he wanted to discount it as an illusion of a sleepy gaze.

But he knew it was not so.

"Do me a favor, will you, lad?"

"Aye, sir."

"Slip down to the deck. Ask the lieutenant to make a careful search into the wind."

"But, sir, my station . . ."

"I'll take responsibility, lad." There it was again. And this time Falconer was ready for it. And the image made it hard to hold to a measured tone. "Hurry now."

The middy glanced doubtfully at the stranger but did as he was instructed.

Falconer held his glass steady south by southwest. Refusing to even blink.

The flash came again. Now he was sure, and the fear crept up his throat.

A leaden line had formed between the ocean and the sky, split every so often by a slash of lightning.

Falconer slapped the spyglass shut. He reached for the rope connected to the crow's nest alarm bell. He rang it, and it seemed as though his own heart pounded with a terror as brash as the bell.

He leaned over the nest's railing and roared with all his might, "All hands on deck! Raise the captain! All hands on deck!"

Before the bell stopped ringing, the poop door crashed open. This time the captain held his coat in one hand and his boots in the other. His nightdress fluttered about his bare shins as he stared upward.

Falconer yelled down, "A blow, Captain!"

"Where about?"

"Ten points off the windward stern." Falconer could see the separation now without aid of the glass. "She's bearing down hard! We've got fifteen minutes, maybe less."

The captain's voice rivaled Falconer's for urgency. "Night watch aloft, rig all sails for storm!"

"Aye, sir!"

"Prepare a storm anchor and await my orders. Lieutenant!"

"Sir!"

"Lash everything double tight!" The skipper looked back up to Falconer. "Have you known tempests such as this?"

"Aye, Skipper, that I have."

"Then I'll thank you, sir, to take charge of the wheel."

"Aye, Skipper." Falconer was already moving for the

ropes. "And please have your steward see to my boy."

"Soap!"

"Aye, sir!"

"Captain's compliments to the owner. Mr. Lawson is ordered to remain in his cabin for the duration. You keep the lad safe." The captain shrugged himself into his coat. "Look lively, lads! Our very survival depends upon it."

Chapter 6

The storm now was visible to all on deck, a beast of the night that rumbled toward them on legs of fire and wind. Its roar, audible at fifty leagues and more, announced the waves coming at them like enormous fists beating against the ship's timbers and flinging their froth as high as the topsails.

Captain Harkness used a canvas trumpet to add volume to his shouted instructions. Sailors raced against the approaching tempest, clinging to ropes high overhead as they hurried to batten down the sails. They clutched the canvas to their chests, drawing their billowing lengths into slivers tight as new moons. Ropes were tossed back and forth in such practiced haste it would have been remarkable to witness had it not been for the monster now claiming all the horizon as its own.

The midshipmen were ordered below—all but the eldest, a lad of seventeen who helped the sailors hammer wooden chocks around all the portals leading belowdecks. When Falconer felt a grinding through his boots, he knew the captain had ordered all the bilge pumps to be double-crewed.

The ship was surrounded by a ghostly illumination. One moment all was black. Then lightning danced upon the waves and the crew's frenetic activity was thrown into garish view. Yet more lightning split the clouds high over-head into great shards of brilliance. The blasts seemed to punch the billows toward them, boiling up and forward at an impossible speed.

Lieutenant Bivens directed the crew to fashion a sea anchor, a double loop of sail that was readied on the stern, there in case the ship lost either rudder or masts or both. The anchor would then be cast overboard to drag the ship about, keeping it from striking an oncoming wave amid-ships. In seas this mountainous, one wave striking the ves-sel sideways would be enough to flip it over and send them all to a watery grave.

The helmsman, assigned to the ship's wheel, shivered so hard his words were chopped into bits. "W-will w-we s-survive this?"

In reply, Falconer unraveled the storm lashings, ropes coiled about the wheel's stanchion. He took a double bite around the sailor's chest and shoulders. "Can you breathe?"

"Aye, s-sir."

Falconer used the second rope to tie himself into a sim-ilar cradle. "Are you right with God?"

The sailor winced at twin lightning strikes, so close there was no space between the fire and the sound. "I-I am, sir. B-But m-my b-baby g-girl, she's—"

Falconer smelled the sulfurous whiff from the light-ning, a scent akin to battle. He forced his voice into an iron hardness. "Focus upon the next wave, the next blast of wind, the next glimpse you have of the compass. The ship and all who sail her depend upon your doing your duty."

The sailor's response was cut off by a sudden shriek of wind. The ship's rigging hummed a frenzied warning. Then the wind subsided for a moment, allowing the ship's crew to hear another sound, a sibilant rush, like a myriad striking snakes. The menacing hiss grew and grew and grew. Falconer watched the sheet of rain flying across the waves, illuminated by lightning on all sides.

The full storm struck.

All the noise and the waves and the rain became one screeching force. The whole ship was tossed into a cauldron whipped to insanity.

Falconer reached one arm around the smaller helmsman so their bodies were melded as one. His reach was longer, so he gripped the wheel spokes just below the sailor's clenched hands.

The waves were often hidden behind the lashing rain, but when an incoming peak was spotted, he and the sailor fought to turn the ship slightly upwind. They could not face the wave directly head-on. They had to steer just off the windward quarter to keep the sails full. Otherwise, they would lose steering and the ship could founder. They nosed the ship into the wave, braced themselves against the shuddering wash of water that spewed over the gunnels, then steered the ship back a notch. Shifting the wheel that fraction of a degree took so much effort the sailor and Falconer groaned with one voice.

The rain came in a sideways wall. The wind strengthened further still and tore the tops off the waves, such that there was no longer any separation between the sea and the storm. Falconer found it impossible to breathe unless he shifted his face away from the full brunt of the blasts. He timed his turns so that either he or the sailor was always facing forward.

One instant the rain was pelting them, the next it had lifted like a curtain and the ship's surface was covered in gray spume blown off the waves. A crewman slipped on the froth and tumbled over the railing. He would have been lost to the sea and the storm except for the lifeline tied to his middle. He clutched the rope and screamed his fear as his mates dragged him back on board.

Whenever their vision somewhat cleared, Falconer and the sailor took aim for the next wave. They now faced a watery mountain the color of a gravestone. They rose and rose, tipped upon the peak, then slid down into the cavernous depths. From beneath his feet Falconer heard the shrieks and wails of the passengers trapped belowdecks. Falconer took time for a single anguished prayer for his boy. Then he recalled his instructions to the sailor and shouted aloud to the wind and the thunder and the storm's ceaseless roar. *Stout heart.* Nothing less would serve them now.

The top of the next wave looked higher than the masts. It broke and sent a massive wall of water tumbling down at them. Falconer and the seaman shouted as one, fighting the sea and the ship both as they met the white water head-on. The ship's deck was completely awash, and for an instant Falconer feared they were lost. But the ship proved stronger than the wave. The nose punched through with stubborn ferocity, clambering up the maelstrom. The ship hung at the peak for a heart-stopping moment, shook off the load of white water, and slid down into the next trough.

Falconer and the seaman gave a wordless cheer. Certainly the crashing storm was not over. Yet Falconer sensed a first hope that they might indeed survive.

Another curtain of rain swept in, and their world shrank down to the next liquid face, the next blast of wind, the next turn of the wheel.

The lieutenant used his lifeline as a guide rope and pulled himself across the deck. He checked each of the hatches in turn, ensuring that they remained watertight.

When he arrived at the wheel, the incoming wave almost tossed him over the side. Falconer released one hand from the wheel, wrapped the lifeline around his forearm, and held grimly on until the lieutenant found his footing again.

"Much obliged, sir!" Bivens was obviously frightened, as were they all. Yet he maintained a wry smile for the crew. "She's a grand vessel, is she not?" he said as he moved to the next checkpoint.

Falconer found himself liking the man immensely, respecting his ability to remain stable and somewhat cheerful in the face of this blow. "Not one in a hundred would have survived that last surge!"

"I was there in Nantucket when they laid her keel," the lieutenant shouted from across the deck. He had to stop then and wait as they crested the next rise and slid down into the enormous valley. "The shipwright claimed she was a singular vessel. I must remember to thank—"

The lieutenant never completed his sentence. From overhead came a resounding *crack,* as loud as a rifle barrage above the storm's savage wail, strong enough to halt work throughout the ship.

The lieutenant cried, "The mast!"

"No!" Falconer had managed one clear glimpse between the lash of rain. "The mid crosstie!"

The captain roared from the quarterdeck. Falconer saw three sailors clutch the rigging and force themselves aloft. The next wall of rain swept down, blinding Falconer. The lieutenant was in the process of drawing his sword when, out of blackness and rain, a wooden pulley on the end of a rope plunged straight at them.

Falconer shifted back and felt the winch whip within inches of his face. The lieutenant did not act swiftly enough, however. The pulley struck his shoulder with the force of a mallet. Bivens cried out and went down hard. His cutlass slipped from numbed fingers and went spinning across the deck.

Falconer released the knot holding himself to the wheel. He shouted a warning to the helmsman, then flung himself at the lieutenant. A wall of water rose out of nowhere, high enough to crash *down* upon the deck. Falconer smothered the lieutenant with his body, ignoring the officer's wail of pain. He gripped both arms about the nearest hatch, hugging the lieutenant between himself and the wood. The wave punched hard at him, so fierce that momentarily Falconer feared his grip would give way. Now that he was freed from the wheel, there was nothing save his own strength that kept him from being washed overboard, along with the lieutenant. But he held fast, the water sluiced off, and the officer was still with him.

Falconer unlashed the man's lifeline and retied it such that Bivens' shoulder remained free while he was now firmly connected to the hatch. Falconer stripped off his own greatcoat and shirt, leaving just his undershirt on, and with frantic haste fashioned a crude sling from the shirt. He tied it tight about the young man's chest and neck to keep the shoulder from shifting and shoved his own arms back into the greatcoat. He spotted the next incoming wave just in time and took a renewed hold upon the injured officer and the hatch.

When the ship shook itself clear once more, Falconer spied two things at once. To his right, the helmsman yelled while dragging at the stubborn wheel. To his left, the sparring from the broken crosstie had tangled about the base of the mast. Rigging and canvas and wood now clung to the ship's leeward side, dragging them about, threatening to turn the ship sideways. Meeting a wave of this size amidships would send them all to the deeps.

Two sailors chopped at the sodden rigging with axes. The captain clambered down from the quarterdeck, drawing his sword as he did so. Falconer spied the lieutenant's lost blade, caught by the railing. He leapt across the deck and snatched up the handle. Raising himself up, he sawed at the nearest rope with all his might.

The ship's railing cracked beneath the strain of the overboard rigging. In the distance, higher than the wind, the helmsman shrieked another warning.

Falconer's rope parted with a savage crack. The captain managed to saw through another. The sailors chopped their way through a third. Together Falconer and the captain began working on the final cord.

The railing gave way altogether. The last remaining rope clamped itself to the deck, humming in taut fury. The captain shouted words lost to the rain. Falconer gripped the cutlass handle with both hands, ignored the looming wall of water that might fling him over the side, and hacked again with all his might.

The rope came apart with a snap as loud as rifle fire. The ship realized it was free and righted itself with such bounding force the nose jammed about, meeting the next huge crash of water with agility.

The incoming wave caught Captain Harkness full in the face, and he went down hard. Falconer released one hand from the rigging, all that kept him on the ship, and managed to catch hold of the captain's sodden greatcoat. The skipper slid with the wash, headed now toward the gaping hole where the railing had once been. Eyes round with terror, the skipper's hands clawed for a hold. Falconer roared with the strain of the captain's weight and the wave's furious strength.

Then it was over. The ship shook off the wave and swooped down the next valley. The captain managed to reach the mainmast and hugged it with both arms, striving to keep his feet beneath him. Falconer struggled upright, massaging the hand burned first by the rope and now by salt. He raced back to the wheel, where he found the helmsman gray with exhaustion. Falconer tied himself back into place, then tore off the bottom of his undershirt, using his teeth and other hand to tie it around his damaged palm.

He managed to grip the wheel just in time to meet the next incoming wave.

It might have been an hour later. It might have been ten years. Falconer reckoned it was closer to the former, but only as time was measured outside the storm.

The sun came out.

The crew was captured by the unexpected shine. They squinted and stared fearfully about, looking like sodden beasts in the amber light. The universal sentiment was expressed by the helmsman, who croaked into Falconer's ear, "What does it mean?"

Before he could reply, Harkness shouted, "John Falconer!"

"Aye, Captain!"

Harkness was back on the quarterdeck. He had lost his canvas trumpet to the storm, but the wind had stilled with the appearance of daylight and his voice carried well. "Is this the eye?"

Falconer used the piece of shirt tied about his right hand to clear his vision. He squinted and peered upward, making a slow circular sweep.

During the time they had been lost in the storm's perpetual darkness, dawn had come unnoticed. The eastern sky was brilliantly clear. To the south and west the rain continued with such force there was a partition between earth and sky.

Falconer turned back to the captain. "I think not."

"Have you seen one before?"

"Aye. Once." Falconer nudged the helmsman. "Can you manage on your own for a while?"

"Not if she blows again, sir."

"I'll be back for that." But Falconer did not think it was going to happen. He was certain enough to unlash himself from the wheel and start toward the quarterdeck.

Simply because it had stopped raining did not mean the going was easy. The seas appeared even more immense in the light of the dawn. The deck was littered with rigging and sails ripped from the masts. Sea froth shimmered in the light and trembled in the lighter wind, slick as oil on glass. Falconer clambered forward using both hands for support, moving swiftly but with caution, for he wore no lifeline.

When he arrived at the quarterdeck stairs, he said, "Permission to enter, sir."

"Don't stand upon ceremony, Falconer. Up with you and be quick about it." When Falconer had joined him, the captain said, "So, you've entered the eye of such a tempest and lived to tell the tale."

"It was not as fierce a storm as this, and we scarcely survived."

The captain motioned to a barrel lashed to the bulkhead. "There's water. Not fresh, but I doubt you'll care overmuch."

Falconer's thirst was suddenly as strong as pain. He hammered off the lid and plunged his head beneath the surface, sucking in water like a dog. He drank until his belly felt distended, then came up blowing hard.

Harkness did not turn from his inspection of the ship

and the wall of clouds. "Tell me why you think we're not trapped in the maelstrom."

"The clouds do not encircle us, sir."

"I'd heard that was the way of the eye but did not believe it."

"It's true enough." Despite the distance the captain had previously maintained from him, Falconer had found himself liking the man. Harkness was a fighter, for only a combatant could have risen from such low beginnings to captain a merchant vessel. Yet this strong, aggressive man did not shy away from admitting what he did not know. "I've heard of eyes so large the leading wall is beyond the horizon. But I don't think that's the case here," Falconer explained.

"And why not?"

Falconer pointed at the massive waves, turned to brilliant silver by the sun. "Inside the eye, the water and the wind both come from all sides. The waves go into a madness. There is no other word for it. Peaks hit both gunnels at the same time. The ship bobs like a cork."

"So you think we've emerged from the storm's far edge."

"The clouds are receding behind us, the wind is gradually shifting to the rear quarter, the waves are half a turn behind them." Falconer nodded. "Aye, Captain. I'd say we have survived the beast's attack."

"For the sake of my ship and my crew, sir, I hope and pray you are right."

"As do I, sir. May I say, Captain, that there could well be more tempests."

"Aye, I've heard that as well, how hurricanes spawn smaller storms."

"They'll sweep out of nowhere," Falconer said. "They will blow hard, pound us with more rain, and disappear."

"The warning is well taken, sir. I'll thank you to resume your post at the wheel."

"Permission to see to my boy, Captain."

"Not just yet, I would beg you. Your strength is still required on deck, sir." Harkness raised his voice. "Bosun!"

"Aye, sir!"

"Tell Cook to fire up the stoves. One watch to stand down but remain on deck. Another to tend the debris. A third to straighten the rigging. Send someone to check on the boy and report back to John Falconer. And send your best man aloft with a glass to eye the horizon. 'Ware more storms!"

Chapter 7

The crew battled their way through two further blows, both arriving with scarce more warning than the hurricane. But now the men were ready. The daylight helped enormously. The ship remained as battened down as the crew could make it. From his station at the wheel, Falconer watched with more moderate unease as both storms grew from black lines upon the horizon to thunderous onslaughts of wind and rain. The rigging shrieked, the rain lashed, the waves tore themselves to shreds. Then the blow passed, daylight returned, and the ship righted itself to less heart-stopping motion. The seas did not return to calm, but the waves were more regular in their ponderous rhythm.

Two hours after the second blow faded, Captain Harkness ordered the watch on duty to stand down. The helmsman lashed alongside Falconer had to be helped belowdecks by two of his mates. Falconer patted the wheel twice, a silent tribute to a trim and trustworthy vessel. When he turned away, he saw that Harkness was watching. Though the captain made no sign, Falconer sensed the captain approved.

When the captain dismissed him, Falconer did not rush belowdecks so much as stagger from wall to wall, allowing the ship's roll to carry him forward. Overhead he heard crewmen hammering out the chocks and granting air to the unfortunate passengers within the fetid holds.

When Falconer arrived at his cabin door, he was greeted by the sound of singing.

"Father John!" The lad leapt from his bed and bounded across the cabin. "Father John!"

"My boy." Falconer lifted the lad and embraced him with all the force he had left in his spent form. "My dear boy."

When Matt's feet returned to the floor, he refused to release Falconer's hand. "Master Soap has been teaching me sea chanteys!"

"He's bright as a new penny, is your lad. And brave as they come." Soap accepted Falconer's hand with a large gap-toothed grin. "Ever so glad to be seeing yourself alive and well, Falconer."

"I am forever in your debt, my man."

"None of that. I was just doing the captain's bidding, as would any able seaman."

"I've been teaching Soap our hymns, Father John!"

"Never thought I'd see the like," Soap said, "a young lad on his first sea voyage, in the belly of a storm as vicious as ever I've seen. And what does he do but sing!"

"God was with us. Isn't that so, Father John?"

"Aye, lad. No question of that." Falconer did not so much lower himself onto his bunk as collapse. Now that his boy was safe there beside him, he could no longer contain the rising fatigue. It came at him in waves as huge as those beyond the portal. He could barely move his lips to murmur to Soap, "It does my heart good to know you were here with the boy."

"A joy, sir, and that's the truth." The grin seemed planted in place. "So we've survived the blow. Had me worried there, I don't mind saying."

"Aye." Falconer did not wish to say more, both because his mouth felt gummed with weariness and because the boy was within earshot. "Help me with my boots . . . that's a good lad."

Matt took hold of one foot and then the other, making a game of pulling off Falconer's sodden boots. Falconer protested mildly but let Soap unwrap his bandaged hand. The steward probed the skin. "Rope burn, by the looks of things. I've seen worse. I'll just go ask Cook for some grease and we'll wrap that proper."

Matt asked, "Shall I sing you a chantey, Father John?"

"That would be fine, lad." Falconer lifted his legs one by one onto the mattress. He smiled briefly at his son and was asleep before he'd drawn a second breath.

The lieutenant himself came to escort them to dinner. "Captain's compliments, sir. He requests your presence in the cuddy."

Soap had already informed Falconer of the captain's intention to invite them to dine with the ship's officers. Falconer had bathed off the crust of salt, washed his hair for the first time since coming on board, and helped Matt don clean clothes. He was in the process of tying his hair back with a bit of blue ribbon supplied by Soap when the lieutenant appeared in the doorway.

Falconer eyed the young man's tightly wrapped shoulder. "How is the injury?"

"Harkness is a fair hand with shipboard ailments—better than most navy surgeons. He's certain there's no break, sir. Claims by landfall I'll be using it again." Bivens glanced at Matt, then added, "You saved my life out there, sir. I'm forever in your debt."

"Shipmates who survive such a storm are not bound by obligations, Lieutenant."

"This one is, and I'd be ever so grateful if you'd call me Rupert."

"My own first name is John, though it is seldom used. You may join my friends in calling me Falconer."

Soap, standing against the cabin wall to make as much room for Falconer's girth as possible, said to Matt, "The entire ship's crew is talking of nothing but how your da saved both their senior officers."

Falconer felt his face grow warm. "None of that now, please."

"Won't do you no good to complain, sir. The crew counts Harkness as a hard but fair man. And Lieutenant Bivens here is a favorite belowdecks. They saw what you did, and they are grateful for the deeds."

Matt's eyes were round and wide. "Are you a hero, Father John?"

The lieutenant replied somberly, "He is in my book, young lad."

Falconer cleared his throat and ruffled Matt's hair. "We shouldn't keep the captain waiting."

"Ah, Falconer. Do come in, though with your bulk we'll scarce have room to breathe." But his welcoming smile belied the words. "And, young lad, how shall I call you?"

"My name is Matthew, sir. I'm Matt Hart."

The captain took his time over the lad, which raised him further in Falconer's estimation. "You do not share your father's name?" he asked, bending down to Matt's level.

"My first father was named Hart, sir. Father John says I should honor his memory with how I am called. And my mother too, of course."

"God keep her blessed soul in eternal peace," Soap intoned, his expression and raised eyebrows sending his meaning.

"Of course. Of course." The captain's gaze was thoughtful as he patted Matt's shoulder. "My steward informs me you survived the storms with your courage intact."

"And his voice," Soap added. "I almost forgot the blow, he sang so sweet."

"Then perhaps you will honor us with a song later."

Matt cast a glance at Falconer, who nodded. "If you wish it, sir."

"Always did enjoy a tune following supper. Do you know hymns?"

"Oh yes, sir. Back in Salem town I sing with the unmarried men's choir."

"How very interesting. Every one of your answers provides another door I'm eager to enter." He straightened and turned to Falconer. "But first there are several matters regarding your father to which I must attend."

Falconer started to object, foreseeing the direction the conversation might take. But at that moment, Lieutenant Bivens managed to catch his eye from his station directly behind the captain. Bivens shot him a warning glance and gave his head a fractional nod.

Falconer held his peace.

Harkness came to attention before Falconer and spoke with somber formality. "Before setting sail I greeted you with less than proper hospitality. You responded with honor. Twice in the night watch I appeared on deck to find you there first, alert as any officer I've ever served with. You were first to sight the coming storm. In so doing, you may well have saved the ship and all who sail her, including the company's owner."

From his place by the rear window, Reginald Langston said, "Here, here."

"Were that not enough," Harkness continued, "you added your own considerable strength to steering our ship through what was the worst blow I have ever encountered. You saved the life of my trusted first lieutenant. You risked your own life in doing so, and then again when you went for the lieutenant's blade and helped free us of the trapped rigging. And finally, you saved my own life."

Falconer felt awkward, both from the compliments and the need to remain silent. Not to mention the fact that Matt was watching him with a face glowing with love and pride.

Harkness paused for breath. "John Falconer, I must apologize for my response to your presence on board. And I salute you as a fellow officer. One of merit. One worthy of both praise and trust."

As the surrounding company applauded, Harkness bowed low, and Falconer returned the courtesy. He was most grateful when the captain turned to the group and announced, "Gentlemen, our meal awaits."

There was smoked fish to start, with real oat bread and cheese sliced so thin it might have been mistaken for butter. This was followed by a leg of goat boiled to submission and spiced with cloves and pepper. For dessert they enjoyed fresh orange slices nearly drowned in syrup. Matt's three portions left him so overfull that when the captain asked him to sing, he piped the words like a leaky calliope.

But the ship's company smiled him through, then bade him a warm good-night as his eyelids drooped upon what had been a truly momentous day.

Harkness bade Falconer remain as Soap steered the lad back to the cabin. He then suggested the other officers retire, all but Bivens, saying their watch would soon begin and they needed their rest. When the door shut behind them, the captain said, "What a truly remarkable young lad you have there."

"His voice is far more winsome than what you heard tonight, sir."

"No doubt, no doubt." But the captain had no continuing interest in such things. "One storm is behind us, another ahead. I would be amiss in denying that I had hoped to lead the charge to rescue Mistress Lillian's son."

Falconer glanced at Reginald, who had remained strangely silent throughout dinner. "I could not possibly object if you insisted, sir."

Harkness fiddled with his dessert spoon. "I awoke this evening to a realization, sir, one that came to me as a prayer gifted from beyond myself. Do you know of what I speak?"

"I have on occasion sensed prayers spoken through me," Falconer told him. "I count them as a true gift."

"Just so. In this case, I saw how you had saved me and my ship by your strength, your experience, and your selfless acts. You were the one who had the knowledge I lacked." Harkness had eyebrows that protruded like gray feathers above an intense gaze. "No doubt you also have familiarity with such pirates as Ali Saleem."

"To my great shame," Falconer agreed, his voice low.

"The Lord of heaven makes good from the worst we carry, if we only seek His will. And I feel the best that can come of my foul greeting is to accept your leadership in what lies ahead."

"I am honored by your trust, sir."

Harkness motioned to where the lieutenant occupied the table's far side. "Young Bivens is more than a fine officer. He is my protégé. I would suggest you trust him as do I."

Falconer nodded in the young officer's direction. "Thank you. Yes, of course."

A communal peace settled upon the four men—Falconer, Harkness, Bivens, and Reginald Langston. Two silver candelabra bathed the cabin in a warm glow. The cuddy, the ship's dining area, was an alcove off the captain's day cabin. The plank flooring was covered in stiff canvas painted a pattern of white and black squares. The wood of the walls gleamed richly in the candlelight, as did the furniture—a table strewn with maps and instruments, a leather sofa, a revolving tray crammed with books, a violin case, a master's chair. Two lanterns swung gently with the ocean's rise and fall. Beyond the rear windows glinted a moonlit sea.

Reginald Langston cleared his throat and spoke at length for the first time that night. "I have a confession of my own to make. When Falconer first determined to eat with the crew and steerage, I intended to confront Captain Harkness and order him to invite Falconer immediately. But there came to me an inner warning as clear as the prayers you describe. So I held back, instead delivering the message as Falconer had wished. When the captain simply accepted Falconer's desire . . ."

"As odious a deed as any I have committed." Harkness's voice was low as he stared into the candlelight.

But Reginald waved it impatiently away. "That is behind us now. The apology has been offered and accepted. I bid you good gentlemen to heed my words.

When you responded as you did, sir, I again started to issue an order of my own. Once more I felt the divine warning, and remained silent."

Reginald peered across the gleaming light at Falconer. "The Bible speaks of David's three mighty men. His most trusted officers, who risked their lives to bring him a gift of water in the desert. I now can see that Falconer's deed has drawn you together into more than just three fine officers. You are a powerful band." Reginald nodded slowly. "Whatever happens, I know with utter certainty that I am gifted with the finest and most trustworthy force available to me on this earth."

Harkness let that settle for a long moment, then turned to Falconer. "Perhaps you would be kind enough to close the evening in prayer."

Falconer leaned over his hands. He stared at the fresh linen bandage wrapped around his right palm. Another scar to add to his vast assortment. But never for a finer reason than this. He closed his eyes.

"O Lord, our God, we give you thanks . . ."

At that point, his throat and chest clenched up tight. He could not continue. He bowed further still, until his forehead came to rest upon his hands.

It was the first time since Ada Hart had become ill that he had said those words. Thanks be to God. Spoken them, and meant them as well.

He had not wept at her passage. He had not wept at her funeral. Now, as he crushed his forehead into his hands, he felt his face scalded by the rush of tears.

The silence held a good while. Finally Harkness thumped the table with both fists. "As fine a prayer as any I have ever heard. What more do we need to hear tonight than thanks?"

"Amen," Reginald Langston intoned, his voice shaky and tight. "I say again. Amen."

Chapter 8

They made landfall at Portsmouth in southern England on a Wednesday. The very same storm that had threatened their survival also shortened the standard journey by six full days, for a solid wind had stayed off their beam the entire voyage. Seventeen days from Chesapeake Bay to England, a time that missed the record by less than thirty-six hours. The pilot who took charge of their final sail into port insisted upon seeing their master documents from the American docks before believing them, then took it upon himself to trumpet the news. Harkness was the toast of the harbor.

He and Lieutenant Bivens remained in Portsmouth while Reginald arranged a swift carriage to London. A new train line was being laid from London to Brighton and then on alongside the coastal road. But it had not yet been completed as far as the port, and Falconer still held serious reservations over the safety of trains. After surviving such an Atlantic storm, he did not wish to lose his boy to a metal beast that ate coal and belched fire and black smoke.

Falconer feared London would be full of painful reminiscences. He had not yet even met Ada when he had resided there with the late William Wilberforce and his young staff. Still, any glance into his past risked raking his heart over the burning coals of regret, sorrow, and lost love. However, he scarcely had time to remember much of anything, for they remained in London only seventy-two hours.

They stayed in the Aldridge residence bordering Grosvenor Square. Samuel Aldridge, who formerly served as a high-ranking diplomat to the court of Saint James, was now Reginald Langston's partner overseeing their European affairs. The two dinners in the Aldridge home were long and crowded affairs, with as many as twenty guests filling the dining hall and cramming the long table to overflowing. Erica Powers, Reginald's sister and wife of the famous pamphleteer Gareth Powers, was in constant attendance. Their entourage filled two entire carriages as they made their way to a variety of official meetings. Though everything was arranged in great haste, seldom were they refused entry. Such was the combined influence of these friends and allies.

They stopped by Bond Street and bought clothes off the rack for Falconer and his lad. They attended a session of Parliament. They met with both the French ambassador and the Spanish, as these nations' Africa holdings were rumored to harbor pirates. They were granted letters of introduction and letters of marque. The documents were signed with great flourishes, dripped with sealing wax, stamped with gold seals of office, and affixed with flowing royal ribbons. Both ambassadors were well aware of the Langston family's power.

Everywhere they went, Matt Hart was agog. He had never seen a big city before. Never seen such grand buildings. Never entered an official residence. Never seen Parliament or a palace or even a museum. The Powers' daughter, Hannah, slipped away from her private school for the first dinner. She and Falconer had become the best

of friends during his first foray in England. She was growing into a young woman whose beauty mirrored her
mother's. Matt fell head over heels in love and later
mourned her departure for two whole hours.

Falconer took time out the second afternoon to go
exploring with Matt. They took in the British Museum
and the royal Portrait Gallery. They walked along the Ser-
pentine and tossed bread to well-fed swans, all of which
were owned by the king. They squandered an hour in a
theater which Mrs. Aldridge had assured Falconer was safe
and appropriate for children. Matt shouted his delight,
while Falconer enjoyed the child's amusement far more
than what occurred upon the stage. They dined at the
famous chop house on Fleet Street, where Falconer paid
extra for the table by the upstairs window, from which
they could watch young runners carry sheets of wet type-
face from the journalists to the printing shops. Matt was so
enthused by it all that he scarcely blinked. He kept a two-
fisted hold on the carriage window the entire way home.
But when the carriage turned back into Grosvenor Square,
he promptly fell asleep. Falconer easily carried him upstairs
and put him to bed.

At dawn the next morning, they were off again for
Portsmouth.

They ate an early meal from hampers supplied by Lav-
inia Aldridge and Erica Powers. Gareth Powers, a former
army officer, had desperately wanted to join them on their
rescue mission. But his pamphleteering efforts, raising
public awareness of slavery's inhumanity, had grown into a
daily newspaper, one with a national readership. He chafed
at his desk and complained loudly at the unrelenting
responsibilities, even though all could see he was a man
born to the task.

Portsmouth lay at the base of the South Downs, a series of steep hills that rose a few miles inland. The air was clear the morning of their return, the fields emerald and afire with spring blossoms, the sunlight gentle in a very English manner. Church spires and ships' masts heralded their arrival. And beyond the harbor's rocky arms, beyond the lighthouse and the harbor fort, the sea beckoned.

When they arrived alongside the ship, a thoroughly unexpected scene came into view. The midshipman assigned duty at the top of the gangway was stubbornly refusing entry to a very agitated woman. The middy stood with the sullen frown of a young man whose temper was held in check only because he was so ordered. The woman's voice carried down the plank walkway and about the stone jetty. Crewmen wrestling hogsheads of fresh produce cast wry grins in the direction of the middy. Falconer did not need to hear their chuckled comments to know they were very glad not to be on the receiving end of this tirade.

"Make way, I pray, madam." The middy did his best to motion the woman aside. "Officers coming aboard."

"I will do no such thing." She wore such a tangled assortment of garments it was hard to judge her stature or her age. A dress, frayed and stained, was topped by unkempt red hair spilling in a tousled mass from beneath a bedraggled hat. Her shoulders were wrapped in a shawl as discolored as a captain's sea coat. Her face was so tanned she might have been mistaken for an Arab or Indian, save for her hair, voice, and eyes. When Falconer grew near, he thought they were the lightest blue he had ever seen, a color one shade off the sky at high noon.

And she was very angry. "There is not one soul upon this earth who has a more vital business on this vessel than I!"

Not even the day's urgency to launch could keep Reginald Langston from offering her a courteous greeting. "Madam, I beg your forgiveness. Might I ask your name?"

"She won't say, sir," the middy replied. "Which is half the problem."

"My name is my own, and my business is with the captain!"

"He's been sent for, sir," the middy added. "But he's been tied up with the chandlers since dawn."

"Then I *insist* upon waiting in his quarters," she announced in tones boding no argument.

"Madam," Reginald said soothingly, "I fear that is impossible."

"By whose orders?"

"My own. No women except passengers are allowed on board one of my vessels. You must understand—" Reginald stopped because the woman's mouth had fallen open.

She faltered momentarily, her face pale. "You are Master Langston?"

"I am."

"Your wife, she is the former countess, mother to the young man named Byron?"

It was Reginald's turn to grow ashen. "Who are you, madam?"

"Thank God, oh, thank the Lord." Her strength dissipated with her ire, such that only the railing kept her from collapsing to the gangway flooring. "I am Amelia Henning."

"Ma'am, forgive me, but your name—"

"I was the first to bring word of your stepson's abduction."

Reginald struggled to shape the words. "You have seen him?"

"I have." All vestige of strength had evaporated with her anger. "Forgive me, sir. Might I sit? I am feeling quite faint."

"I have spent four months fighting against an uncaring, unlistening world." Amelia Henning's trembling fingers held fragments of the bread and cheese supplied by Soap. "I have been living at the seaman's mission run by my husband's church. I have spent days seeking aid from the navy and the government. All to no avail."

"Samuel told me . . . That is, Samuel Aldridge, my friend and partner. He informed me that the messenger— who turns out to be you—had simply vanished."

"It was a mistake. I see that now. But your man insisted upon taking such a measured course. And his constant questions nearly drove me insane."

Which was how she looked to Falconer's eye. A woman on the border of insanity. Her movements were jerky. Beneath that ragged hat, her face was blistered with sun and taut with hunger and nerves. Yet through all the disarray, she was an uncommonly attractive woman, in a rather half-starved and desperate fashion. Amelia Henning sipped from her cup, rattling it against the saucer when she set it down, then turned back to the plate of bread and cheese.

"I could not wait. Not for an instant. And Mr. Aldridge insisted upon doing nothing until you arrived from America. You or your trusted man." But she did not say this in other than a matter-of-fact tone.

Reginald had adopted a pose of utter patience. He nodded in agreement at everything the woman said and spoke to her as he would a woman of position. "I apologize most profusely, madam. But Samuel merely acted as I had requested. We had received so many frustrating reports, you see. One after the other proved false. People who had heard of our son's disappearance sought to profit from it."

"Do I seem to you a woman after gain?"

"No, madam. Nothing could be further from the truth I see before me and hear from your lips."

"Yet your Mr. Aldridge peppered me with his questions and offered no help at all!"

"Again, my sincerest regrets over any distress he might have caused. Won't you have more cheese?"

"I am rather famished." She could scarcely lift the fragments of bread to her mouth. She ate a bite, then a crumbled segment of cheese, then took a tiny sip from the cup. Her gaze was never still.

Footsteps rumbled down the outside passage. Harkness and Lieutenant Bivens entered the cabin, then crowded to a halt. "What's this?"

"Captain Harkness, may I have the pleasure of introducing Amelia Henning. We were just having a most remarkable conversation. Mrs. Henning, would you mind terribly if they joined us?"

"Of course not." Her voice was both weary and petulant. "Why should I, since I've spent the entire day trying to meet him?"

"Of course. Most foolish of me."

Falconer sensed a sudden chill race up his spine. All of a sudden, the entire situation came into brilliant focus. Eyeing the sun through a telescope could not have been more shocking.

He interrupted the introductions. "Mrs. Henning, may I ask why you did not tell Samuel Aldridge all that you know of this situation?"

The hand rose and fell, a bit of bread, a sliver of cheese. "And you are?"

"My name is John Falconer. I am Reginald Langston's trusted man. We have known one another for years, and I can assure you, whatever Master Langston says is far more trustworthy than most men's gold locked in a steel vault."

"I will testify to that as well," Captain Harkness said.

Falconer leaned forward in his chair. He could not say why, but he was certain enough to speak his thoughts aloud. "Madam, forgive me for saying this. But I fear you and I suffer from the same malady."

The hand stopped in midair.

"We have both suffered a grievous loss, is that not true?"

The hand began to tremble more violently.

"I mean something beyond the death of your husband. This Ali Saleem. He took someone dear to you."

She whispered, "His men attacked the village where I carried on my late husband's mission."

Falconer lowered his voice to a murmur. "There is something more, I believe. Something you have kept hidden away. It tears at you, though. I know, Mrs. Henning. I know because I have been there myself."

A tear coursed down the sun-blistered cheek. "He has my daughter. If she is still . . ."

Falconer reached across the impossible distance and caught her hand with his own. "We shall pray with you, madam. And if we can, with God's help we will see the two of you reunited."

"Amen," Reginald echoed.

But the words merely drove the woman to straighten her spine. She spoke to Falconer directly. "I am after more than comforting words, sir."

Falconer felt the bond between them, of loss and the drive to overcome sorrow for another's sake. He searched the woman's narrow features and decided. "You wish to come with us to Africa?"

"I insist upon it." At this she turned and stared meaningfully at the captain, as fierce a challenge as Falconer had ever seen.

Harkness began a rumbled reply, but his protest was never fully formed. Out of the corner of his eye, Falconer saw Reginald Langston abruptly signal to the skipper and then say, "Proof, Mrs. Henning. It is a terrible word, and I am certain it has caused you offense. But we have received so very many false reports, I have no choice but to ask if you have any to offer."

"Your stepson carries a scar on the inside of his left forearm."

Reginald's voice quavered slightly as he asked, "Did Byron happen to mention how he received it?"

"He spoke of climbing out of a dormitory window his last year at Eton."

"It is he," Reginald whispered. He sank into the seat next to Falconer. "How did he appear to you?"

"Terrified," the woman replied curtly. "Exhausted. He was kept in Ali Saleem's underground dungeon, with no glimmer of daylight and very little air."

"Did he say anything that I might pass on to his mother?"

A flicker of compassion registered deep in the widow's shattered gaze. "Only that he was sorry. That he begged her forgiveness. And beseeched God and your good self not to leave him to rot away without light or hope."

Reginald covered his eyes and spoke no more.

Falconer took over once more. "So Ali Saleem showed you Byron."

"One of his captains did. I never set eyes upon the pirate prince." The words came with a force shocking to her hearers. "The captain himself hauled me into the dungeon. He said my daughter would live if I delivered the message. And if you brought gold."

"This much you told Samuel Aldridge," Falconer said, speaking low and calm. "This captain, did you catch his—"

"Yes, I told Mr. Aldridge. But I saw what was behind his questions." Despite Falconer's soothing strength, her voice rose once more to a frantic pitch. "He was going to take all that I knew and then leave me to wait in England! He would not promise to give me a berth! And I will *not* wait here a thousand leagues from my daughter! Catherine—" her voice broke—"is all I have left in the world! Do you hear me, sirs? I will *not be left behind!*"

Chapter 9

They sailed the next morning with the outgoing tide. Captain Harkness made no further objections to Amelia Henning's presence, and the crew said nothing directly to the officers about it. But Falconer's years of experience belowdecks aided his interpretation of the mutterings and the scowls he heard and saw. Not all of the sailors were men of faith, and some of those who were still had not fully cast off common seamen's superstitions. Falconer caught the men's grim predictions that a woman who was not an official passenger would only bring them all bad luck.

Yet their sailing could not have been finer. The skies remained clear and the wind fair, a steady blow from the east that powered them southward across gently rolling seas. By their second evening on board, they had passed the Channel Islands and entered the deep waters marking the Bay of Biscay.

Captain Harkness and Lieutenant Bivens included Matt in their sailing instructions as they did the middies. They taught about charts and compass bearings, and they let him sight the sun through the sextant. He held the captain's chronometer when a crewman cast the log along the leeward side to measure the ship's speed. Falconer watched with pride as Matt counted the knots in the log rope, halting when the clock's second hand swept through the minute and then correctly reporting the ship's speed to the captain. Falconer observed how Harkness played stern but fair when Matt mangled the finicky calculations to determine precisely where the ship lay. The boy grew strong, sun-browned, and fit, and though he scarcely ever smiled, he drew pleased grins from the toughest of sailors.

Amelia Henning sat upon a poop-deck chair, one lashed to the railing alongside the water barrels. She carried a book of psalms in her dress pocket and often drew it out. Although she seemed to ignore the crewmen, Falconer was certain she was aware of their hostility. Whenever Reginald or Captain Harkness addressed her, she responded fully. Now that she was shipboard and headed toward the Mediterranean and her captured child, she gave freely of what information she had.

Whenever the men stepped away, the woman stared to the south, peering over the waters at a daughter only she could see.

The person who was able to reach her was Matt. They took to reading a psalm together each morning. The two heads, one red haired and gaunt, the other towheaded and lively of countenance, squinted against the brilliant sun and traded verses. Since Matt had become a favorite among the seamen, his growing closeness to Amelia Henning gradually erased the sailors' grumbling more than anything the captain might say.

Falconer was watching the two of them study the Book when Harkness invited him onto the quarterdeck, the captain's private domain. "What can you tell me of these pirates, Falconer?"

Reginald moved forward at a beckon from the captain. The owner had legal right to any place on the ship, but a happy crew was one where customs were maintained. And an owner could not sail the ship. Reginald Langston was a man who chose his skippers carefully, then was himself careful to treat them as leaders in their own right. He did not enter the captain's bailiwick unless invited.

When Reginald had joined them, Falconer replied, "I have not fought these particular Barbary louts myself, so everything I know about them is hearsay."

"Forget that for the moment. I too have heard of them for years. What I want to know is the general cut of a pirate's jib. You have gone up against pirates, I suppose."

"On three occasions. Once off the Malacca Strait. Twice in the Indian Ocean."

Falconer found himself distracted by the sound of Matt's voice and glanced to the lower deck. Matt stood like he'd been born to the sea, legs well spaced and his body rocking easily to the ship's motion. He stood beside Amelia Henning's chair and sang. Falconer recognized the hymn as a favorite of Ada's. A number of the sailors had turned from their duties to observe the boy and hear a voice as clear as the sea air.

"I am waiting, sir." But Harkness did not sound impatient.

Falconer turned back to the skipper. "They are brutal fighters and show no quarter. But they lack discipline. They are raiders. They prey on weakness. They fear a stronger foe."

Harkness gripped the lapel of his greatcoat and tugged. "And this captain the woman mentioned, what is his name?"

"La Rue. Philippe La Rue."

Reginald asked, "Is that an African name?"

"More likely French."

Reginald was shocked. "In this day and age a citizen of

a civilized country would become a pirate?"

Harkness replied, "I have even heard of Americans among the Caribbean raiders."

Falconer added, "The French have a division of their army which is open to anyone. Prisoners, deserters, men of any stripe or nation. The foreign legion, it is called. A brutal force, with the harshest discipline on earth. Many who survive it become mercenaries."

Harkness tugged harder upon his lapel, the act of a fighter impatient for action. "How, pray tell me, would you go about this maneuver?"

"We first must stop in Marseilles," Falconer explained, glad to be discussing plans. "Make it known who we are and why we are there. An agent for the pirates will contact us."

"How can you be so sure?" Reginald demanded.

"An agent will seek us out," Falconer repeated. "And then they will test our mettle."

"What, you mean attack?"

"Seek to steal our gold. Perhaps seize some of us for ransom."

Reginald cast an anxious look from one man to the other. "What are we to do?"

"That is simple enough," Harkness replied, his gaze steady upon Falconer. "We prepare."

The third evening after leaving Portsmouth, they dined as usual in the captain's cuddy. Harkness had invited Amelia Henning to join them, but she had politely declined. The officers were well aware of Matt's presence at the table, and they tempered their discussions about what lay ahead. After a dessert of green English apples and fresh figs, early fruits gathered in the Portsmouth market, a subtle shift in the wind caused Harkness to rise and move to his doorway. He returned a moment later and sat back down in his chair with a nod to Bivens that all was well. But his mind seemed to be elsewhere, such that he said to no one in particular, "Late in yesterday's night watch, I heard weeping from the lady's cabin."

To their surprise, Matt spoke up for the first time during the meal. "She fears for Kitty, sir."

"Who?"

"Her daughter, Captain Harkness."

"I thought the lass was named Catherine."

"She has been known as Kitty since birth, sir. She had a habit of mewing like a newborn cat that charmed everyone who heard her."

"Did she indeed." Harkness pushed his dessert plate to one side and rested his elbows upon the linen tablecloth. "What else did you learn?"

Matt finished chewing his bite, then said, "They were missionaries to a tribe south of a desert they called something like the Great Burn. The tribe worshiped all manner of things. The Earth, the sky, the sun, the clouds, certain trees. Reverend Henning and Mrs. Henning told this tribe about the true God. About His son Jesus Christ."

Falconer watched in new amazement at his son's confidence, poise, and insight. He knew Ada had spent many hours reading with Matt, which practice Falconer had carried on when possible. But this maturity went far beyond those books and discussion of ideas.

Harkness did not respond immediately but settled his chin upon his fists, mashing his lower face into a massive scowl of concentration. "How long were they there?" he asked finally.

"Five years, sir. I believe she said Kitty was four when they arrived in Africa. Then the good reverend caught a fever. After he died, Mrs. Henning decided to stay on and continue her husband's work."

"So this makes the daughter about nine now. What more can you tell us?"

Matt put down his fork and folded his hands on the table. His hair was burnished by the candlelight. His cheeks and forehead were chafed in places by the sea and sun. His eyes were clear and as somber as his tone. "To the north and west was another tribe. They were Muslims and herders. They coveted the wells of the tribe where the Hennings made their home. One day they swept in at sunrise. They overran the tribe's defenses and carried them away. They all marched across the desert for seventeen days. The elderly and the weak did not survive."

Harkness cast a single glance at Falconer. The captain's query was clear. Falconer resisted his first impulse, which was to tell the boy he should stop speaking of such terrible events. He said softly, "They sold them to slavers."

"Yes, Father John. In the port where the pirate captain lives."

Falconer looked at the upturned face for a moment. "I would rather the lady had not spoken to you about such things."

Matt's gaze was steady. "It made her feel better to speak the words aloud, sir. She told me so. Afterward we prayed for her daughter. I prayed for her peace. I said God had reached into my heart and offered peace. Even when I miss Mama the most, I know God is with me. I know this. She said that offered her more hope than anything she had known in all the weeks since Kitty was taken."

Several of the men around the table found it necessary to clear their throats. Falconer among them. Harkness said gruffly, "And what a good lad you were to try and comfort her."

Falconer felt his own heart swell with love. "You're a

long way from Salem town, my boy."

Matt must have understood what Falconer meant. "All my life, I heard Papa Brune and other elders speak about the evils of the outside world. And how we are to be a people set apart for God. But the world comes in anyway, Father John. We help slaves to freedom. The elders, they worry about what the Carolina government will do about us and our way of life. They think the children don't understand what they say, but we do."

One of the officers scraped his chair, pushing back from the table. The lantern squeaked softly as it rolled with the sea. A beam creaked. Overhead the ship's bell clanged the hour. Otherwise the cabin was utterly silent. Behind Matt, the steward and a crewman acting as his second had stepped through the open doorway to listen.

Matt went on, "The world enters in, Father John. And so does evil. Being inside Salem did not keep me from losing my father and my mother."

Falconer said softly, "You have given this much thought."

"I want to be a man of God, just like you, Father John. But I don't know if I want to be that man back in Salem town."

"It is your home, lad."

"It was Mama's home," Matt corrected. The unspoken sadness almost made him chant the words. "I don't know where my home is yet. I pray to God for guidance. I pray that He will be with me each day, wherever my home is."

"Oh, yes indeed, well said." Harkness lifted his chin so that he could use one fist to lightly thump the table. "What a wise and brave lad you are."

"I have a boy of three," Lieutenant Bivens said. "I can

only hope and pray he grows into a person with your share of wisdom and faith."

Falconer waited until the burning in his chest and eyes faded a trifle, then said, "I feel certain our God will answer your prayers."

Chapter 10

Lieutenant Bivens took to practicing swordplay with the midshipmen to restore his injured arm. He held a heavier cutlass in his weakened left hand, and the middies used smaller rapiers, their blades so thin they whipped like springs. Even so, Bivens grimaced as their blows landed upon his own blade. Falconer heard the clash of steel upon steel ring like a call of former days. Matt watched the middies and the sweating lieutenant, but did not join in. When not involved in his lessons of seamanship, he continued to remain near Mrs. Henning, reading to her from the lady's book of psalms and singing the occasional hymn.

During their journey south along the coast of Portugal, Reginald Langston spent a good deal of time in his cabin, working through a box of papers he had collected from his London offices, reading from the Good Book, or resting in his bunk. He confessed to Falconer that the journey was a healing balm, as he gradually set aside the tensions and cares that had been building over recent months. He shared this news almost diffidently with Falconer. The journey had forced Reginald to accept how little control he had over events and timing. He was learning to release his tomorrows to God, and in so doing was sleeping better than he had in half a year.

The wind remained favorable, and squalls were few. On the sixth morning they came in sight of the cliffs that marked southernmost Portugal and the end of the Iberian Peninsula. The captain ordered the men aloft and turned the ship eastward on a heading for the Strait of Gibraltar.

Captain Harkness had assigned Matt duty with the middle watch, treating the lad as just another middy in every manner save pistolry and swordsmanship with Bivens. In these the captain silently accepted Falconer's lead and allowed the boy to chart his own course. That particular day, as the ship swooped through the course change, the wind shifted with them.

Bivens noticed it as well. He lowered the musket he was priming and called over the cluster of midshipmen up to the quarterdeck. "Wind has gone ten degrees to the north, Captain!"

"Bosun, pipe the watch aloft!"

Falconer did not say a word as Matt scrambled up the ropes with the other two middies of that watch. But his heart constricted as he looked aloft. He knew full well that the higher up the masts they went, the more every motion of the ship was magnified. On numerous occasions Matt had been as far as the maintop, a platform and staging area where the lower mast was joined to the upper. The upper one was a single seasoned tree trunk, usually pine. The lower masts were formed by several trunks bound together with iron bands. This time Matt gripped the main shrouds and clambered higher. These shrouds were heavily tarred, which added strength to the ropes and also granted the seamen a better grip. In many cases the boys clung to the shrouds by their knees while using both hands to manage the sails.

The two middies and Matt, however, were stationed where guide ropes, known as ratlines, connected to the mast. A second circular station was set there for the watch-men. The middies were supposedly sent aloft to direct the topmen, but these sailors knew far more about setting sails than any young midshipman. In truth, the middies were there to learn the ship—bow chaser to stern anchor and every rigging in between.

A voice spoke softly to Falconer's left, "It appears a ter-rifying height from here."

Falconer nodded in a brief salute to Amelia Henning, then returned his attention to the small figure above. "It is far more frightening up there."

"Does your son know fear?"

He glanced down once more. "Ma'am?"

"Oh, it is a silly question. But he is so remarkably calm. I know he is just a lad, yet I feel able to talk with him of nearly anything that comes to heart and mind." Her focus followed Falconer's to where Matt clung to a ratline, stand-ing upon a perch that looked smaller than a halfpenny. "How will he get down?"

"That is part of the test. If he still has strength in his limbs, he will go out the crosstie and come down the outer sheet."

"Test?"

"It's part of a midshipman's training, ma'am. Learning to maintain one's strength and courage where there is both risk and danger."

"Oh, there they go." Her voice raised an octave. "He looks so awfully small."

Indeed he did, a blond-headed waif perched impossibly high, two full sails above the deck, upon a tossing sea. Matt followed one of the topmen out along the wooden boom, another middy behind him. They were all barefoot. The topman was an experienced mate. Falconer could see the sailor smile reassuringly as he talked the middies out to the crosstie's narrow end. There the topman clambered onto the rope ladder, scarcely as wide as Falconer's thigh. He climbed up higher, so that the middies moved onto the ladder with him holding the upper ratline and keeping it stable. As stable as any rope ladder could be, high above a wave-tossed deck, with three bodies moving slowly earth-ward.

Falconer resisted the urge to race over and steady the ladder. He had been tested in the very same manner, and knew the lad had to make it on his own. But Falconer remained so tightly poised to spring if the lad's grip slipped that he could not breathe.

His chest did not unlock until Matt's feet touched the deck. Harkness had obviously felt the strain as well, for when the second middy stepped from the ladder the skipper's voice cracked slightly as he called down, "Well done, the pair of you! Ye'll be old salts before you know it."

Falconer pressed a fist to his chest, forcing his lungs to drink in a breath. His heart thudded as loud as a hammer on teak.

Mrs. Henning sighed audibly. "I admire your calm, sir."

"On the contrary, ma'am." Falconer found it necessary to lean against the railing. "I was merely frozen solid with fear."

Matt did not skip across the deck, though he might as well have. "I was high as a mountaintop, Father John!"

"Indeed you were." Once more Falconer resisted his urge to wrap his arms around the boy. "Yes, indeed," he said again. "I couldn't have done better myself."

Matt took hold of Falconer's hand, and Falconer could feel the gummy tar upon the lad's fingers. Matt craned up and traced the line he had just taken. "I was so afraid, Father John. I prayed ever so hard."

"Courage comes from acting in the face of fear, lad."

Matt kept his gaze upon the rigging overhead. "I have been very afraid for so long, Father John."

"Of what?"

Matt shrugged. "I did not even know—didn't know it was fear until just now. Is that strange?"

This time, Falconer gave in to his impulse. He squatted down beside the boy. "I will tell you the honest truth that resides in my heart. I have no experience with lads. None. But I think you are remarkable, both in what you think and in your deeds. So I shall answer you as I would a man. Which, I think, you are."

Matt dropped his gaze to Falconer's. He had his mother's eyes, clear as smoke from a holy fire.

Falconer went on, "You are more alone than any lad ever deserved to be. You have lost both mother and father. Yet you remain a good lad, not giving in to rage or useless grief. You pray, you sing, you care for others. Your fear is natural. Your pain is what makes you human just now. But I am certain . . ."

Falconer's throat clenched tight. He used his free hand to brush at the boy's hair where it fell across his forehead. When he could speak again, he continued, "I am certain that you are well on your way to wholeness—body, soul, and spirit. And that neither your fear nor your loss will conquer you."

Falconer had forgotten the woman was nearby until he heard movement. He glanced over and saw how her shoulders were bowed, her head supported by her uplifted arms resting on the railing. He knew he should go to her, but not before he was finished with the business at hand.

He took Matt's shoulders in both his hands. "I am very proud of you, my son."

Late that afternoon, as they passed Cape Trafalgar, a British frigate appeared on the horizon and greeted them with a round of cannon fire.

"Captain Clovis sends his compliments, sir," Bivens said as he read the signal flags through his telescope. "He asks our business and our destination."

Captain Harkness bristled at the challenge. "Respond that our destination is obviously the Mediterranean. Our business is our own."

Falconer spoke loud enough to cause the lieutenant to hesitate as he sorted through their own chest of signal flags. "I beg you to reconsider, Captain."

Harkness jabbed a finger at the warship as it hove to a half dozen leagues away. "No popinjay frigate flying British colors has the right to demand anything of an American merchant vessel."

"Permission to join you on the quarterdeck, sir." When Harkness waved him forward, Falconer climbed the stairs to where Reginald Langston had now joined them. "We are entering alien territories, sir," Falconer said gently. "I would suggest we seek allies in every quarter possible."

Harkness glanced at Reginald. But the owner was clearly not intending to offer any opinion. "What do you advise?" the captain asked, looking Falconer full in the face.

The American ship's longboat covered the distance in half an hour. The waves were steep and the wind fresh, such that they arrived at the British vessel fully drenched. Falconer and Bivens climbed the rope ladder, saluted first the foredeck and then the ship's colors, and requested a private word with the skipper.

A middy led them to the captain's day cabin. This being both a smaller frigate and a warship, the quarters were not nearly as large or ornate as upon the Langston vessel. A good deal of the day cabin was also taken up by twin eighteen-pounders, the numbers denoting the size of shot the cannons fired.

Captain Clovis was a stubby, barrel-chested man with a beard that spilled over his navy uniform jacket. He accepted their salutes with a nod, invited them to sit, and directed his steward to serve coffee. While the mate bustled about, Clovis said, "You're sailing one of those new-fangled clippers."

"Aye, sir," Bivens replied.

"British made?"

"Boston."

"I hear they are fast."

"Chesapeake headwaters to Portsmouth docks in seventeen days and three hours, sir."

That news turned the steward around. Clovis was a proud man, bearing as he did the imprint of the British navy. He tried but did not fully succeed in hiding his astonishment. "Not much to her abeam, not much at all. What's your armaments? Twenty guns?"

"Sixteen, sir."

"Not but sixteen, is it?" The captain sniffed. "Fourteen amidships, one in the forecastle and a single stern chaser, why, that would scarcely disturb an infant at rest."

"We merchants prefer to leave the fighting to your good selves," Bivens said politely.

"Nice to hear a merchant acknowledge our place upon the waters. Why, many's the time I've been snubbed by you Yankee merchants. Snubbed!"

Bivens cast a glance at Falconer. "Indeed, sir. Not good judgment on their part, I would say."

"Drink your coffee, man. It'll go stone cold on you." Clovis was clearly mollified by their attitude. "Now then. What brings you on board my vessel?"

At a nod from the lieutenant, Falconer said, "Might I ask, sir. Are you part of the Gibraltar squadron?"

"That depends on who's doing the asking."

"John Falconer is a senior official within the Langston merchant empire," Bivens replied. "Reginald Langston, the owner, is on board."

"I've heard nothing but good things about yon Langston and his vessels," Clovis said, settling further into his chair.

Falconer pulled the oilskin pouch from beneath his coat and used his napkin to dry off the exterior. He then untied the strap and removed the folded documents. "We carry official requests from the French and Spanish ambassadors to the Court of Saint James for all possible assistance. And another from the Admiralty."

Clovis inspected them carefully. When he lifted his chin, his tone had become less guarded still. "What do you seek?"

"Counsel and allies, Captain." Swiftly Falconer recounted their mission.

When he finished, Clovis rose from his chair and stumped to the rear windows. He released the bottom latch and used the rope pulley to winch it open. The salt air was fresh and tangy. "The pirate La Rue has taken to calling himself an admiral now. Ali Saleem has given him control over the entire pirate fleet."

"You know him?"

"Know of him, sir. Never met him personally. If we had, he'd not be sailing these waters ever again. Of that I can assure you most confidently."

Falconer chose his words carefully. "The war against the French is over . . . the Mediterranean is open waters."

"The northern sea is free and open," Clovis corrected, addressing his words to the stern waters. "The south is a political quagmire. Do you wish to know why we permit this man to prey upon the helpless? Well, then, I shall tell you. Because we have no choice, sir. Because we are *ordered* to leave him be, by the same powers that signed your document! The French and the Spanish and the Whitehall officials tie the Admiralty's hands!"

Clovis began stumping back and forth between their chairs and the stern windows. Even seated, Falconer was almost at eye level with the skipper. "Ali Saleem is a prince," Clovis went on. "Not any made-up title. A genuine prince of the desert realm. La Rue is his most trusted deputy. Ali Saleem has entered into a treaty with both the French and the Spanish, who by all accounts are well paid for this patronage. In return, La Rue is free to inflict his suffering upon the innocent. So long, I might add, as he is not caught in international waters. Five times I have chased him, sir. Five times! At least I have caught sight of his vessel and given chase—whether or not he was on board I cannot say for certain. Each time he has slipped into one of his harbors, where I am ordered not to enter."

Falconer glanced at Bivens and took a breath. "I would like to tell you of our plans."

As Falconer spoke, Clovis returned to his seat, fixing a glare at Falconer that might have melted a lesser man. When Falconer finished, Clovis continued his fierce inspection. But when he finally spoke, it was to say, "I should like nothing better than to come to your aid and join you in your quest."

Chapter 11

Captain Harkness had never had occasion to visit Marseilles. Falconer had been there once and Bivens three times. Together they inked out a crude map, mainly the port area and the old town. Though Reginald Langston had never reason to call on his company's new offices, he had read enough reports to offer some aid, at least in regard to the upper-class market areas where neither sailor had set foot. Captain Harkness used the largest paper on board for his map—the reverse side of the South Seas anchorages. The map became the centerpiece for their final dinners on board. They plotted with the care of a small frigate entering enemy waters. With meaningful looks from Falconer, they kept their discussions veiled until Matt had gone off to bed.

Amelia Henning was repeatedly invited to dine with them. Each time she begged permission to take her meals in the solitude of her cabin. The final night before their arrival in Marseilles, however, Harkness turned to his first lieutenant over coffee. "Ask the lady to join us, Bivens."

The young officer rose from his chair. "Aye, sir."

"If she declines, insist. As gently as possible, mind. But make it clear we need her presence this time."

Bivens saluted and departed. Harkness turned to Falconer

and said, "You showed an uncommon way of communicating with the lady, sir. I would rather you handled this."

"If you wish."

Harkness nodded. "You know what's to be done."

The woman obviously did not argue, for they waited scarcely three minutes before Amelia Henning appeared. The officers rose as one, and Harkness stepped forward to greet her. "Thank you for attending us, Mrs. Henning."

"You are welcome. Your man made it sound urgent."

"Indeed so. You should find that chair comfortable. Will you take coffee?" Harkness waited for his officers to resume their places, then motioned to Falconer.

The lady was seated between Reginald Langston and the first lieutenant. She was dressed in the same threadbare garments, but at least they had been washed as properly as shipboard life allowed. Her wayward hair was controlled somewhat by a pair of tortoiseshell combs. The blisters which had marked her face were healing. Falconer found himself reducing his earlier estimate of her age by a decade, down possibly to her late twenties. Were it not for the internal wounds she carried, Falconer realized, Amelia Henning would be a remarkably attractive woman.

"We arrive in Marseilles with the dawn," Falconer told her. "Our preparations are nearing completion. We must discuss your role."

Her chin lifted into a fiercely stubborn line. "I shall remain with the ship's company and retrieve my daughter."

Falconer possessed a voice that could reach the highest watch in a storm. Now, however, he spoke so gently his breath did not disturb the candles anchoring the map's near side. "The ship's company shall not proceed further than the African coast, madam."

She blanched. "What—what do you mean?"

"I cannot say for certain what will happen. Everything

we hope to do depends upon what we discover in Marseilles. For the moment, we feel our tactics are as sound as we can make them. We move forward with stealth and determination. Which means limiting the number of people who will enter into harm's way. Who will require protection."

Amelia Henning was reduced to a trembling form. "You are asking me to trust you with my daughter's life."

"Madam, you have no choice. None of us do." Reginald Langston spoke as gently as Falconer. "I too have been reduced to the role of observer. These men are fighters. They have traversed such waters before. You and I know nothing of it."

"But I have been there."

"To take you would risk everything," Harkness said. "Would you have other lives on your conscience?"

Reginald went on, "I have fought and I have begged and I have searched my way through almost a year of sleepless worry. Now I must trust in these men, heroes all. Men I am certain God has brought together as an answer to my and my wife's fervent prayers. I suggest, madam, you do the same."

Harkness added, "We carry in our holds the gold the pirates have demanded. We shall insist upon your daughter's release before handing over the first payment, even before we seek the release of Reginald's son."

The woman studied the candlelight for a time, then asked Falconer, "What of you?"

"I shall become the shadow." He waited long enough to be certain she would object no further. Then he asked, "What can you tell us of La Rue's hideout?"

"It is no hideout, sir. It is an entire harbor city. The port of Tunis, it is called nowadays. Tunis proper lies some ten miles inland from the African coast. Ali Saleem rules his fiefdom from there. La Rue controls the port from his castle."

"Describe it please, if you will."

"A fortress from beyond time. It was old when the Romans arrived. The Phoenicians named the town Carthage, and they wrested this very same fortress from a barbarian race whose name no one remembers."

The table was so still even the candle flames stopped trembling. The ship creaked and rocked upon steady seas. Inside the cuddy, however, the assembly remained locked upon the woman and her softly spoken words.

"The castle," Falconer gently prodded.

"There are no windows in any chamber I entered. Just arrow slits. It is a man-made cave with walls two paces thick. Rock and iron and doom. The dungeons are endless. My daughter . . ."

Falconer raised one finger, offering her something to help refocus upon the matters at hand. "What do you remember of your time in Carthage?"

"Everything of what I saw."

"And please, what did you see?"

"The slave yards. The castle's entry chambers. The dungeons."

"The port," Falconer said. "Did you catch even a glimpse?"

Amelia Henning was silent so long they assumed she was imprisoned by her memories. Then she murmured, "Ports, plural."

"I beg your pardon?"

"I recall seeing two ports. Is that possible?"

"Not only possible, ma'am." Harkness spoke in a voice that sounded over loud. "It is a standard harbor of old. One small port within a larger, separated by a second breakwater. This gives greater shelter from storms. From intruders."

She shrugged away this information. "Two ports," she repeated, more certain now. "The slave yards were a stone-lined arena west of the ports. The slavers lived in a small tower between the inner and outer harbor."

"Slavers, ma'am? Not soldiers?"

"Soldiers, slavers—I saw no one in uniform. I only know the men who controlled the slave yards went there to sleep and eat."

Falconer shared a glance with the officers. A harbor keep holding slavers meant the city was so comfortable and seemingly safe its security might be lax. He asked, "Anything else you might be able to describe for us?"

She frowned into the candlelight. "There was a market on the port's other side. Camels, spices, food. And taverns. I saw the merchants there." She was quiet for a time, then, "I don't believe I recall anything further."

Falconer leaned forward. The map crinkled beneath his elbows. He shifted the candles to one side and waited until Amelia Henning met his gaze. He waited longer still, until he saw the question register in her wounded eyes.

"My son has told us that your daughter Catherine is known by all who love her as Kitty. Is that correct?"

Her nod, though scarcely a tremble, was enough to dislodge a tear.

"We must have something that will help us to recognize her. No matter what she might be wearing."

The unspoken rose into the shadows and clustered about them, looming reminders of the woman's greatest fears. She required a long moment to reply. "She has a birthmark."

"Where?"

"On her left shoulder. The size of your thumbprint. It

is purple and shaped like a ripe plum with the stem pointed downward."

Falconer leaned back. Harkness met his eye and nodded approval. Falconer felt the woman's sorrow like a stone set upon his own heart. "Madam, I shall do everything in my power to bring your daughter home."

"I suggest we close upon a moment of prayer," Harkness said. "Mr. Langston, will you do us the honor?"

Chapter 12

After Amelia Henning said her good-nights, the others remained in the cuddy until well after midnight. As tired as he was, when Falconer finally lay in his bunk he found he could not sleep. His restless impatience brought back memories of other sleepless nights, other dangers he had met with ferocity and an utter absence of faith. He tried to pray, mainly to reassure himself that he was a different man now, but the silent words seemed to fall like pebbles to the creaking floor. Falconer quietly left his bunk, made sure Matt was asleep, slipped into his clothes, and walked up on deck.

The night officer saluted him and spoke of the wind. When Falconer did not respond, the young man saluted again and moved off. Crewmen were trained by life on board to respect their shipmates' need for privacy. Falconer took an oilskin cloak from the pile by the wheel. He flung it over his shoulders, stepped to the windward railing, and let the night wrap him in its veil.

The wind blew from the north. The deck and railing were damp from a passing squall. The wind tasted of rain yet to come. There were no stars. Falconer could smell land up ahead. Cities always had a peculiar scent sailors could detect after spending weeks at sea. Land-starved

sailors hungered for what lay beyond the horizon, yet a
city's smells always seemed too big for the air. Falconer
breathed in deeply, searching the wind and the coming
rain for any hint of danger.

Instead, he heard a woman's voice say, "Would you
mind if I joined you, Mr. Falconer?"

The truth was, he could not say. So he merely bowed
briefly and replied, "Shall I find you an oilskin, ma'am?"

"Thank you, but I have my own cloak." Amelia Henning stepped to the railing beside him. "Will it rain
again?"

"Soon, I think. Would you not be more comfortable
in your cabin?"

In reply, she pulled the cloak more tightly about her.
"Your son has spoken about you in a manner that has left
me deeply moved, John Falconer," she finally said to the
wind.

"Most call me Falconer, ma'am. You are welcome to
do the same."

She did not respond to the invitation. "Matt adores
you, and he counts you as the reason he has survived the
loss of his mother. I feel that I have come to trust you also
by what he has said. With your permission, I no doubt
shall speak far too frankly for a stranger."

"Shipboard life inspires a remarkable level of confidence, ma'am."

"That first day in the captain's cabin, you said something that at the time I could not address," Amelia Henning continued slowly. "You said you and I were bound by
something other than our loss. At the time, what I most
remarked was how you spoke to my heart. But I wish to
know now what it was you meant."

"I think you already know, ma'am."

"Still, I ask that you tell me."

He smelled the chill, clean spice of rain. Falconer addressed his words to the approaching squall. "We have both been struck by the world's casual brutality."

She shuddered, and yet did not draw away.

"We have not merely lost our most precious possession. We have had it stripped away in a manner that has deepened the wound. We have been rendered utterly helpless. Our strengths and convictions have been made to seem as empty as . . . as old smoke."

He waited for the question. The one he knew lay behind her approach in the middle of this dark night. As he waited, he sensed that likely here was the reason sleep wouldn't come.

She asked, her voice low, "Do you rage at God?"

Falconer listened to the hiss of rain striking an unseen ocean. "The Scriptures tell us of Elijah, a man of God who so despaired over his own brutal world that he fled to the desert. God found him there, huddled upon a rock, like a man who had gone in search of his tomb. And what did the man do when God spoke?"

Amelia Henning's whisper was almost lost to the wash of rain. "He covered his head."

"He pulled his cloak over his face like a shroud," Falconer agreed. "A man so disgusted with life he wanted nothing but the grave. God's presence meant nothing to him. Yet God was there still. Urging him back into life. Into the life that God wished to bestow upon him." He turned his head slightly to look into her face.

Her only response was to release the hood of her cloak, lift her head, and allow the rain to join the tears.

Falconer raised his own face. The rain had a chilling effect, washing away the world beyond the horizon and all the responsibilities he must face with the dawn. Instead, the image that had driven him up on deck flashed before his closed eyes, more clearly even than when he had first awakened. It had come and departed so swiftly it could hardly be called a dream at all. More a fleeting memory that slipped through his sleep like a dagger between his ribs.

"Just before yesterday's dawn, I dreamed of our church back in Salem," Falconer said to the night and the squall. "It was on the day of Ada's funeral."

"Ada was your wife?"

"Of eighteen months. I had long thought I was fated never to know either love or family. Both had been granted me, the miracle so complete some mornings I could not find room about my full heart to breathe. Joy was mine. And completeness. I thought eternity was captured by the sight of her face in the dawn light. I thought we would be together for all time. Yet now, when I look back . . ."

Amelia Henning picked up the thought in a broken voice, one awash in months of tears. "Now the days are mere seconds. The perfect life is a myth. And nothing lies ahead but darkness and rain."

"No, ma'am. I am sorry. But in that you are mistaken." Falconer gripped the woman's shoulder through her shawl. The lady seemed as insubstantial as the unseen dawn. He turned her toward the east. "You do not see it. But in less than one hour, the sun will rise. Though the rain falls. Though we endure a storm not of our choosing. Even though we might not be able to see it this time, the sun shall come again."

He dropped his arm and turned back to the north and the city beyond the horizon. The city and the duties and the life ahead. He said, as much to himself as to the lady, "At the time I was so broken by loss that I could not mourn. Yesterday I dreamed of that loss and felt anew the

114

pain. Yet there was a difference. The pain is gradually moving into my past. I sensed that its passage made way for a new future. I have duties. I have friends who need me. I have a son who relies upon my strength and my love."

Falconer stopped. He was not given to such talk. He had a warrior's ability to look outward and see almost nothing within. Or rather, it had been so until every breath and every thought became colored by his inner wound.

He looked at the woman beside him. There was not so much a rising dawn as a lessening of the surrounding dark. She had lowered her head so that her rain-swept hair hid her face. Falconer said, "I stand here beside you, ma'am, as a man who has walked the same rocky path as you. I tell you this with all the strength remaining in my heart. I cannot say what we will find in the Tunisian port. I cannot speak for your daughter. But this I know. God is. And before you expect, perhaps before you are ready, He will speak to you. He will call you into the future He has prepared for you."

At dawn's light, the city of Marseilles appeared a haven for ancient mystery. Their ship passed the Frioul Islands and the fortress of Château d'If before dawn. This timing freed Falconer from explaining to Matt how the medieval prison's infamy was tavern talk from the Spice Islands to Brazil. The two forts which guarded either side of the harbor entrance had been old fifteen centuries ago. Before sailing to the African wars, Roman soldiers had garrisoned there and offered sacrifices to Saturn at the hillside temple where a church now stood.

Falconer entered the harbor standing in the ship's bowsprit, there to shelter Matt, though the lad needed neither his strength nor his balance. Matt's gaze was everywhere, his questions constant, for the port held a realm of forbidden mysteries. Falconer was weary from his night of meager sleep. But the boy's eager questions were a boon stronger than many nights of quiet rest.

"There, Father John—did you see that? A beast with humps!"

"It is called a camel."

"Is that a French beast?"

"The animal comes from the deserts of Africa. The humps are used for storing nourishment. It is said they can go for weeks without drinking."

The lad mouthed several words, each of them laden with their own mysterious treasures. *Camel. Desert. Africa.* "Have you seen deserts, Father John?"

"Beyond the borders of some ports, yes. They are yellow or red or some color in between, and vast as waterless seas. And extremely hot." And he was destined to visit such a land. Incongruously the thought chilled even this dank and sweltering sunrise.

Matt's youthful vigor was back in earnest, along with a hunger to know everything and do even more. His gaze tracked along the approaching quayside to the ancient forts. He named them correctly. "Fort Saint Jean is there to the north and Fort Saint Nicholas to the south, and beside it the church of Saint Victor. Captain Harkness says the emperor's troops are garrisoned there, whenever they go off to war and when they return."

"Indeed." Falconer had been present when the captain had told the middies what little he knew of the French port. He hadn't told them that Marseilles was France's central port dealing with their African settlements.

"Yes, Father John. The captain said there has been either a temple or church on yonder hilltop for more than two thousand years. That seems ever such a long time."

They passed a pair of African sailing hulks with yellowed lateen sails. Young boys in filthy djellabas lifted net sacks of fish and shouted a price Falconer could not understand. Within the harbor walls the darkish water smelled of old refuse. The quayside lanes were a jumble of people and noise. Every manner of dress and speech was present in the harbor market. Another vessel tied to the quayside disembarked a steady stream of live beasts, either in wheeled cages or lashed upside down to stout poles. The animals shrilled their protest and their fear. The din grated on Falconer's teeth.

The sky was empty of the night's rain. Already a yellow veil of dust and smoke clung to the city's rooftops. The smells, thick and pungent, were of woodsmoke and fish and ancient spices. Falconer searched the approaching dockside and silently fretted about the perils ahead.

The steersman knew his craft and drew the ship alongside the stone quay with scarcely a bump. Captain Harkness bellowed, "Make fast stern and aft! Lieutenant Rogers!"

The second lieutenant was a pale young man, twenty-seven years of age but looked scarcely eighteen. He probably still did not shave more than once a month. Yet Harkness had often professed to Falconer the young man's potential. "Aye, sir!" came his shout.

"The ship is yours!"

"Aye, Captain!"

"Gentlemen!" Harkness bellowed with a strength amplified by what was yet to come. "To your stations, if you please!"

"I must go now," Falconer said to the lad.

117

"All right, Father John."

"You will do as we discussed?"

"I will stay on board, help the middies with their duties, and not go ashore until you return." Matt recited this without taking his eyes from the shoreline. He took a deep breath. His obvious pleasure was too great to do more than sigh the words. "Is this not the most beautiful and mysterious place you have ever laid eyes upon, Father John?"

Chapter 13

Falconer stepped up on the quarterdeck just as Reginald Langston emerged from his cabin. The company owner was dressed in such fine garb the captain commented admiringly, "You seem ready to go riding with the King of England, your honor."

"Ready to do my bit, for a change." Reginald nodded and tugged upon his dove-gray overcoat. "When do we depart?"

"Swift as we can. Soap! Ah. There you are. Good man." The steward, smiling still, was holding up the captain's finest jacket. Harkness shrugged off his salt-stained sea coat and donned the one with glittering braid and polished gold buttons.

"Shall I touch up the skipper's boots?" Soap asked.

"No time for that. We'll be moving too quickly for them to remark on my shoes, eh, Master Langston?"

Reginald agreed. His hearty coloring did not permit him to become wan. Yet his features were so pinched the skin about his mouth and eyes had gone pale. He asked Falconer once more, "Are you sure our meager number will prove sufficient?"

"Our safety comes from speed and surprise," Falconer reminded him.

119

Their plan was simple. The gold needed to be shifted to safety ashore. Their best plan lay in doing so immediately upon making landfall. Hopefully their foes would still be amassing information about their weaknesses. There was a risk they would be attacked in this first foray. So they had planned a feint of their own. Two parties would leave together, then split apart, leaving their attackers uncertain which carried the gold.

Harkness nodded to the second lieutenant, now commanding the ship, then said to the others gathered about him, "Ready yourselves, gentlemen."

Where the entryway to the stern cabins blocked the view from the quayside, Lieutenant Bivens remained poised above three sailor's packs. The packs were fitted so as to ride high upon their backs. Bivens hefted one and fastened it into place, as Falconer did the same for Soap, who had begged and pleaded for the chance to serve. Falconer had reduced Soap's load by a third, to take the additional weight himself. Even so, the steward staggered slightly as he took the sack's weight.

Falconer took the third sack upon his own shoulders. The steward had sewn one canvas bag into another and attached leather security straps which they now bound across their chests. The sack's contents clinked softly as he fitted it into place. They took spare oilskins and slipped them down between the canvas and their spines, then looped them over the bags such that they hung down behind. The cloaks left them looking rather deformed, but it hid the sacks from more careful inspection. They hoped to move too swiftly for anything further.

Speed and surprise were their greatest allies.

Harkness motioned to the bosun, who whistled softly. Four handpicked bullyboys came up from belowdecks. Muscular and battle-scarred, their fierce expressions signified men hungry for conflict. Two men bore oilskin-covered packs, but theirs were filled with cotton batting. In their hands were wooden billy clubs. The two other sailors were unencumbered save for long wooden staffs.

"We're off," Harkness announced.

They took the stairs to the main deck. The bullyboys slipped into line behind them. Harkness led them down the gangplank, piped away by the oldest middy. Falconer glanced at Matt but did not smile. Nor did he ask if Soap could manage the weight. The man had not a single ounce of quit in him.

Once on the crowded quayside, Harkness asked the nearest man holding the staff, "You're sure of the way?"

"Been over the map with Lieutenant Bivens and the master both," the sailor confirmed.

"Then lead off, and make all speed," Harkness said. "There's a gold sovereign for each of you at the end of this day's escapade."

The sailors needed no further impetus. They flitted to the front of the entourage, bellowing, "Make way!"

"Close up ranks," Harkness barked. "Quick march."

Make way!" Voices accustomed to being heard above a storm parted the crowded quayside traffic. People and animals alike bleated and jumped aside. Before they could recover, the nine of them were past. Two of the sailors, then Harkness and Reginald Langston, followed by Falconer and Soap and Bivens. Then the two sailors with their billy clubs and empty sacks making up the rear guard.

The entourage passed a corner marked by street signs. Falconer saw they traversed the Quai du Port, a cobblestone lane littered with refuse from the waterfront market. The smell of fresh-caught fish was strong. Customers and stallholders alike turned to observe their passage.

The strengthening day was humid, both from the sea

and from the previous night's rain. Under his burden and cape, Falconer sweated heavily. Ahead, Soap's face was wet with perspiration and his bow-legged limp growing more evident. The canvas straps bit deeply into Falconer's shoulders, his load weighing in excess of one hundred and sixty pounds. It was not possible even for a man of Falconer's strength to trot while carrying such a load. He made do with a quick shuffle. His boots scraped across the cobblestones as he pushed himself hard, around the bend at the harbor's most inward point, and then back out again. They faced seaward, away from the rising sun, out of the market bustle and upon a broader and more orderly lane. Falconer shook his eyes clear of gathering sweat and saw from a passing corner sign that this new road was called the Quai de Rive Neuve.

"Here," Bivens gasped from behind Falconer, each word a severe effort. "Turn here."

They turned onto a lane broader than the quay and passed a palatial building. Above the expansive staircase and the trio of giant doors, Falconer read the two words chiseled into the stone facing. *Opera Municipal.* Beyond that rose an even grander building, the one he had been looking for, the one that announced itself to be the *Theatre National.*

"Go," he said, the one word he had breath for.

Reginald Langston cast him a worried glance but did as Falconer said. Rising from the corner just beyond the theater was a long building whose ground floor was wrapped by broad wood-framed windows. And above each window were gilt letters spelling out *Langston's.*

The sailors executed as tight a maneuver as any Falconer had seen. One of the men holding a staff and one of those with a sack peeled off with Reginald Langston and the captain. The other two bunched more tightly still about Falconer, Bivens, and Soap.

Falconer managed to ask, "Can we increase the pace?"

Ahead of him, Soap could not spare the breath to respond with more than a quick nod.

The lane was immensely crowded. Carriages and pedestrians, women in broad hoopskirts and tradesmen pushing barrows on tall metal wheels, hawkers and children and mules. The lead sailor kept up a steady call for those ahead to give way. But this rather well-heeled crowd proved less willing to step aside. Falconer steadied Soap as he stumbled over a curb. The man's body trembled. They all did.

"There," Bivens gasped. "To your left."

It was then, with their destination in sight, that the attackers struck.

The assault was lightning swift. A trio of men, perhaps four—Falconer could not risk a glance about to be certain. They slipped from a narrow alcove, either a servants' entrance or a constricted alley. Falconer was almost blinded by the sweat pouring from his hair and brow. But he saw the metal glint in the sunlight and bellowed with what strength he could spare, *"Attack!"*

Two villains armed with wicked clubs took aim at the man on point. The sailor parried the first blow but took the second on the muscle where his shoulder met his neck. He grunted and went down to one knee, managing somehow to raise his staff and deflect the second strike.

What the villains clearly had not expected was for the last man in their little line to spring forward so swiftly. The billy club rose and fell like wooden lightning, and two blades clattered to the street.

"Run!" Falconer could scarcely recognize the voice as his own.

Bivens shouldered past a carriage that had chosen this

moment to halt alongside their walkway. Or perhaps it was part of the attackers' scheme. Falconer had no idea. He merely knew that Soap would have sprawled headlong into the horses' traces had Falconer not been there to steady him.

An attacker lifted a stave or pike and tried to jam it into Falconer's face. Falconer merely turned himself so that the blow landed upon his sack. The pack clinked and cushioned the blow, though the additional weight almost pushed Falconer to his knees. Then another set of hands gripped him from the other side and plucked him back aloft.

A woman to Falconer's left screamed. Or perhaps it was a bucking horse. Falconer could not spare a moment's glance. For all he knew, the villains were still on them. He heard fighting behind him and more voices raised in fearful protest. Falconer, Soap, and Bivens remained gripped in tight unison and shoved their way across the street. A horse rose up on its hind legs at their sudden appearance and a man yelled at them in what Falconer assumed was French. They mounted the curb and three round steps that formed a rising curve around a broad street corner. A guard shouted at them in the same unknown tongue. They shoved him aside, pushed through the doors, and entered shadowed coolness.

Falconer cuffed his eyes clear of sweat and peered about. Somehow the fracas out on the street seemed louder here in the quiet and the cool. The guard scrambled through the door behind them and angrily protested their arrival.

Soap muttered, "What do we do now?"

Falconer rounded on the guard. Whatever the man saw in Falconer's face caused him to step back. He turned the name Langston had given him into a question. "Sancerre?"

Ignoring Falconer's query, the guard picked up his tirade again.

Falconer inflated his lungs as far as the leather straps permitted and roared, *"Sancerre!"*

Another voice rose. "You seek Monsieur Sancerre? He is not here."

Falconer saw a slender man in a black topcoat and neatly trimmed beard. "His office?"

Despite the heavy accent, the man's English was excellent. "There at the rear. But you cannot—"

"Forward, men. On the double."

"Monsieur! You cannot enter without—"

Attention flashed away from them, however. For at that moment the corner door crashed back, admitting two sailors. One held the broken half of a wooden staff in his hand and bled profusely from a cut to his forehead. The other held a billy club high overhead, as though searching out the next villain to strike.

This time Falconer was certain the screams came from women.

The bleeding sailor roared, "Lieutenant!"

Bivens called over his shoulder as he shuffled down the length of the bank behind Falconer. "All clear, Sailor. Stand guard!"

"Aye, sir." The sailors formed up back-to-back and lifted their weapons to the ready.

Falconer shouldered his way past a cluster of bank officials, opened a door at the rear, and shouted, "Bring me Sancerre!"

Chapter 14

The young banker's name was Bernard Lemi, and he treated Falconer's arrival as grand entertainment. The Marseilles bank was a branch of a Paris-based establishment whose tendrils extended from South America to the Spice Islands. Monsieur Sancerre, director of the Marseilles branch, was away for a fortnight in Paris, they learned from their host in accented but perfect English. Bernard Lemi was the youngest son of the company's chairman, acting head in Sancerre's absence.

Over coffee, Lemi readily admitted to despising his job. "It's a dreadful bore, good sirs. Except for events this morning," he added with a mischievous grin.

Falconer had insisted upon the two sailors remaining on guard outside the office where he and Bivens now sat in high-backed chairs. Soap had declined the offer and taken up station in the corner behind Lemi's chair, from where he rubbed the kinks from his back and legs. Falconer could hear querulous protests from the main hall, no doubt over the two brutish sailors on guard outside his door. "The city or the bank is boring?" he now asked Lemi.

"This position. Marseilles is a gateway to mystery. But alas, as a banker all such doors remain closed to me. As my dear papa has often said, a banker is paid to be respectable.

Do take more coffee, good sirs. You must be parched after your encounter with the ruffians."

The cup was delicate china and so tiny Falconer could not fit his finger through the loop. He held the cup by its rim, as he would a thimble, and permitted the banker to add to the treacly black contents. "Your English is excellent."

"I studied in London for a year and a half. My father wished to establish connections with British merchants. I confess to loving the British, sir. They are a most adventurous race."

Bivens set down his cup and rubbed the shoulder injured in the storm. "Is it common for villains to attack in full daylight?"

"This close to the port and Le Panier, anything is possible." Bernard Lemi wore standard bankers' garb of black and gray, but with a somewhat raffish cut. His striped gray trousers had the shimmer of silk, as did his gray waistcoat. His half boots were shiny and pointed, with a row of buttons up each ankle. "But no, I must confess that such a massive show of force as you describe, and in broad daylight, is shocking." But the banker did not sound shocked, appearing delighted with the break in his routine.

Bivens said, "Le Panier, that is the city's old quarter?"

"Indeed, sir. It lies within the medieval walls northwest of the port. A greater den of wickedness and danger does not exist anywhere," the banker noted with relish.

"You know it?"

"I confess to having ventured there on occasion." Lemi hesitated, then added, "Though if my father knew as much, I would instantly be brought home."

Falconer had a warrior's trust for his gut instinct. But this was not his decision alone. Which was why he looked at Bivens as he said, "Mr. Lemi, I wonder if I might entrust you with a secret and a mystery."

The banker's voice rose an octave. "Nothing you could possibly say would bring more joy to my day, sir!"

Bivens hesitated a long moment, then nodded his agreement. Falconer settled back into his chair, wincing at how the motion pained his shoulder. A welt was rising where the sack's straps had cut into his skin. "The sacks you see there hold five thousand gold sovereigns."

The suave banker couldn't help his gape at the bulky canvas bags, half covered by the oilskins. "But that is a fortune!"

"A heavy one," Soap muttered.

"Three hundred and twenty pounds in weight," Bivens agreed. "At least, it started as such. By the time we arrived here it must have weighed ten times that amount," he said wryly.

"Five thousand sovereigns," Falconer repeated. "Ransom money."

The banker's eyes gleamed with an almost feverish light. "Ransom for what?"

"A young girl of nine and a gentleman of twenty-seven."

"Kidnapped?"

"So we have been informed."

"By whom?"

Again Falconer glanced at the young lieutenant and once more received a confirming nod. "Ali Saleem."

"Ah." The banker stroked the tip of his neatly trimmed beard. "You mean, of course, Saleem's trusted friend and deputy, Admiral La Rue."

"You know him?"

"I know of him, sir. We have of course never met. But there is a client of this bank who is said to be La Rue's representative in France."

Bivens leaned forward. "A client? Here?"

"Indeed so. And I must tell you, sir, that it is your great

good fortune Monsieur Sancerre is away. For this gentleman—his name is Raban—is my superior's closest friend."

Harkness had ordered them to report back immediately upon depositing the funds in the bank. Instead, Falconer sent Soap with news of their discovery and intentions. He and Bivens then set off with the two sailors and Bernard Lemi. The banker explained that they should walk, as the distance was less than a mile, and a carriage would only draw further unwanted attention.

They did not return to the harbor, but instead cut down a series of side streets. The closer they came to Le Panier, the more constricted grew the lanes and the denser the foot traffic. It was good they had elected to walk, for once inside the crumbling old walls the lanes narrowed to little more than alleys. They were forced to walk single file and had to take considerable care not to become separated.

The lanes were cooler than the city's wealthier quarters, for sunlight seldom penetrated. The air was thick with odors and woodsmoke and spices. Falconer found himself drawn back to days he had thought lost and gone forever. No longer in a French city, his memories took him back to Africa. Back to a world of danger and menace. Back where every passing stranger might hold a dagger or a pistol or both.

He could not say whether he disliked the way his blood ran faster or his muscles bunched with the danger-tension that had saved his life on so many occasions. Only that it was so.

A new man, he silently repeated. One created in a higher image.

He hoped and prayed that when challenged, the words would prove true.

They paused at a point where the alley began a steep

incline. A crossroads permitted a sharp lance of sunlight, strong as a golden pillar. In the blinding light Falconer made out a series of stalls where young boys sat and pounded brass into a myriad of bowls and saucers and carafes. The scene was drawn from a hundred other ports, down to the dusty djellabas the boys wore, and the hats called fezzes worn by the overseers. Even the Frenchmen he saw wore the Arab hats. At least, Falconer assumed they were French.

One of the sailors muttered, "Never thought I could be this lost this close to the sea."

"The harbor is a thousand paces directly behind you," Bivens told him. "If we lose contact, use the sunlight as your compass and aim south by west."

"Aye, sir."

The banker pointed into the sun-splashed lane. "Directly across from here is Raban's café. His office is the rear corner table, beside the door leading to the upstairs rooms."

"What happens upstairs?" Bivens asked.

In reply, Bernard Lemi simply looked at Falconer. Falconer grimaced his understanding. The banker was no longer smiling as he asked, "Shall I proceed and introduce you?"

"I would rather keep our alliance a secret," Falconer said. "At least for now."

The banker looked somewhat relieved. "When shall we meet again?"

"Tonight," Falconer decided. "Join us on board for dinner, if you will."

"With pleasure." He cast another glance across the thoroughfare. "Be on your best guard in there. When it comes to the beast known as Raban, little is as it seems."

Chapter 15

The café's exterior was like most buildings Falconer had passed in the Panier district. The second floor was rimmed with wrought-iron balconies. The building's ancient stone was cloaked in centuries of yellow dust. He spied the top floor's adornment and stopped at the edge of the thoroughfare.

"What is it?" Bivens demanded.

Falconer pointed across the lane. "They call that a harem perch. I have never seen them outside Arabia. I would say this is confirmation that Raban is our man."

Falconer and Bivens squinted at the long balcony silhouetted against the sky and encased in intricately carved wood. Slender slits permitted whoever sat inside to observe the world and remain unseen. The lieutenant's features were taut and sweat stained. "My gut tells me we're walking into the dragon's lair."

Falconer heard the sound of a man in pain. "What does your shoulder tell you?"

"That I carried too much too soon after the storm," Bivens confessed. "I fear my injury has been aggravated."

The nearest sailor, a rock-solid man of few words, said, "Told you to let me shoulder that load, I did."

"And you were right." Bivens gave the sailor a half

grimace, half smile. "You'll have to watch my weak side in there."

"With my life, sir," the sailor replied, and meant it. Bivens was well liked by all the men.

Falconer asked, "Does your gut tell you that we should go no further?"

Bivens, taking the question seriously, gave the harem perch another careful inspection, his focus so stern he might pierce the shadows. "I shared the skipper's promise to bring Byron home. The little girl too. Even if it means fighting a hundred dragons."

A hand signal from Falconer was enough to plant the two sailors inside the café's front door. The café lay just three steps below the street, yet it felt to Falconer as though he entered a man-made cave. The windows were high and curved like half-moons, and the sunlight filtered through faded, dirty curtains such that the interior was in a constant state of gloom.

The café was drawn from a distant land. Falconer walked down the carpeted central aisle and felt himself entering a realm of veiled women and daggers shaped like scythes.

All conversation ceased at their passage. Men in robes sat or lay upon low divans. Wooden shutters carved in arabesque designs separated the tables, forming the suggestion of alcoves. The air was pungent with the fragrance of mint tea and tobacco smoldering in water pipes.

The man they sought sat in the café's only Western-style chair, which was drawn up to an octagonal table inlaid with mother-of-pearl. At first glance, the man looked ordinary enough. Of slender build and wearing a pale suit with a white shirt buttoned to his neck, his ring with a diamond the size of a fingernail caught even the dim light. His eyes were cold and so gray they appeared as colorless as his close-cropped hair. A conical Arab hat with a flat top rested upon the table beside a thimble of coffee and a beaker of water. He tapped the ring upon the table-top as he listened to the man standing on the opposite side. The man whined an entreaty and tugged at the shapeless hat in his hands. Raban appeared to nod at the man's words, but his eyes remained upon Falconer and Bivens. He halted the supplicant with an upraised finger. He spoke one word. The man's whine rose an octave.

The seated man murmured a single word. In response, another man took a step out of the shadows behind the table. Falconer was astonished he had not noticed the man before.

The guard was as tall as Falconer and outweighed him by a hundred pounds. His arms were as large as the suppli-cant's thighs. His wrists were banded by broad sword guards of burnished copper. His neck was as thick as a tree trunk, his head carefully shaved. He wore a leather vest across his massive chest, and two jeweled daggers were tucked into a broad belt. The belt's buckle was white jade and the size of Falconer's palm.

Falconer addressed Bivens so softly that the supplicant's final whining pleas hid his words. "You do the talking."

They stepped to either side of the supplicant, who stumbled as he backed from the table, still beseeching Raban. But the café owner was no longer listening. He addressed them in English. "Let me see. You must be Lieu-tenant Bivens, yes? Second-in-command of the Langston vessel. But you, sir, I have yet to know your name."

Falconer did not answer. Instead, he stepped around the table and slipped into the shadows. The same shadows into which the guard had again vanished. Falconer did not look at the giant.

135

The guard growled a warning in a tongue Falconer did not need to understand.

Raban raised the same finger. The guard subsided, grumbling. Falconer could feel the enormous man's menace like heat.

"Never mind," Raban said. "I shall know your name soon enough."

The finger rose another notch. Instantly a waiter appeared. Raban spoke, his words a sibilant rush. The waiter bowed and backed away. Falconer understood only one word the waiter said. It was the same as the title repeated by the supplicant. *Effendi.*

The waiter returned with a chair for Bivens and a water pipe for Raban. The waiter used tongs to hold a burning coal over the copper bowl as Raban drew hard upon the carved ivory stem. Only when the pungent smoke clouded the air between them did Raban say, "Make yourself comfortable, Lieutenant."

"Thank you. I shall stand."

"Sit, stand, it is of no consequence." The water in the hubble-bubble seethed more smoke. "I see the young banker chose not to join you. That man speaks of adventure but fears his own shadow."

Falconer felt the guard's eyes shift over and take his measure. Falconer remained utterly still. He had positioned himself such that his scar was on the side of his face nearest the guard. Out of the corner of his eye he saw the guard take a half step away, and Falconer turned slightly, ready for the attack. Good, Falconer said silently. A worried man might hesitate.

Bivens asked, "Were you behind the attack on me and my men?"

"My good sir. If I had attacked you, we would not be having this conversation." The words seeped out with the smoke. "Why ever should I create a ruckus, since you will bring the gold to me of your own accord?"

A snake, Falconer decided. A viper in a fine desert suit. A man who cared less than nothing for the lives of others.

Bivens said, "You know why I am here."

"Remind me."

"If you have what we seek, I do not need to."

The water pipe bubbled for a time. Bivens responded with his best parade-ground stance. His eyes were steely, his gaze fastened slightly above Raban's head. As detached as the seated merchant. And as fierce.

Raban gave first. "Is that pestering woman with you?"

"Which lady might that be?"

"The missionary." He softly spat the word.

"Again, such information is yours only if you are the man with whom we need to speak."

"I believe a sum of money was mentioned."

"Was it?"

"Five thousand sovereigns. In gold."

"Such numbers are meaningless unless we have clear evidence, sir."

The pipe bubbled for a time longer. Then Raban spoke in a language Falconer did not understand.

The guard reached for the blade at his belt.

Falconer sprang at him with a roar.

Falconer gripped the guard's arms by his wristbands and held on for dear life. The guard shouted his fury and bucked like a human bull. Behind him Falconer heard the table overturn. Patrons and waiters shouted protests. Another voice shrilled in panic. Falconer could only hope that Bivens protected his back. Every shred of his strength was required to keep hold of the guard. Twice the giant tried to head-butt Falconer. Twice Falconer shifted his head in time to take the blows upon his shoulder. His arm was going numb from the strikes. He did not know how much longer he could maintain control in this frantic deadly dance.

"Hold! Hold!" Raban's voice had risen to that of a frightened woman.

"Call your man off!" Bivens roared.

"I never . . ." Raban switched to Arabic. At least Falconer thought it was Arabic. The giant's dark eyes were inches from Falconer's and burned with molten fury. But his struggle subsided.

Falconer released his hold and backed off a step. Another.

Bivens held Raban facedown upon the table. The coffee thimble, the water carafe, the pipe, all lay in shambles. The two sentinels by the door were now stationed between them and the others within the restaurant, all of whom were now on their feet. Bivens had a pistol planted deep into Raban's ear. His voice was a seaman's roar. "You have one chance, do you hear me? One! Give me what I want or I will—"

"No, no! I was telling my man to do just that!" He squirmed futilely against the officer's hold. "You're *hurting* me!"

"One chance!" Bivens ground down harder. "Is the young man alive!"

"Yes, yes, of course!" Raban frantically babbled further in Arabic. The giant glanced warily at Falconer, then reached slowly with one hand for his belt. Falconer tensed but remained where he was.

The guard pulled two small hinged boxes from a secret pocket inside his belt. Both were of silver chased in some ornate design. He reached forward and set them on the table beside his master's face.

Bivens and Raban both tracked the giant's hands.

Falconer's grip had been so tight the copper wristbands were both crumpled, and one was broken and hung by a slender chain.

Raban whined, "There, you see! A gift! That's all—"

Falconer addressed Raban for the first time. "And the girl?"

"What?"

Falconer stepped forward. "The missionary's daughter. She is alive?"

Raban sought to draw Falconer into focus. "Of course!"

Falconer nodded to Bivens. Bivens uncocked the pistol and slipped it back into his belt. He released the man and stepped back. "You will send a man to the ship at midnight. He will speak English. We will discuss how the exchange will take place."

Now that he was released, the viper's hiss returned. "You will pay for this insult." The empty gray eyes sought out Falconer. "Both of you."

Chapter 16

The clouds began gathering a half hour after the sun melted into the western seas, so low as to crimp the earth with their shadows. The sun's final rays turned them into a sulfurous yellow. Harkness stood upon the foredeck, joined by Bivens and Falconer and Reginald Langston, frowning at the approaching storm as he would a foe. "What say you, gentlemen? Is this a celestial warning or merely another passing squall?"

"I would call it a gift," Falconer replied.

The three men turned about, but the captain's response to Falconer's remark was interrupted by a vague piping from the main deck. Falconer had returned to the vessel to learn that Matt had been assigned duty at the gangplank. Matt had not yet mastered the pipes, and his signaling of the visitor's arrival sounded like an injured bird. Bivens hid his grin behind his hand. A sailor chuckled from the rigging overhead. Harkness coughed hard.

Matt's voice was almost as high as the pipes. "Visitor for Captain Harkness!"

Bevins said, "It's the banker Falconer and I spoke to you about. Bernard Lemi."

Harkness called down, "Have him attend us on the foredeck."

141

"Aye, sir!" Matt was dressed for the occasion in the coat of another middy, a boy so large the coat's edge scraped upon the deck and Matt had to sweep the arms up to free one hand for a salute. "Welcome aboard, sir."

Reginald Langston had ordered fresh provisions from his company's larder, and they ate well enough. Matt ate with the midshipmen in a small alcove behind the galley. In spite of the fine meal, dinner was a subdued affair. Not morose, rather the reflective quiet of men uncertain of this newcomer. Amelia Henning had elected to join the captain's table, dressed in what clearly was a new frock from Langston's local emporium. High-necked and without adornment, it was saved from appearing severe by its soft silk fabric and dove-gray color.

Bernard Lemi must have sensed the men's uncertainty. Yet their guest made no attempt to break through their reserve with loud banter or familiarity. Harkness asked a few questions of Lemi's background, which he answered fully. Otherwise, he accepted the silent hospitality with a calm of his own, clearly content to wait for whatever might come.

Over a first course of fresh trout and eels, Amelia Henning said, "I cannot thank you enough for your generosity, Mr. Langston."

"It is nothing, ma'am. A mere trifle. I am delighted you find the frock appealing."

"I was not speaking of the dress, though it is perhaps the nicest I have ever worn." Indeed, Amelia Henning looked a proper lady this night. The worst of her sunburn lesions were healed over, and her hair was determinedly tied back with a length of gray ribbon that matched her new dress. "I meant for everything. You face your own trials and loss. Yet you have remained a gentleman and more."

She took in the men seated at the table with her eyes and her words. "A true saint in the company of saints."

Harkness murmured, "My dear lady."

"You have put up with my solitude and my worries, and done so without protest. You have asked nothing of me save what was required to unite me with my daughter." Her eyes glistened like rain-washed gemstones. "I have nothing to offer save prayer, but this do I offer you with a sincere and trusting heart. You shall all be counted among those I bring before God. For the rest of my days."

The silence was finally broken by Captain Harkness, who said, "Madam, were you to plant a chest of jewels upon my table, I could not feel wealthier than I do in this moment."

"Nor presented with a gift I less deserve," Reginald agreed. "Though which I accept with heartfelt thanks."

"Amen," Bivens echoed. "I say, amen."

"We share in your own distress as well," Falconer said. "And pray for your swift reunion with your child."

"Daily," Harkness agreed.

Bernard Lemi showed genuine confusion. He stared at one face after another. Falconer glanced over, but not for long. He knew the young man's bewilderment all too well. It was not so long ago that he would have felt the same. In the company of men who stood and acted like warriors. Yet who spoke of a higher discipline and a greater calling. And who used such words as *prayer* and *hope* with the same confidence as they might comment upon the rising sun.

Reginald asked, "Where are you from, Mrs. Henning?"

"Philadelphia. My father was a pastor and then taught at seminary. My husband's family were missionaries in the province of California. We met when he came to do his seminary training."

They spoke of inconsequential matters through the second course, a stew of lamb and potatoes and fresh vegetables from the local market. While Soap and another sailor removed their plates, the steward said, "Begging your pardon, sir. But the gentleman guest brought a great box with him and said I should serve it up as your dessert."

"I hope that is permitted," Bernard Lemi said. "I thought you might like to sample some delicacies of Marseilles."

They finished off the meal with perhaps the finest sweets Falconer had ever tasted, small tartlets of some feather-light pastry filled with an astonishing variety of flavors—blackest chocolate, lemon custard, vanilla, cinnamon, cherry. They exclaimed over one essence after another, and still they came. When they could eat no more, Harkness ordered the rest to be shared with the midshipmen. "Never knew a lad who could not eat his own weight in sweets."

Captain Harkness then fiddled with his coffee, clearly uncertain whether to ask the banker to let them discuss the matters before them in solitude. Falconer remained silent. This was the captain's decision.

As though in response to the unspoken, Lemi asked Falconer, "Did Raban know I brought you?"

"He did."

"No doubt he accused me of cowardice."

Falconer hesitated, then confirmed, "In a manner of speaking."

The cabin's oiled woodwork shone ruddy in the candlelight. The faces about the table were cast in taut shades of light and dark. All eyes remained upon the banker as he flattened the tablecloth with a slow sweep of his right hand.

"My best friend—my only friend in these parts—he is in terrible debt to Raban. You do not . . . you cannot imagine . . ." He hesitated, then lifted his gaze to the woman seated across from him. "Forgive me, madam. I should not speak of such things."

"We are a company who have been made close through common wounds and weaknesses," she replied. "As for myself, what I have endured over the past half year has left me immune to shock, monsieur."

Bernard Lemi nodded slowly, as though the motion helped him absorb what he had just heard. "I paid off my friend's debt. Once, and then again. But he is addicted to the dice. And the dice have made him Raban's slave. I confronted Raban. I threatened him, demanded satisfaction in a duel." He glanced at Falconer. "You met his guard?"

Bivens said to the captain, "A veritable beast of a man."

"Raban said if ever I spoke to him again, he would set his guard upon my friend." Another apologetic glance at Amelia, then he added, "The giant enjoys inflicting pain. Raban . . ."

There was no need for Bernard to finish the thought. Falconer saw Harkness and Reginald exchange both a glance and a nod. He took that as his cue. "With your permission, Captain?"

When Harkness waved assent, Falconer reached into his coat pocket and withdrew the two silver boxes. He set them in the middle of the table. "Raban gave these to Lieutenant Bivens."

Bernard Lemi blanched. He said nothing as Reginald reached over and opened the first box, though Falconer could see that it required all the young man's strength not to turn away.

Reginald Langston pulled up a lock of dark hair tied with a bit of gold chain.

"Hair." Bernard Lemi sighed the word and slumped down into his chair. "Only hair."

The second box held the same, except that the hair was blond. The entire table watched as Amelia Henning reached out and accepted the fragment with trembling fingers.

She declared softly, "It is Catherine."

Harkness cleared his throat. "Forgive me, madam. But a simple bit of blond hair could—"

"Do you think I might mistake a lock from my own daughter's head?" The woman seemed utterly unaware that she was weeping. "It is feather soft, just as hers. And you see this curl? No, Captain. This belongs to my Kitty."

"Very well." Harkness looked a question at Reginald. "Sir?"

"I wish I could be so certain, but I can't," Reginald replied. "I haven't seen Byron in several years, and we were never close. All I can attest to is that Byron's hair was this color."

"We will take it for the moment as confirmation," Harkness decided. "We have little choice."

Reginald turned to the banker. "Did you know my stepson?"

"Not well." Bernard hesitated, then added, "Byron did not . . . well, he did not get along with your agent, sir."

"That is putting it mildly. Speak your mind, I beg you. Whatever you might say can hardly be worse than what the agent told me this afternoon."

Bernard took a long breath, then confessed, "Your son hated any form of labor. Your agent lives for nothing else. Their quarrels were legendary. They once came within a hairsbreadth of exchanging blows inside our bank."

Falconer guessed at what Bernard was not saying. "And Raban?"

"Byron spent more time than was healthy in the chambers above Raban's café," Bernard allowed.

Reginald said to Falconer, "My agent was a senior clerk in London. He is a man who devours ledgers as others might a fine meal. He is narrow in his build and narrow in his habits. He and my stepson would have nothing whatsoever in common."

"I fear you are correct," Bernard agreed.

Thunder rumbled through the rear windows, this time more than close at hand. Falconer rose from his chair. "With your permission, Captain, I would like to borrow Soap and a few other men."

"For what purpose?"

In reply, Falconer asked the banker, "Would you think Raban is watching our vessel?"

"I have no doubt of it whatsoever. Raban feeds on information."

"I think it is time we turned the tables on our foe," Falconer said to the captain.

Chapter 17

Thunder continually rolled across the horizon where the sun dropped into the sea, streaking the clouds with reflections from the city's ruddy colors. When the rain finally arrived, Falconer was ready. He and his small band moved swiftly.

The deluge was just what they needed. It turned the narrow lanes behind the Hôtel de Ville into cobblestone rivers. The quarter was empty save for rain and the sound of nighttime revelry from behind shuttered windows, and Falconer might as well have had the entire Panier district to himself. Falconer took refuge beneath the largest cloak he had found on board their ship—one so vast it covered his head and shoulders like an oilskin tent. He signaled to his team. Soap and the two sailors who had guarded their back that afternoon turned and raced off. Falconer quickly stepped into a shadowed alcove, hoping that anyone who had been watching was following the larger band. When he could identify no one else through the mist, he hurried away in the opposite direction.

Their plan was simple enough. The weather had merely improved their chance of success. The sailors were to lead Raban's spies on a merry chase around the Panier district at a trot until any chasers were weary and then head back to the ship. Falconer, however, had another purpose in mind.

Falconer arrived at Raban's café and slipped into the alley opposite the main entrance. He crouched in a doorway and studied the main thoroughfare. A trio of sullen donkeys pulled empty carts. The drovers were huddled far down within their cloaks and blind to all save the road ahead. Four men emerged from the café, shouting words Falconer could not understand. Rain poured in a steady stream over Falconer's hideaway.

An hour passed. Falconer could not decide whether he was pleased with how easily he returned to the old ways. All he knew for certain was that patience was crucial for a hunter. And toward the end of his second hour in the doorway, his waiting was rewarded.

A narrow-faced man with the deep-set scars of a former prisoner stepped from a door opposite Falconer's hideaway. The open doorway revealed a hallway and stairs. The giant guard Falconer had bested that afternoon filled the hallway behind the first man. Falconer crouched lower, huddled within the cloak, hoping the shadows and the veil of rain would keep him invisible. The narrow man slipped a hood over his face and stepped into the rain. The guard who followed gave the rain no notice at all. He was dressed as he had been that afternoon—the same leather vest, the same pair of curved blades tucked into the broad belt. Only the copper wristbands, the ones Falconer had crushed, were gone.

The giant stepped into the rain, his shaved head and bare arms instantly awash. He followed the narrow man down the alley and out into the thoroughfare, where they turned toward the harbor and the ship. Falconer had the confirmation he had sought. Raban's messenger was headed to the ship, with Raban's private guard as his protector. Which meant Raban was exposed.

Falconer waited another ten minutes, fifteen. Then he rose from his crouch and slipped across the alley. He tested the door and found it locked as he had expected. But the yellow brick which formed the doorframe was ancient and crumbling. Falconer took a two-fisted grip upon the iron ring which made the door's handle. He lowered his shoulder until it was flush with the sound of the rattling lock. He heaved.

The door crunched free of its lock. Falconer could not tell how much noise it made, his heart thundered so. He had retained his grip on the center ring to keep the door from crashing back against the wall. He entered the flagstone hall, shut the door, and let his oilskin drop to the floor. He waited with his mouth open, breathing shallowly, listening.

The hall was empty and lit by a series of oil lamps fastened to the wall. The café was beyond the wall to Falconer's right, and from it came the raucous sound of men making merry. He heard an Arabic lute and pipe and drums, and the clink of finger cymbals. The men began clapping and shouting louder still. A belly dancer, Falconer decided, assuming the café's din must have been enough to mask his entry.

He made his way soundlessly up the stairs. The steps were pickled oak, pale as smoke and hard as iron. Twice Falconer heard a rise in the café's noise level, for the wall between the stairs and the café held small spy holes masked as peaked wooden carvings. From the café side they would appear as mere ornaments set high above the action. Yet from this vantage point all could be observed in utter secrecy.

At the second-floor landing, the stairs curved around a closed door. He passed further spy holes which emitted pungent odors, the clatter of dice on wood, and the brittle sound of women laughing.

On the third-floor landing, the stairs opened into a domed foyer, painted as in an Arabian palace. Falconer slipped through the curtained entrance, his footsteps silenced by layers of Berber carpets. He moved swiftly, hunting now with his ears as much as his eyes. He passed through one room, another, a third, each larger and more ornate than the last. All were empty.

Then he heard birdsong. And a gasp. A tray clattered to a wooden floor. Falconer flew in the direction of that sound and came upon a servant in the act of pulling a pistol from his cloth belt.

"Easy now." Falconer did not test the man's strength. He did not need to. The servant was wide-eyed and trembling with terror. Keeping his voice level but stern, Falconer said, "You would not want that to go off and hurt someone."

He doubted the man understood him. Nor did it matter. For the fight was not in him. Falconer removed the pistol, a long-barreled gun with a handle chased in silver. He held the waiter by his collar and trained the gun at a figure seated in a thronelike chair. The ivory mouthpiece of another water pipe dangled from an astonished open mouth. A young woman in Arab dress of balloon leggings sought enough air to scream. "Tell her to be quiet."

But Raban was too astonished to speak.

"You. Come here." When the woman did not move, Falconer instead pulled the servant forward by his collar. The servant protested weakly, but only until Falconer glared a warning. He forced the servant behind Raban's chair. With the gun trained on their master, he used his other hand to press first the servant and then the young woman down until they were seated upon the floor.

"You . . . you can't be here."

"But I am." Falconer stepped back until he rested against the side wall, able to observe both the trio and the entrance. "Keep your hands where I can see them."

"My men—"

"Are on their way to the ship. Where they will engage in some scheme you have cooked up." A bird with a bell attached to one claw flitted about a gilded cage. The cage was suspended from a ceiling beam, between two silver oil lamps. A lute rested on the wall beside a cushion, where no doubt the young woman was intended to sit and entertain her master. Falconer could not help but ask, "Is she a slave?"

The eyes hooded over. "Don't tell me you are one of those." Raban obviously was trying to gain control of the situation.

"I take that as a yes."

"What an utterly wasted sentiment. She is quite happy as she is." When Raban adjusted himself in his seat, Falconer's pistol followed every movement.

He resisted the urge to argue further. "To the matter at hand."

"Indeed." Raban's hiss returned, no doubt now certain Falconer was not there to do him harm. "I assume you are here to make plans to enrich yourself."

"On the contrary. To enrich you." Falconer slipped out a leather purse and tossed it over. Raban squealed in genuine fear until he heard it clank when it hit the carpet at his feet. "Open it."

The merchant untied the knot and released a stream of gold into his lap. His robe was ornate and chased in silver thread, though pale in contrast to the coins in his lap.

"Two hundred and fifty sovereigns," Falconer said.

Raban let the coins clink between his fingers. The

young woman murmured softly. Raban smiled in her direction, a humorless gesture, one that boded ill. The woman either did not notice or chose not to care. Raban glanced at Falconer, his gray eyes scornful. "Here, I shall show you how happy are my little band."

"Slavery is outlawed in France."

"But this is not France, John Falconer. This is Le Panier." Raban handed out a coin each, first to the servant and then to the girl. Raban allowed the young woman to capture his hand and kiss it in gratitude. "Do they appear sorrowful to you, John Falconer?"

Falconer's voice grated with the strain of keeping his anger tamped down. "Either you will return my gold or you will agree to my terms."

"But of course, John Falconer." He turned Falconer's first name into the French counterpart, Jean. "Only tell me what you wish. If it is within my grasp . . ."

"How long will it take you to get word to La Rue?"

"Three days, four at the most." He returned his attention to the young woman, stroking the side of her face, mocking Falconer with his eyes. "Why?"

The young woman's eyes were as void of life and hope as any Falconer had ever seen. His former sorrow and guilt and rage now fueled a cauldron within his heart. "Tell La Rue exactly this. We will rendezvous with him ten miles off the coast of Tunis. He will bring the two captives. We will exchange them for gold."

Raban continued stroking the woman's face as he faked consideration. The woman stared into the nothingness before her, her face a thousand years old.

Raban said, "La Rue will not come alone, John Falconer."

Falconer gave no indication this was exactly what he was intending. "We will then pay you the same amount again upon our return, so long as the two captives are safe and unharmed."

Chapter 18

The next six days passed pleasantly enough. Harkness permitted his men to disembark to go into Marseilles in groups of at least two, preferably three, when not on watch. The officers, as well as Amelia Henning and the master, never set one foot on land alone. Sailors could not bear arms in a foreign port, but no one could force them to give up their billy clubs or working knives. These they wore in plain view. Ordered to remain outside the Panier district, they all were able to avoid trouble.

Each day Falconer took Matt out for a walk about Marseilles. They visited the emperor's museum, which was largely given over to prizes taken from Napoleon's various conquests overseas. They visited ancient churches. They ate in a trio of restaurants. They watched the people. On the sixth day, their last but one at port, Falconer packed a rucksack with provisions and told Matt he would walk the young lad's legs off. Matt took it as the challenge that it was, responding with a brilliant smile, the first since they had docked in the city. The expression drew Ada into a clarity Falconer had not known for several weeks, sharp and strong enough that he felt anew the dagger of loss.

Four of them left the ship, father and son accompanied by Soap and Bivens. The two sailors claimed nothing would suit them better than a chance to walk in a straight line until their strength gave way.

They left the city by the so-called northwestern gate, though in truth the city's medieval walls were little more than crumbling relics. Owners of outlying homes had stolen stones from the fortifications, leaving holes big enough to send armies through. Beyond the gate was yet another market, this one for regional farmers who displayed heaps of late fruit and bleating animals and ropes of fresh-made sausages. There they purchased a loaf of rosemary-scented flatbread, a chunk of glistening cheese, and fresh-churned butter. They followed a road that ran through a copse of trees before joining with the first of the neighboring slopes. They finally halted when a pair of hills and valleys separated them from the port. The day was clear, the clouds shepherded by a wind fresh enough to dry Falconer's sweat as soon as it was formed. They took their water from a swift-flowing stream that meandered through the valley.

The meal completed, Falconer and Matt left their friends lolling beneath an elm and started slowly up the next slope. Sheep bleated in the pastures to either side of the road. Further east, flax grew upon the hillside beneath a crest of blooming myrtle. At least Falconer thought it was flax, with its silver face revealed under the rising wind. Falconer reckoned it late for the myrtle to be in full bloom, but the months ran differently here, he thought. Falconer had sailed the Med any number of times and knew it possessed a woman's lovely ability to reveal an astonishing variety of moods and seasons.

Falconer waited until Matt selected a seat upon a likely looking log to say, "There's been something I've meant to ask you about, lad." He planted a boot on the log beside his son. "But shipboard life means that private conversations are hard to come by. If you don't mind, I'd like to speak about it now."

He knew he was speaking too formally. But truth be told, he had no idea how to broach such a subject with the boy. It was one of many areas where he sorely felt his lack of experience with children. "The day you climbed to the topsails, when you came down, you spoke of harboring fears. Do you remember that, lad?"

Matt squinted into the distance. The earth dropped away from their perch, tumbling down to where a creek glistened silver and a dusty road climbed the next hillside. He might have nodded. Or perhaps he simply drew himself in more tightly.

Falconer plugged forward determinedly. "I was wondering—that is, would you care to speak with me about the fears you hold?"

A bird not far different from a robin took up station in a neighboring oak. Falconer hoped the birdsong would not be the only response. Finally the boy spoke in a voice that blended with the wind. "Sometimes I don't know why I'm afraid."

"And other times?"

"I remember losing Mama."

"Are you afraid I'll leave you alone, son?" Falconer resisted the urge to take Matt in a massive embrace. "I have given my word to Reginald Langston that I would try and help free Lillian's son. But I have other oaths that I must fulfill. Some to God, others to Ada. I confess that it is difficult at times to balance them. This has become one point that I pray most over. That and a true answer to our quests, most especially the one you and I share together. But say the word, son, and I will retreat from the quest to rescue the prisoners."

Matt turned and looked at him. "Has God ever spoken to you, Father John?"

Of all the things he might have expected to hear from Matt, this was not one of them. "Aye."

"What was it like?"

Falconer took his time walking around the log. He slowly settled down beside his son. "Do you remember Serafina? Of course you do. I once asked her the very same thing. She told me that God spoke to her most clearly in the small, quiet moments of life, and the most ordinary parts of her day. I do not think I ever heard God's voice any clearer than in the love your dear mother gave to me every day of her life on earth."

Matt rubbed at his eyes, two swift motions. "I've been so angry with God."

"I can well understand that, Matt."

"At first I thought the bad storm was because of me."

Falconer comprehended the boy's words all too well. He selected his words carefully. "If God chose to punish us for all the times we fail to act as we should, especially when life delivers its blows, I would be the first to reap the whirlwind."

This time, Matt's nod was more fully formed. "I knew it was wrong to think like I did. Master Soap, he was scared too. That's why I sang. And I saw I couldn't be angry or scared and still be able to sing. I could be one way or the other. Not both. Master Soap thought I sang for him. But I sang for me, Father John."

Falconer found it necessary to clear his throat. "Is that why you sang for Mrs. Henning?"

"No . . . well, yes. In a way. In the storm, I saw how singing helped me push away the anger and the fear. No, not push . . ."

"You made a choice," Falconer suggested. "The singing held you to your chosen course."

"I sang for Mrs. Henning because I wanted to help her hold to God in spite of her worries over Kitty." Matt glanced over, his tight gaze fashioned by staring toward the westering sun. "Did I do right, Father John?"

"Indeed you did, lad."

"But one night, I heard her crying in her cabin."

"One night of worry does not make a life, son. We all have our moments of human weakness. Some nights just seem darker than others. I feel certain Amelia Henning has held fast to her faith and her hope, and that your company has aided her." His throat felt raw from the effort it required to keep his tone steady. "Sometimes we plant seeds of hope in others. But only God can see when they bring forth fruit."

The lad said nothing further for a long while. Falconer felt he had given a very bad answer, such that it had pushed Matt away. He resolved to remain as he was until the lad was ready to leave.

Finally Matt spoke into the wind, still facing the lowering sun. "I became very frightened the day we first arrived here, Father John."

Instantly he knew enough to fill in what his son had not said. "When I went to help the captain and Reginald?"

Matt nodded. "When you left the ship, I saw how the sailors watched you. They were worried. I knew it was dangerous. I went into the cabin and . . . and I cried."

"Oh, my dear, sweet son. I would never want to cause you sorrow."

"I prayed to God. And God spoke to me. At least I think He did."

Falconer turned from the boy and also stared into the sunlight. "Now I understand your question. The answer is yes, God spoke to me once. It was in the weeks before I met your mother. A time of great distress, in a manner of speaking. One different from what we faced with your mother's passing. But distressing just the same."

He knew he was expressing himself badly. Matt had no idea of those days, when Falconer's entire world revolved around Serafina and the fact that she would never be his. He had certainly loved her. But Ada had revealed to him something else entirely. The gift of a mature woman's heart, a strong and independent soul who gave freely and totally. It was a form of love beyond anything Falconer might have imagined. No, it was not right to compare. But what he had felt for Serafina had at the time been very real. As had been the moment God had spoken.

"How did you know it was God, Father John?"

He realized Matt was watching him. Falconer stood and took a measured pace away from the log. He addressed the distant hillside. "The message was something that could not have come from myself. It was granted with an unearthly power. And it was in harmony with my study of the Scriptures. All these things came to me over time. At the moment, I tell you honestly, there was no room for such questions. God spoke and I listened."

"Will the Lord speak to someone as young as me?"

Falconer looked at his son. "For all children everywhere, I cannot say. When I look at you, though, I see a lad who has faced down great fears, who has even greater reasons to rage at God for all your life long. I tell you in all honesty, Matt. Your wisdom astonishes me. You make me very proud."

There was a change to the manner of silence between them, a comfortable union that went far beyond the setting or the circumstances. Falconer returned to the log, sat, and draped his arm around the boy's shoulders. They listened to the wind and the sheep and the birds until a halloo from below signaled the others' readiness to return.

Only when they started back down the path did Falconer ask, "What did God say to you, son?"

"That He would hold you close and bring you back safely."

Falconer took hold of his son's hand. "The comfort in those words will take me through whatever comes."

Chapter 19

Admiral La Rue's answer arrived late the next afternoon, a single word written in bold print.

The brigand's response was delivered by Bernard Lemi. The banker arrived with the sunset, grim and alone. He doffed his hat to the middy on duty by the gangplank, then a second time to the captain. He waited until the other officers were gathered before handing over the sheet to the captain.

Harkness looked at it a long moment, then gave the parchment to Reginald Langston, who had returned from his offices a few minutes earlier and appeared as grim as the banker. He stared at the message. *Agreed.* Beneath that was a date four days hence.

Lemi informed the group, "My superior returned from Paris last night. He ordered me to appear before Raban and apologize. He threatened to write to my father and complain of my behavior. He described you as little more than simple ruffians, British and American louts who had no place in French society. All but you, good sir." Bernard nodded in Reginald's direction.

"Naturally," Reginald replied dryly. "Monsieur Sancerre would fear losing my company's trade."

"He described you, Monsieur Langston, as deluded by

the presence of these hooligans." Bernard Lemi's words were bitten off in angry precision, his accent made thicker by his rage. "Raban kept me waiting since eight this morning. When I was finally permitted to enter, he sat at his table at the rear of the café." He gestured at the paper Reginald still held. "I was given this note."

Harkness drew out his pocket watch, observed the time, and said to Bivens, "We have until midnight to depart with the outgoing tide. How many men do we have on shore?"

"Less than half the watch. The bosun's been ordered to keep track of their whereabouts."

"Have him fetch them back, if you please."

Bivens touched his forelock. "Aye, Captain."

"Tell him to do so quietly." Harkness clicked the watch shut. "Though Raban will no doubt know of our actions long before we leave harbor."

"Aye, sir."

Harkness said to Bernard, "We are indebted for your service as messenger. Join us for dinner, if you please."

Lemi bowed his acceptance, then added, "La Rue will have developed a scheme, Captain. Mark my words, he will be out to trap you."

Harkness shared a look with Falconer. "That is indeed our fervent hope."

"The Barbary sailors called themselves privateers," Bernard Lemi explained, "because they carried letters of marque from the princes that ruled the North Africa coast. But the princes were brigands themselves, and the letters were meaningless. They were nothing more or less than pirates."

Seating at the captain's table was cramped that evening, for Harkness had invited the midshipmen to dine with them. The four youngsters, the banker, and Amelia Henning took the seats opposite the skipper, who this night was seated closest to the door. Behind Lemi the harbor glinted a dullish copper in the fading light. In the distance, torches were lit around the keep of Fort Saint Jean.

"The Barbary pirates have been a scourge for over five hundred years," Lemi continued. "The term Barbary came from the largest coastland tribe, the Berbers. The correct name for the coastline is Maghreb. The pirates attacked ships ferrying your knights to the Crusades. Fifty years ago, they controlled over a dozen ports along the southern Mediterranean coast."

"Weren't they defeated some time back?" Bivens asked.

"Indeed so. Their stronghold at Tangier was destroyed by the Gibraltar fleet in 1816."

"Then who, pray tell, is this Ali Saleem?"

Bernard shrugged with his entire upper body, a particularly French gesture. "A brigand, for sure. But also a prince. He is secure enough in his power and his alliances to take up the habits of his predecessors."

"He is not alone," Falconer added. "There are similar pirate princes operating in the Somali lands of eastern Africa. Others rule fiefdoms in the southern islands, especially Mauritius. Still more further east, around the Malay Peninsula."

"You know this for a fact, do you?" Harkness demanded.

Falconer unthinkingly traced the scar on his face. "I do indeed."

A church bell sounded the hour. Harkness checked the time against his pocket watch, then clicked the face shut and returned his attention to the banker. "You were speaking of this Ali Saleem."

"He gains most of his wealth from trading in slaves,"

the banker explained. "He cares nothing for current treaties. He also takes great pride in Christian slaves, particularly Europeans. In his twisted logic, as a Muslim, his taking Christians as slaves justifies his acts. Regardless of the fact that most of his victims are drawn from other regional tribes."

Amelia Henning protested, "But my daughter is a hostage held for ransom, not as a slave."

Bernard Lemi bowed in the woman's direction. "Indeed so, madam." But as he straightened, he shot a glance at Falconer. One look was enough for both men.

The look was also not lost upon Harkness, who said, "I have heard tales of castles built entirely by Christian slaves."

"The tales, I fear, are true. The largest was the fortress of Moulay Ismail, on the Morroccan coast."

Bivens demanded, "How do you know so much about these men?"

Bernard's features looked haggard in the twilight. "Because, sir, my bank has been involved in their despicable trade for a long time."

Reginald Langston was shocked. "I had no idea."

"It is a fact the bank seeks desperately to hide," Bernard said apologetically. "But it is true nonetheless."

Harkness said to Bernard, "This explains the alliance between Raban and your superior."

"Precisely." Bernard Lemi leaned across the table. "Take me with you," he implored. "Let me perform some small penance for centuries of foul deeds. I shall do whatever you ask of me. Anything."

The ensuing silence was broken by Reginald's pushing his chair away from the table. "I cannot permit my business to remain with that bank for another moment!"

"The tide," Harkness said. "There is not time—"

"My conscience! My convictions! My commitment to God!"

As though in response, there came a knock on the wardroom's door. "Begging your pardon, Skipper," Soap said. "Bosun's compliments, and the tide has gone still."

Harkness opened his watch, but more to give his hands something to do than check the time. He asked Reginald, "Where then would you have us place the gold?"

"We did not take it to my offices because we knew neither my agent nor his security." Reginald's tone was determined. "But the man is trustworthy, and you have seen the safe with your own eyes."

"How long would it take to transfer the gold from your bank to the Langston safe?" Harkness demanded.

"With me at your men's side," Lemi responded, "a matter of minutes. Otherwise it could take days, perhaps weeks. Monsieur Sancerre does dearly love gold, even that which is not his."

Harkness looked from one face to the next. "Very well." Harkness snapped the watch shut and stowed it away. "Soap, gather your hearty sailors. We must shift some bullion, and be quick about it. Falconer, you would be so good as to lead them?"

"Of course."

"Lieutenant, order the bosun to lower the longboats. The harbor wind is so fitful with the surrounding hills we shall tow the ship into open waters."

"Aye, sir."

Harkness turned to the company owner. "What say you of the banker's request to join our band, sir?"

"I can hardly refuse such a request—not when Falconer also holds a desire to offer penance for past deeds."

Bernard Lemi followed the master's gaze across to where Falconer sat. "You were . . . a slaver?"

"To my eternal dishonor," Falconer replied.

"Not eternal, good sir." It was Harkness who countered Falconer's words. "Not when the Savior gave up His blood so that we might all be washed clean."

Falconer's nod was deep enough to be a half bow. "I stand corrected, Captain."

Once more the banker was silenced by words he scarcely comprehended. As he looked from one face to the other, Amelia Henning asked, "Am I to sail with you as well?"

"Unless you prefer to wait on land, madam."

"But I thought you said I was not to be brought along. That we, the ship, that is . . ."

"What I said was true." The captain's tone gentled, as it often did when addressing the lady. "We sail fearing that La Rue's agreement is a lie."

Her voice rose to a very soft wail. "Then what of my daughter?"

"My dear lady," Harkness replied, "we have prepared a few surprises of our own."

When the captain was about to dismiss the group, Falconer decided they had all watched Bernard fret long enough. "There is clearly something else which disturbs you this night."

Bernard shot him a look from beneath furrowed brows. "You have enough troubles of your own without hearing of mine."

"More than you are aware of," Falconer solemnly agreed. "More than I would wish upon anyone. But I also have allies. People with whom I can entrust my woes and who offer their strength when my own is not enough."

"There is nothing anyone can do," Bernard muttered to the candlelight.

Amelia Henning stirred on the table's other side. "Sir, forgive me, but you are wrong not to hope. Despair such as yours is as bleak and wearying as the grave. It saps your will, it defeats you long before the battle begins. There are only two answers to such desolation. One is prayer. The other is trust in the strength of true friends."

Bernard lifted his gaze and studied the woman. He seemed to be working through the words and their softly spoken challenge. "My friend has been taken," he finally said, "and it is my fault."

"This is the gambler?" Falconer asked.

"Yes." Bernard returned his attention to the candles. "City guards took him at dawn. He has been pilloried."

Amelia Henning protested, "That dreadful practice can't possibly still be in use—not in a civilized land."

Harkness replied, "France brought it back during the Revolution. Some towns still keep a pillory on hand."

Bernard continued to address the flickering flames. "He has been accused of running from his debts. The truth is, Raban knows I am aiding you. He wants your gold, and he knows my father's power. So we are safe, but my friend is not. Raban hurts me by hurting my friend."

There was a moment's silence, then Harkness said, "Forgive me, sir. But we are pressed into action by the tide's timing. Will you aid us in moving the gold to the Langston safe?"

"Of course, but won't you require it as ransom?"

Harkness glanced at Reginald, who replied, "We brought double the amount demanded. Just in case part was stolen or the demands changed."

The young banker pushed his chair back from the table. "I see you know our foe well."

Bernard's concerns were so great he was not conscious of his own words, *our foe*. But the rest of the table took note of how he had joined with them. Harkness gave Falconer a hard look from beneath his heavy brows and said, "You will take charge of this duty?"

"Aye, Captain. That I will."

"How long will you require?"

"Not an instant longer than necessary."

Harkness dismissed them with, "Make all possible haste. And beware the unseen reefs."

Chapter 20

Transferring the gold to the Langston building took less than a half hour. The bank manager tried in vain to at least slow things considerably. A rotund little man with tiny feet, he protested and fluttered like a ballerina in dark broadcloth. He repeatedly pointed at his watch and waved them off, demanding they return during normal business hours. When that failed, he issued dire threats in Bernard Lemi's direction, particularly when the sacks of gold began to gather upon his office desk. But Bernard was beyond caring. When the myriad objections failed to halt them, Monsieur Sancerre sought to take hold of the bags. Falconer planted himself next to the banker, bent in close, and scowled. The banker's features turned greasy with genuine fear. His intended protest came out as a squeak, and he went utterly still.

Reginald's local director was an unsmiling bloodless man, far better with numbers than people. The Langston safe was in fact a windowless cellar room, with an interior casing of concrete and a steel door so thick the key was longer than Falconer's hand. The former clerk sniffed over the gold and offered them a stamped chit. Clearly the manager thought the gold should have gone there in the first place and thus saved everyone a good deal of bother.

Outside the company offices, Falconer asked Bernard, "Where is he?"

"Who?"

"Your friend. What is his name?"

"Pierre. But the sheriff's men—"

Falconer gripped the banker's shoulder. "Did you hear the captain speak of the tide?"

"Yes, of course. But . . ."

"We have no time to lose." To the sailors, he said, "Stay close and be ready."

Bernard looked at the hardened men, saw how the sailors grinned with anticipation. Even the older Soap looked pleased. Bernard asked Falconer, "You would do this for me?"

"I told you before. It is the least we can do for a friend."

Once again Falconer and his small band skirted the quayside, following Bernard through a maze of alleys that grew increasingly cramped the deeper they moved into the Panier district. Beyond the Hôtel de Ville, the quarter started up an incline, becoming steeper the further they traveled. Most of the houses were medieval in age and design and offered a narrow façade to the streets—usually only one or two windows wide. The balconies were rusted iron over crumbling bricks and flaking paint. The support timbers were angled and as twisted as the original trees. On any other evening, the visit might have been a pleasant diversion. Tonight, however, Falconer pushed himself and the men hard. He had to achieve their goal before enemy reinforcements arrived.

The quarter's main streets were paved in the ancient Roman manner, with two curved wagon tracks framing central brick steps. The men were all puffing hard from the strain of trying to run up a steep cobblestone hill. Finally Bernard waved them to a halt beside a curved brick stanchion that might well have dated from the era of Vandals.

"The Place des Moulins," the banker puffed as he pointed.

The square was rimmed by sputtering torches and a series of open-fronted taverns. A decrepit windmill rose from the square's far end, its limbs motionless in the still night air. The patrons drank and laughed and ate and jeered at the man imprisoned at the square's center.

The pillory was set upon a circular platform in the shape of a sundial. The wooden structure had five openings, all bordered in leather. The young man's wrists, ankles, and neck were trapped, and he sat morosely upon a narrow bench. His features were streaked with debris tossed by the tavern patrons. He had been turned ancient by his ordeal.

Falconer glanced behind. The empty lane dropped off so steeply he looked over the rooftops to the two portside fortresses. The moon was almost full. The sea glistened black and silver, out to where a watch fire burned upon the Château d'If. Falconer saw no one stalking them.

"Guard my back," he said, and raced forward.

He headed straight for the pillory. The young man, fearing another taunter, watched him approach with genuine fear. "We're going to get you out of there, lad," Falconer told him.

He doubted Pierre understood the words but hoped he was at least able to catch the tone. Falconer studied the two massive padlocks, both of them from another era.

"A hammer and a chisel," he muttered to himself. "You should have thought of this long before now."

All of Falconer's senses were at full battle readiness. He could slice the seconds into a myriad fragments, each holding its own crystal clarity. He heard the imprisoned young man whimpering in pain and confusion. He heard footsteps clatter across the cobblestones and knew without turning that those who approached were friends. He heard Bernard speak words of assurance to Pierre. Then he heard the first roar of opposition. Bernard and his pilloried friend both blanched with genuine terror.

Falconer, however, took it as his cue.

He turned and raced toward the man now rising to his feet. The night's shadows made Raban's guard even larger and more fearsome than when he had been inside the café's confines.

Raban's beast recognized Falconer and overturned his table and half-finished meal with one angry sweep. Patrons shouted and scampered.

Then the man's hands swept to his belt. One hand came up with a pistol, the other with his long curved dagger.

Falconer had one chance. A man of that size was accustomed to opponents hesitating. The giant was used to having the advantage, the one who dictated the terms of battle.

Or so Falconer fervently hoped.

Falconer did not hesitate. Instead, he powered faster still, racing as fast as the slick cobblestones allowed.

He saw the beast's eyes widen in surprise. And knew he was right to charge.

As he passed the café's periphery he grabbed an overturned chair. He added his forward momentum as additional force to the two-handed swing, wielding the chair as a club.

The beast was caught completely off guard. He tried to deflect the chair with his forearms. The chair splintered, but the beast lost both his weapons.

Raban's guard bellowed and went down on one knee.

Falconer spun about by the force of his own attack. He gripped a table and continued to spin, making a complete circle and gathering speed as he did so.

When he let fly, the table shattered into a thousand fragments, and this time the beast went down on all fours.

Falconer gripped another table and brought it crashing down upon the man's head. He went prone at Falconer's feet.

But Falconer was not done. He kept moving, his force carrying him from one table to the next in the space of two heartbeats.

The two guards backed up against the tavern's side wall. Typical sheriff's deputies, they were chubby characters accustomed to bullying their way forward, their official titles the only defense they required. Now they recognized a force beyond their ability to counter. They held their pikes in trembling hands and wailed protests Falconer did not need to understand.

Falconer effortlessly plucked the weapons from the guards' fingers. He tossed away one of the pikes. He stripped the pistols from their belts and flung them into the night. He silenced the men with a single look and ran back to the pillory.

"Stand aside."

He hefted the borrowed pike and used the spearlike end to smash first one and then the other padlock.

As the sailors lifted the pillory's upper gate, the guards shouted a feeble protest. Falconer turned and silenced them with a single glare.

The two sailors brushed Bernard aside and hefted the limp and whimpering man. Now that his rescue was imminent, his cries became half-formed words.

Falconer was in the process of ordering his men back to the ship when an image struck him with the force of a branding iron. He saw again the lifeless gray eyes of the young woman enslaved to Raban and heard her whispery voice. He recalled Raban's hand stroking her face, one robbed of all hope. Just another den of iniquity. He had known many such places, and sinned in them many a time, blind to all the sorrow his gold helped fuel.

But this night would be different.

As Falconer led his men from the square, he wrested a flaming torch from its stanchion and said, "All of you would be far better off taking yourselves back to the ship."

Soap understood him correctly, for the old sailor said, "And leave you to battle the fiends alone? My mother didn't raise her son to fall into any such nonsense as that, sir."

"This has nothing to do with our quest or the captain's orders," Falconer said. "I have a task of my own to fulfill."

"That don't change a thing. I'm your man," Soap said fiercely.

The bullyboy whose forehead remained scarred from the attack at landfall agreed. "As are we all, your honor, sir."

"Then grab torches for yourselves and follow me!" Falconer pointed to Bernard. "You get your friend to the ship. We'll join you soon as we can."

"With respect, I must refuse." Clearly Bernard understood what Falconer intended. "I can show you the swiftest way to the café, and as I speak the language, my help may be required."

Falconer heard the captain's timepiece ticking away the seconds in his mind. "Make haste!"

They clattered down the way. Falconer took Soap's torch so the older sailor could help Bernard bundle his friend down the slope. They moved at such a pace that the freed prisoner skipped upon the cobblestones, his feet taking virtually none of his weight. Neither Bernard nor Soap minded the burden. The sailors had the battle gleam in their faces. Bernard's features were alight with a fierce joy.

At a sign from Falconer, they propped Pierre against the wall across the lane from the café's entrance. Falconer handed Soap his torch and said to Bernard, "Stay close. You lot, we are after speed and mayhem."

The bullyboys were grinning broadly. "You've got the right mates for that, sir."

"We'll start on the ground floor. Light what burns. Clear out the place as we go. No one is to get hurt this night, most especially yourselves."

"None save Raban," Bernard hissed, glaring at the top floor hideaway.

"You stay close at my side. I need you to translate."

"What am I to say?"

In reply, Falconer raced across the lane. He struck the café's front doors with a force so explosive both were burst off their hinges, flying far back into the café's gloom. He roared a single word, *"FIRE!"*

A trio of musicians seated upon a raised dais midway back froze in comic unison with the belly dancer. The café's patrons halted in mid-cheer. Falconer hefted a table in the hand not carrying the torch and smashed it against the side wall. He continued in his sweep, using the torch now to light the damask curtains and one empty set of cushions. *"FIRE!"*

His men spread out, roaring and smashing and spreading fiery chaos as they flew. Bernard's shrill warning rose in French, pointing at the door and imploring the patrons to escape.

The café exploded into a crashing, banging, screaming mob. Falconer stepped further from the doorway and shepherded them along with his torch and his club. One of the sailors rushed past, supporting a guard who nursed a welt on his head and complained in a whining voice. The sailor booted him out the door, cast Falconer a merry grin, and rushed back for more.

Falconer shouted over the din, "Bernard! Come with me!"

They headed for the side stairs, the ones which mirrored the hidden stairs leading up to Raban's quarters. Falconer crashed through the middle floor's door as though it were paper. He entered a sweetly scented din of soft lighting and screams. *"FIRE!"*

There was so much to burn on this floor. The gambling tables and the soft cushions and the draped alcoves all begged for his torch. The layers of misdeeds and misery added to the smoke and the flames.

He waited until Bernard had sped on their way the last of the screaming patrons and servants, then yelled, "Upstairs!"

His boot took care of the bar set upon the door's other side. Together with Bernard and one sailor, Falconer leapt up the final set of stairs.

He spied the servant just in time. *"Down!"*

He flung himself upon Bernard and pummeled the banker to the stairs just as the servant fired his pistol. The sailor behind them was more accustomed to close-quarter fighting and had not needed any further warning. The bullet whined safely overhead. Falconer jumped to his feet and took the final steps in one bounding leap. He caught the servant in the process of aiming his second pistol. He ripped the pistol away and flung the man against the wall. The man crumpled.

Falconer used a favorite warrior's trick then. He sprang into the room and just as swiftly sprang back. Which meant Raban's ready pistol fired and shot nothing but the wall. Instantly Falconer bounded back into the room, crossed the space in two great strides, and smashed his club across Raban's trembling arm. The man squealed as the second pistol went spinning across the room.

Raban's gun landed at the grinning sailor's feet. The sailor knew good loot when he saw it. He slipped the gold and bejeweled pistol into his belt and said, "Thank you kindly."

"You," Falconer said to the crouching young woman. "Flee now."

The woman rose uncertainly to her feet. Raban hissed a single word but went quiet when Falconer jammed the torch within an inch of his face.

"Wait." Falconer turned to Bernard. "Ask her if she knows where Raban keeps his treasure."

The sudden glint in her eyes was all the response Falconer needed. "Tell her she can take all she can carry, and may it help her recover a semblance of hope and life."

The young woman flung herself at Falconer's feet until Bernard was able to coax her up and away. They remained thus, surrounded by ever thickening smoke. The sailor whistled as he walked from room to room, lighting everything in his path. Finally they heard the woman shrill a further thanks as she fled down the stairs.

Falconer tossed the torch onto the cushions. He gathered up the unconscious servant, tossed the man over his shoulder, and said to the cowering Raban, "Stay or flee. It is all the same to me."

"We are all done here," he said to the men who watched him.

Chapter 21

Before they finally left Marseilles behind and headed out to sea, they deposited Pierre upon the lone Frioul island which was inhabited. The fishermen's harbor, was too small for the clipper, so she laid anchor in protected headwaters while Pierre was rowed ashore. Reginald Langston and Bernard Lemi accompanied the two sailors who stretchered the young man across the beach and into the rough-hewn fishing village. Reginald saw the young man safely into the island's only decent inn, woke up the innkeeper, and paid in gold for two weeks' food and lodging. More gold was left for a new set of clothes and for the innkeeper's wife to see to Pierre's wounds—at least those to his body. The rest they could only leave with the Almighty.

When they were again on board, a perplexed Bernard Lemi sought out Falconer and reported, "Langston asked my friend for his word that he would never gamble again. He also said that the rescue was a gift. He urged Pierre to find God, and through God find the strength to free himself from his vices."

"That sounds a solid bargain in the making," Falconer replied with a nod.

The rosy hint of breaking day illuminated the banker's

confusion. "When Langston bid me farewell, I begged him to let me come along on this voyage. He said I was welcome but that I owed him nothing at all, that he had not done this for me. He also said his strongest ally had been forged in similar depths of confusion and woe, and that I should speak with you."

Falconer directed his words to the brightening eastern sky. "I was once a slaver."

"You told me that before, and I still do not understand."

"How I came to be here? Or why Reginald treated your friend as he did?"

Another breath, then, "Both."

"They are one and the same answer. The friends I have here with me, we share not just this mission but a faith in the God of miracles and grace."

Bernard worked on those words for a time. "I hear your words, but I do not fully understand."

Falconer felt a certain reluctance to continue. "Perhaps one of the others could help you comprehend more fully what it means."

From behind them, a woman's voice said, "No, I think not, John Falconer."

"I did not hear you approach, Mrs. Henning."

"But you did hear what the gentleman said, yes?" Amelia Henning spoke with a different voice, somewhere between a whisper and song. "Reginald Langston sent him to *you,* not another."

Falconer dropped his head. "Since my loss, most of my prayers have fallen like clods of winter earth from my mouth. Perhaps this same absence of Spirit is why Bernard does not understand what I have said."

She rested her hand lightly upon his arm. "John Falconer, do you think God hears only those who are whole in heart and mind? Tell me this and I shall throw myself overboard, for the last shred of hope I have will be lost forever."

He had wept only once since he had put Ada in the ground. Yet here he was, fighting against eyes that burned like coals. "I do not know what to say, madam, except that it feels as though anything I say to this man is only half the truth."

"Tell him why, and let him be the judge." Slight as she was, her gentle pressure was enough to turn him around. "Speak, John Falconer."

He tore a ragged breath from the salt-laden air. "My wife died last February. A love I waited a lifetime to find, gone like that." Thumb and finger clicked her passing as Falconer looked into the man's face.

Bernard Lemi's gaze shifted from one to the other. The fighter who stood a head and more taller than himself, and the slight woman beside him. "I can only offer my sincerest regrets, sir."

"You heard what I have said to the lady. I feel as though my wounds have left me unable to speak with the same strength of conviction as before."

A multitude of questions working through the young banker's mind played across his features. "And yet, when I hear you talk, I feel as though a door opens before me. One through which I am invited to enter. Though I understand not what lies on the portal's other side."

Falconer glanced back at Amelia, pleading now.

She revealed to him an uncommon change. Peace and trust shone in her face so that her own wounds, visible in eyes and expression, diminished. "Answer him the best you can. Leave the rest to God."

Falconer stared at the eastern sky, out to where the sun was moments away from appearing. "Some time back, the year I captained a slaver, I met a man of faith. He spoke to me of a Savior. He spoke words I had never heard before, or perhaps heard yet never thought could apply to the likes of me."

Bernard was silent through a trio of waves that crashed against the oak timbers beneath them. "And those words?"

"Salvation." Falconer felt his voice crack, though he could not name the reason. "Healing. Eternal hope. Heaven."

Bernard's hunger to understand was so great he did not seem to notice Falconer's distress. "I have lived among the churched all my days and never heard words spoken in such a manner as this. As though . . ."

When he was unable to explain, the woman on Falconer's other side offered, "As though the words are not now spoken to your ears and mind, but rather to your very soul."

Bernard took a long moment to murmur, "Indeed."

"Ask him, John Falconer," Amelia said.

He gripped the railing with both hands, as though wrestling with the wood helped him take that vital step beyond his own internal questions. "Would you care to pray?"

The day passed in the steady cadence of life at sea. The watches changed, the sails were shifted to meet the vagaries of wind and tide, the decks were holystoned, the meals served. Amelia Henning joined the men for dinner and even managed a smile at the tale they served up with the main course, of the heroics at the top of a cobblestone hill. The officers renamed it the Skirmish of Windmill Square.

After dinner she waited for the assembly to depart before turning to say, "Your prayer this morning, John

Falconer, with the young French gentleman moved me. I think it moved him as well."

He stared into her face and saw the fire rise strongly enough to quench momentarily the pain in her gaze. "I can scarcely remember a single word I spoke."

"Some of the finest prayers I have ever known were formed just like that."

"I could not have spoken those words, madam, had it not been for your urgings. You were right in all you said."

"It is strange how I found the strength to speak only by looking at you." The smile, though tiny, warmed them both. "I was thinking it might do us all good to begin a time of study and prayer. Captain Harkness has been good enough to offer us the use of his day cabin. Would you care to join us after breakfast in the morning?"

"Mrs. Henning, I could think of nothing more welcome." Falconer found the smile remained imbedded on his heart long after she was gone.

———— ✍ ————

They made an odd assortment the next morning, or so it seemed to Falconer as he entered the room and glanced around. Amelia Henning had taken the captain's chair, dressed in her threadbare frock. Sunlight flooded through the great stern windows, illuminating the pinpoint of sadness at the core of her gaze. Yet this strange and lovely woman, who had not spoken a dozen words for days on end, who had initially refused to dine with the ship's company, now smiled a greeting and bid them welcome in the Lord's name.

Reginald Langston, owner of a worldwide system of ship and trading, was seated beside the widow. Then Matt, then Bernard, then Soap. The wizened steward was clearly uncomfortable seated in the master's cabin. Falconer found a place next to Soap. One of the barrel-chested sailors who had aided Falconer in Windmill Square was next. Another of the midshipmen made eight. Captain Harkness and Lieutenant Bivens stood at the corner chart table, their heads almost touching as they softly discussed tides and depths and wind.

Amelia Henning looked at Falconer and asked, "Would you like to lead us in an opening prayer?" When he hesitated, she pressed gently, "A gentleman is seated among us this morning because of you. Prayer in such times is a recognition of God among us, John Falconer."

He invited the others to bow their heads. He spoke the words, and felt a stirring resonance within his own heart. When he lifted his head, he found Amelia Henning gazing at him. "My late husband," she said, "may he rest in God's eternal peace, often said that some of the finest confessions he had ever heard were spoken out of the depths of wounding confusion. Because only then did the strong among us come to accept their desperate need for God. Would you care to confess your own confusion, John Falconer?"

Had he known this was where she was headed, Falconer might have refused to come. As it was, however, he found a faint yearning call rising within him. As though some part of him had wanted this very chance to speak, though his mind might have rebelled at the prospect. "My wife, Matt's mother, passed away last winter," he started, speaking to the floorboards by his boots. "For much of the time since then, my heart has been a stone. Many of my prayers have seemed so empty they have felt almost like fables. I prayed with Bernard yesterday because Mrs. Henning requested it. But I feel I did a disservice to him, because though I spoke of God's abiding love, I felt it not."

To his surprise, it was Matt who spoke up then. "But you love me, Father John."

"Aye, lad. That I do. No question about that."

"The Good Book says God is love."

Amelia Henning spoke in a voice Falconer did not recognize. "It does indeed, young sir."

"If you love me, Father John, doesn't that mean God is still close to you?"

To that, Falconer had no answer.

Amelia Henning asked the table at large, "Would anyone else care to confess a weakness, a need that remains unfulfilled, a wound that troubles them greatly?"

"Aye, that I would, ma'am." To their surprise, it was the young lieutenant who spoke. Bivens shifted around and opened his coat, revealing a sling. "Against the advice of both the skipper and Falconer, I insisted upon carrying my share of the gold yesterday. My injury from the storm has worsened to where I can scarcely lift a fork."

Harkness said, "I ordered him to shield the wing for a fortnight."

"Which means," Bivens said, "I cannot accompany Falconer on his mission. I feel I have let down the brethren because of my stubborn nature."

Soap came to seated attention. "I'd count it an honor to go with you, sir."

"You have no idea what you're saying," Falconer replied. "Or what lies in store."

"Don't matter a whit, sir. I'm your man."

Bernard Lemi said, "I would beg to be included in your company as well, sir. I have never been in battle, but I am known as a fine shot with both pistol and musket."

Amelia Henning softly tapped the table. "I suggest we

leave further discussion of plans and weapons for when the lamp of prayer is not lit."

"Well said, madam." Harkness stumped across the cabin. He directed Bivens into the one remaining chair and pulled over a footstool. He waved Soap back into his chair. "Well said indeed."

Amelia Henning said, "Would anyone else care to speak of unanswered need?"

It was Reginald Langston who spoke up next. "All who know me realize I am a man of action. I love nothing more than a hard day's work followed by a night of good friends, my family, and good cheer. I love life, I love a good table, I love my church. I have never been a man of great intelligence and it has never bothered me at all. I have given everything I have to whatever task is before me. Until this time, it has served me well enough."

His gaze had gradually lowered until his eyes rested upon the hands clasped on the table before him. "Yet now my power as a merchant and a man of action is brought to nothing. In the months leading up to my departure from Washington, my dear wife often slipped from our marriage bed so that her sobs would not wake me, or so she thought, as she mourned over her son. But my helpless state had already robbed me of sleep. I have been forced to learn what it means to do nothing but wait upon the Lord. And this act of waiting has been the hardest challenge I have ever faced. I have sought to study. At some times the words seem illuminated by my powerlessness. At others, my mind makes neither head nor tail of what I read. One moment I find peace, and the next I am so frustrated and worried my peace seems but a lie. And in those dark moments, my prayers . . ."

Falconer found himself speaking for his friend, "They are but dust that falls from our lips."

Reginald sighed to his hands, and nodded once.

In the silence that followed, a young boy's broken voice struggled to shape the words, "I miss my mama."

Amelia Henning's hand came to rest upon Matt's. She cast a glance around the table, and when no one else spoke, she said, "You are all far too aware of my own troubles. Yet in the midst of my own dark hour, when my daughter seems lost to me . . ."

It was the lady's turn to stop and take a very hard breath. "I find I question many of my most cherished memories. I felt God leading me to remain in Africa and continue my late husband's work. I have no family in America, no one to care for us or miss us while we are away. It was just Kitty and me, and my daughter loved Africa more than I, if that were possible. Yet in my darkest night since leaving my daughter in that foul dungeon, I have wondered if perhaps I listened to a different voice, one that spoke of selfish yearnings to remain where I was needed, where my life had meaning, and thus put my own daughter in grave peril."

A strong flame rose in Falconer's chest. He clenched himself hard, bunched a fist, and pressed it fiercely onto his ribs. He was a man of the sea. A soldier. Such people as he were not brought to tears by a woman's words.

Amelia Henning went on, "God is showing me again what it means to be open in weakness. How to speak when I have no answers. When I am blinded with pain, and understand nothing that has happened to me, still I am called to *choose*."

Bernard Lemi took a breath that was midway between a gasp and a sob. He covered his eyes.

"And this above all else I know," Amelia Henning said.

"God is here. With us. This day. Though He seems distant, though our weakness and our pain are all we might see." She looked to the ceiling, far enough to where the tears were released. "Our God is here with us."

Chapter 22

Hours were spent each day in meticulous planning and preparation. Perhaps Harkness insisted upon such discussions because he was to remain with his ship. But Falconer did not think that was the case. Harkness might skipper a merchant vessel, but he possessed a true leader's eye for exactitude. They went through the plan in scrupulous detail. When they were finished, they did it again. By the third repetition, Falconer's rough concept had been reformed into a strategy of stealth and possible success.

The fourth morning after their departure for the north African coast, Harkness ended the now-daily prayer meeting by inviting the company to join him on the foredeck. Only Matt could not do so, as it was his assignment to stand watch. Lieutenant Bivens stared at the empty yellow wasteland beyond the passing shoreline and said, "I have heard tales of galleys rowed into battle by men chained to their oars."

Falconer watched Matt cluster with the other middies. They took a shot of the sun with a shared sextant and quarreled mildly over the calculations. "The rumors are true enough."

Bivens watched him intently. "How do you fight such a foe?"

"Such vessels cannot carry the same weight of arms as we do," Falconer replied. "Nor are they well disciplined. They strike when their foes are weak and flee before reinforcements arrive."

"That may all be true," Harkness muttered, peering through his telescope at the southern vista. "But I'll never let one of them draw to my windward side. With us relying on sails, they'd have me as trapped as a monkey in a barrel."

Together they stared across miles of water to the realm of yellow heat. The ocean met the shore in a series of steep hills, the sea of water giving way to a sea of sand. Falconer used Reginald's telescope to study the terrain. The merchant's spyglass was of etched brass and the outer rim circled in Spanish leather. The glass was the finest Falconer had ever used. Even so, he found no sign of life—not a tree, not a movement of any kind. Just sand and yellow rock and a rising ribbon of heat.

Amelia Henning protested, "But we are not here to battle anyone. We are here to rescue our children."

Captain Harkness slapped his own spyglass shut. "We are also dealing with pirates, madam."

"And what, may I ask, do you mean, sir?"

The captain turned from the desert to inspect the woman standing beside him. Harkness was as blunt in his features as his manner. His graying beard was chopped off like a spade. His features were sun-darkened and deeply lined. Falconer knew from Reginald Langston that the captain was forty-one years old. He looked sixty.

Yet his eyes were as clear as illuminated crystal and his voice was gentle as he said, "I have been deeply affected by your lessons these past mornings, madam."

"Here, here," Reginald agreed.

"You have not merely overcome a grievous loss. You have turned this tragedy into illumination."

Amelia Henning dropped her gaze. "I have done very little, if anything, Captain."

"You have allowed God to work in you. You did as you have been urging us to do, to *choose*. Only then can God work in the midst of life's chaos." He paused a moment, then said, "Your husband, may his soul rest in eternal peace, was blessed by having you at his side."

The widow's tone was very subdued. "You are telling me that I must not allow my fears and my distress to take control once more. I must trust you to do the best you can. The best *anyone* can." She sighed. "You are right, of course."

The captain extended his spyglass and returned to inspecting the shoreline. "A wise woman indeed."

Bivens and Falconer spotted their goal at the same moment. The two cried, "There!"

"I see it." Harkness scowled. "The heat causes all the markings to swim so, I might as well be peering beneath the hull."

"Shall I order us closer to shore?" Bivens asked.

"No, we've attracted enough attention as it is." He glanced at Falconer. "Tell me again what the Englishman said we'd find—what was his name?"

"Captain Clovis," Falconer replied without taking his eye from the glass. "A ruined city has been turned into a roadside resting place, which the desert folk call a caravan-serai. Four towers marking a city all but smothered by the desert. Two of the towers are crumbling; the others belong to a mosque at the city's heart and not at the walls. The ruins spread out eastward, beyond the old fortifications, and are used as corrals. Bedouin tents rise beyond them."

Bivens added, "Clovis also said the fortress walls are of brick and not stone."

Harkness scowled at the danger beyond the horizon.

"How the man saw the nature of those walls is beyond me. Did he make landfall?"

"Not he." Falconer shook his head. "Two of his men."

Bivens glanced at Amelia Henning, then added, "Captain Clovis stated that these corrals are used not just for animals."

"I know that." Harkness stiffened as the heat waves momentarily cleared. "Yes. There. Four towers. Two in ruins. Lieutenant, you may order the bosun to make way."

They turned east and sailed toward Tunis. As they traversed the shoreline, they studied intently the knolls rising behind the caravanserai. Forming a backdrop to the road, the hills grew in height the further eastward the ship sailed. Midway between the caravanserai and Tunis, the cliffs reached a height of several hundred meters, paralleling the shoreline and about half a kilometer inland. Falconer watched a train of camels and donkeys and men parade in a slow desert cadence along the road running between the sea and the ocher cliffs. The hills were so close to the road as to frame the caravan in shades of yellow and auburn. Falconer was the first to sight a curious formation atop one hill, one that Captain Clovis had instructed them to identify. A pair of stone fingers rose half again as high as the hill itself, frozen in timeless salute to the sun and the heat.

Harkness shut his glass once more. "All right, I've seen enough. Lieutenant, bring us about. North by northwest. Take us well over the horizon."

"Aye, sir. North by northwest it is."

Harkness focused intently on Falconer. "If we take on this plan alone, we'll be hung out like my dear wife's laundry, flapping in the wind and open to attack. All I can say is I hope your English skipper is a man to be trusted."

Falconer handed Reginald his telescope. "I hope so too, Captain."

They were in position twelve hours before the scheduled meeting. First they sailed almost within hailing distance of the Tunis port. Harkness ordered that a brace of cannons be fired. In response, the ancient Carthage walls boiled with men. Falconer watched the sun spark upon curved scimitar blades and muskets chased in silver. The fortress guns boomed their reply. While Harkness had fired with powder alone, the fort's guns used round shot and elevated their guns to the maximum. Even so, the balls arced high into the air, then fell harmlessly into the sea.

Harkness brooded by the quarterdeck railing. Falconer stood to one side, Amelia Henning and Reginald Langston to the other. Harkness said to the widow, "Tell me again what you know of the lay of the land."

"Beyond this port area are a series of low hills."

"Aye, I see that."

"Beyond the hills is a giant lake. Or perhaps it is a third bay—I have no idea. But I did not see a connection to the sea. And beyond that is Tunis proper."

The hillsides formed a distinctly desert scene. Low houses were surrounded by stone walls of the same color. The houses and the walls and the lanes all blended into the desert. Yet dotted among these were huge Bedouin tents, some larger than the more permanent dwellings.

"And the citadel?"

"You see it there."

"It looks half destroyed. Or half finished."

The fortress appeared so old it had melded with the northern cliffs. The southern side tumbled into a pile of rubble, the rubble disappeared into the slope of a dune, and the dune fell into the inner harbor. There were, as Amelia Henning had described to them earlier, no windows that Falconer could see. Spaced around the outer wall were tight arrow slits.

Amelia Henning's voice had grown as low as the wind moaning through the rigging. "It is as dark and old as unmarked graves."

Harkness lowered his telescope. "My dear Mrs. Henning, I am well aware this is extremely trying for you. But I must ask you to brace yourself. These questions are critical to the success of our venture."

She straightened her shoulders with genuine effort. "Ask what you will of me, please."

"Thank you." Harkness returned to his inspection as the cannons fired again. "What say you, Bivens?"

"The gunners are either lazy or ill trained, sir." Bivens handed the timepiece back to the skipper. "Four minutes between rounds. And the cannons do not track more than thirty degrees."

"What does that mean?" Reginald asked.

"It means they are old guns, sir. Very old. It means that the man who occupies that keep is secure in his treaties and not his arms."

"But we are not intending to attack!" the woman wailed, then covered her mouth with her hand.

"Even so, it pays to know our enemy, does it not?" Harkness cut off any reply by asking the lady, "You mentioned before that you entered the inner keep."

"Two chambers only." They all could see she was making every effort to hold to calm.

"From what I see, sir," Bivens said, "the inner fortress could hardly hold much more."

Falconer agreed. The fortress might have once been a far grander affair, but he doubted it. He had visited such desert-style keeps during his checkered past. The ancient builders did not intend to make palaces. They sought a strong room, a secure hold for their booty, and little else. The true palaces would be further inland, where their masters could live surrounded by the desert's security.

"I spy one harbor only," Harkness said.

"It only seems that way." The woman's voice was quiet but now as determined as the set of her spine. "There is a narrow spit of land, scarcely broader than the road which runs along its crest."

"A road, you say."

"Yes." Her features were as taut as the wind-filled sails overhead. And as pale. "It runs from one side of the harbor to the other. Ringing that are the slave corrals and the fortress. The slave keepers' quarters are in the stubby tower you see there."

Harkness raised his voice, addressing both the young officer beside him and the crew on watch. "Lieutenant Bivens!"

"Aye, sir."

"Come about and head us back along the shoreline. Stay well clear of the gunner's range, mind."

"Aye, sir. Ready about!"

The ship wheeled its graceful curve, the sails refilled, and they began their steady progress back toward Tunis. Harkness directed his company to the deck's opposite railing and resumed his careful study. "Madam, I must ask you again about the dungeons."

Clearly she had been expecting this. "Massive. Endless. Dark. Terrifying."

"Be so good as to describe all you can remember of your approach."

"I was bound as a slave, my arms and hands behind me, the rope reaching up to encircle my neck." She could not erase the tremors from her words. "I met with some smirking official in the keep's first chamber. The great doors were open, and I saw La Rue seated in the other, holding audience. The official gave me the message for Master

Langston. I did not speak with La Rue directly. I was then taken downstairs."

"The stairs opened from the outer chamber?"

Her features tightened further and she drew her lips together as she strained to remember. "There was a door bound in iron. No . . . wait, I remember. We crossed a small space back toward the outer walls. I thought we were done and that I was being taken back to the pen holding the women."

"The doorway was attached to the wall?"

"No. It was in a small house—maybe a shed."

"To the right or the left of the main entrance?" Falconer asked.

"I don't . . . yes, to the right."

"You are certain?"

"Leaving the inner keep, we started toward the fortress gates, and then I was pulled off to the right." Her voice raised a notch. "How is it possible I would forget this until now?"

"You were exhausted, you were terrified for your daughter. Of course your memories were chaotic." Falconer pointed to the shoreline, redirecting her attention back to the recollection. "So they took you to a small house and you entered through a stout door sealed with iron strips. Was the door shut?"

"Yes." Her voice was firmer now. More confident. "There was a guard. He stood away from the door. No. He leaned against the wall."

"In the shade," Falconer softly prompted.

"Not for that reason. Well, I suppose. But as we approached there was the most horrid stench. Oh, I have nightmares about the smell."

Falconer saw the tears forming. "We will do all we can to rescue your daughter from that place, Mrs. Henning.

Now tell me. Were the stairs straight?"

"Winding. Stone. Broad at the top. There was a table and chairs inside the doorway, but they were empty."

"Shoddy way to run a keep," Harkness mumbled.

"The stairs narrowed further down," she went on. "The dungeon was a straight line running off in two directions, perhaps more. I only saw two. Dark as caves, lit by torches. Perhaps it was once a cave, because the walls were coarse and rough hewn."

"Roman by design, most likely," Harkness commented. "I have seen the same once before. With small caves or alcoves as both cells and strong rooms, and doors of wood."

And no light within, Falconer finished silently, unless the prisoner had access to funds to buy lamp oil. "Were there many guards down below?"

"One at the base of the stairs. And the jailer. He bore a great ring of keys upon his belt."

"No one else? Just the one guard?"

"None that I saw." She turned away from the shore and inspected the men's faces. "Why is that important?"

None of the men spoke, save in the examination they gave each other. Grave and determined and ready for what they all were certain would now come.

Chapter 23

At twilight, Falconer approached Amelia Henning and Matt, who were seated on a bench fashioned by two planks roped between water barrels. Their backs rested upon the wall alongside the quarterdeck stairs, shielded from the wind that grew chillier with the sun's descent. Amelia had draped a stiff blanket about her shoulders. Many women as fine as she would reject the horsehair as both scratchy and unbecoming. She, however, wore it as another might a fashionable shawl. She held a prayer book in her hands.

When their heads lifted from the book, Falconer said, "I hope I'm not disturbing you."

"On the contrary, you are most welcome, John Falconer." Her gaze had cleared since the morning's ordeal. Now the sunset and the wheelman's torches illuminated eyes that were full of a light all her own.

"I can stand if you wish to sit, Father John."

"Remain where you are, lad." He pulled up a stubby bench used by the sailors when repairing canvas. "It is not my habit to leave important things undone." He looked into her face, then away. "I have not thanked you for your lessons these past mornings."

"I too have found great comfort in this company of wise and caring men."

His finger absently traced along the scar ringing his wrist, then down the deeper one across his palm. "I have never been one to look much within myself. And such words do not come easily to me."

"Which makes them all the more cherished, John Falconer."

Perhaps it was her tone. Perhaps the usage of both of his names. Whatever the reason, he felt compelled again to lift his gaze and meet her own. "I have never truly been able to mourn the loss of Ada—of my wife." He reached out a hand to Matt, who grasped it with both of his own.

She shook her head. "Simply because you don't weep does not mean you have denied your sorrow."

He stared at her more intently. "How can you know such things?"

"My husband was a bookish man. His greatest strengths were his mind and his voice. Many might have thought of him as weak. Yet he held many traits similar to your own." She paused a moment to contemplate the book in her hands. "He was tempted by his intelligence to stand away from God. He had perhaps the most remarkable mind I have ever known. He had memorized not merely verses of the Bible but entire books of the Scripture. When we were packing for Africa I asked him why he did not carry a pastor's library, shelves of reference volumes and teachings. He replied that he did, and tapped the side of his head."

"I am sorry I did not know him," Falconer murmured.

"You are quite different from him," she said. "And yet there is a great similarity. When wounded, you and he do not become angry with God. You retreat. You question whether God truly exists for you. And you condemn yourself for this questioning. You cannot see yourself as others do, John Falconer, and neither could he."

"I am not a pastor," Falconer protested.

"But you have a heart for God. Even when that heart is so hurt it is wrapped in veils of remorse."

"Even when too many of my prayers seem empty? Even when the Scriptures read alien as a foreign tongue?"

"This too shall pass."

Her softly spoken confidence permitted him to say, "Your words in the morning prayer time have moved me to the core."

She shut the prayer book and set it to one side. "Perhaps because we share the experience of grievous loss, you are permitting yourself to see what still lies within your own heart."

Matt sniffed loudly and wiped his face with one sleeve. Falconer reached over and put his hand on top of Matt's. "Perhaps."

"Perhaps also this is happening because it is *time*. It is *time* to move beyond, John Falconer. And this can only happen when you offer up your pain to God."

Falconer's throat felt raw as he forced the confession from his lips. "I do not know how."

Amelia Henning responded as though she had awaited this since the moment he sat down. "Speaking with your son has illuminated my own path, Brother John. His songs have soothed my spirit to where I can listen again for God's own breath." She reached out one hand toward the two of them. "Perhaps you will permit me to return this gift and allow me to speak the words for you this day."

He did not answer because he could not, save to join his and Matt's hands to hers. Nor in truth did he hear more than the soft cadence of her words of prayer. Instead, he felt her voice wash over him, reaching down into the depths of his being, stripping away the shadows and the veil.

But the clearest image of that too-brief time was the pressure of her hand, the long slender fingers intertwined with his and Matt's.

Falconer lay on his bunk fully clothed, his senses on full battle alert. Though the only sound in the cabin came from the creaking timbers and the soft patter of sailors' bare feet overhead, he knew Matt was awake. Finally he slipped from his bunk and crossed the room. As he sank onto the floor, he heard the rustle of his son's bedclothes.

Two arms reached out into the black and wrapped themselves around his neck. Falconer held the boy for a time, then said, "Would you like me to light a candle?"

Matt released him, and Falconer shifted across the plank flooring until he came to the small cabinet beneath their porthole. He struck the tinderbox, then lit a candle and placed it in the pewter holder. He returned to his son's bedside and sat on its edge.

Matt watched him with dark and somber eyes. Falconer stroked the side of the boy's neck. "Say the words, lad, and I will excuse myself from this mission."

It was a hard challenge to set before one of Matt's age. But Falconer felt he had no choice. He had said as much earlier. But this was on the eve of a far more dangerous adventure than their recent encounters. "It is something I would have said to your mother, if she were here. I know I am speaking to you as though you were a man. That has been one of my great failings, you see. I have no experience in raising lads. So I have always felt as though I could speak to you as a grown-up. Which you are, in so many remarkable ways."

Falconer knew he was going on in uncommon fashion. But he needed to fill the void between the moment and the coming departure. "The words Amelia Henning spoke to me, the ones that had such a powerful effect, she was able to speak them because of you."

The boy shifted on his bunk and remained silent.

"I know you did not shape the thoughts, lad. But you granted her the ability to look beyond her own grief."

"I like her." The words emerged as almost a whisper.

"As do I."

"Do you think . . . ?" He didn't finish his question.

"You do not need to hesitate to ask me anything, lad. Or speak your mind on any subject. Not now, not ever. I want nothing but trust between us."

"Do you think you might like her as you did Mama?"

Falconer hid his surprise as best he could. "I both liked and loved your mother. But I also understand your question. The answer is, I have no idea whatsoever."

"She's very pretty. And nice."

"Aye."

"Is it wrong to think like that, Father John?"

"No, lad. But you shouldn't get your hopes up on that score. We're both recovering from grievous wounds, she and I." Falconer continued to stroke the soft down below the boy's hairline. "Is there anything else you wish to say to me?"

A moment's hesitation, then, "Can I go on deck with you when it's time for you to go?"

"Aye, lad. If that's what you wish."

"Can we pray first?"

"Of course. Why don't you—"

"I want to hear you pray, Father John."

Falconer told himself he had prayed with Bernard Lemi. But this was different and he knew it. With his son there was no disguising the hard truth. "You know I feel . . . I feel very distant from God."

Matt swung his bare feet to the floor beside Falconer. "Please, Father John."

Falconer could not deny his son. He breathed in so long he might have been using it as an excuse to avoid doing the impossible. When the breath ended, and when he had refilled his lungs, he shut his eyes and bowed his head over tightly clenched fists. "Lord in heaven, I pray to you though I feel you are too distant to hear my feeble words."

Falconer stopped. Matt had placed one hand upon his arm. He felt the stone of his flesh under his son's touch and realized it was not just his hands that were clenched, but his entire body. Falconer breathed again, this time forcing his chest to unlock. God's presence rested upon his tightly clenched heart. "Thank you for the gift of this wonderful son, Lord. Thank you for bringing Matt and me together. I do not know why you had to take Ada from us . . ."

He stopped because his son was sobbing so hard he could not take a decent breath. Falconer shifted Matt's limp fingers to his opposite hand so he could reach around and draw the boy closer still. His beloved boy cried for them both.

When Matt grew silent, Falconer finished simply, "Keep my wonderful dear son safe, Lord. Keep me safe. Not just now, but always. Make me a better father. In the name of your Son I pray. Amen."

He remained as he was until he heard the soft knock upon his door. "I must go, lad."

Matt rose silently from his bed and donned his clothes. At the door Falconer stopped. His hand upon the latch, he turned back. Even though the candle was burned down so it disappeared into the pewter holder, the light was enough to reveal the expression on Matt's face. Falconer understood all too well. "Lad, I want you to take what I'm about to say and tuck it away safe, so in the years to come you'll be able to draw it out and remember it well. You are not weak for having cried. You have a strength I do not possess. The strength of an open heart, one not scarred by all the wrong choices I have made. I am eternally grateful for the gift of your tears."

The boy wiped his face again and said nothing. But Falconer could see Matt had calmed from the words, even though he might not have clearly understood.

The knock was louder this time. Falconer opened the door and said, "We are ready."

Chapter 24

Falconer was the last man to climb into the longboat. Though the wind was mild, the seas were running strong, which indicated a storm somewhere beyond the horizon. He timed his motions to the boat's sway, such that he touched down easily.

Bivens said, "One can always tell a well-salted man by the way he handles the ropes. Cast off there, Bosun."

"Sir. All right, me hearties. Pull hard!"

"And keep your voices down," Bivens instructed. "We're running silent and swift from now on."

The young lieutenant, his arm still in the captain's sling, seated himself beside Falconer and studied the rising sun. "Not long now."

Falconer did not respond. His attention remained caught by the image of two figures standing by the lee railing. Amelia Henning rested one arm around Matt's shoulders. The lad bravely waved him away.

Falconer lifted one arm in farewell. To that, Amelia Henning raised one arm and Matt two. Falconer felt as though he could still hear the woman's whispered farewell.

He remained warmed by his last moments on deck. Amelia Henning had drawn him and Matt to the side of the vessel away from the longboat and the activity, off to where her actions and her words were as hidden as anything could be on a sailing vessel. "I shall pray for you and your safety and your success, John Falconer. As hard as ever I have prayed in all my life."

"I as well, Father John," Matt said with a small catch in his voice.

Amelia Henning's gaze held a light stronger than the dawn. "Whatever happens, I want you to know that you are a dear and good man to take on this mission. I trust you, John Falconer, and more. If it is possible, you will do this. I have *confidence* in you. I am entrusting my daughter into your care. I wish I could express what it means to be able to say that. . . ."

Then she abruptly reached forward and embraced him. An action so swift it caught them all by surprise. She released him as abruptly and stepped back, her face aflame.

Falconer covered his confusion by turning to his son. Matt clung long and hard to him. But the words of remorse he had expected, or the plea that he could not deny, did not come. Instead, the lad whispered into Falconer's ear, "When I grow up, Father John, I want to be brave like you."

Falconer had waited until the lad relaxed his grip, until he could look the boy straight in the eye. "You already are."

Lieutenant Bivens' voice interrupted Falconer's reverie. "Steer us straight east, Bosun."

"East it is, sir."

"We want to remain hidden by the rising sun."

"If they come at all," the bosun finished for them.

Neither Falconer nor the lieutenant responded. They watched as their ship gradually vanished beneath the horizon. When the topsails were all that were visible, Bivens said, "That should do it. No, keep your oars in the water, men. Hold us steady. We will wait."

Though there was no one to hear them, they held to silence. An hour passed. Then two. The sun was fully above the horizon now. To the south the heat rose in endless ribbons into a cloudless sky.

"There," Falconer muttered, pointing. "South by southwest."

"I do not see them."

"Further toward the shore. Wait. The mast I spotted has disappeared now."

A sailor rose from his bench. "Down, man," Bivens said.

Falconer said, "You may be missing out on a real fight, accompanying me like this."

"I think you were right in your predictions," Bivens said, squinting as he searched the tossing sea. "They will probe but not attack."

Falconer grinned at the younger man. "So you would have forsaken me if there had been a better chance of a quarrel?"

Bivens turned his attention from the water. "Do you know, I believe this is the first time I have ever seen you smile."

"I see them, sir," the bosun said.

Bivens returned his attention to the sea. "Where?"

"Wait for the next rising wave, sir."

Falconer let the smile slip away but remained warmed by its reason. Levity had been lost to him, he had thought forever. Yet now he smiled, not at the lieutenant, but rather at the arms he could still feel about his chest. How was it possible to ache over the loss of one woman and find joy in another's words? It was a puzzle that remained beyond him.

Bivens muttered, "Oh my . . . what . . . ?"

This time, half the oarsmen were in the process of rising when the lieutenant rebuked them softly. "Down, I say."

But it was hard even for Falconer to remain seated. For arrayed across the southwestern horizon was not the single vessel that had been the agreement.

Admiral La Rue had arrived with an armada.

The sea's horizon boiled with sails.

Bivens muttered, "How many do you reckon?"

Falconer shook his head. Forty, fifty, sixty, the number did not matter. Too many for one lonely merchant ship, no matter how well armed or manned, to fend off. "Take note of how they sail."

Bivens set one knee upon the gunnel and steadied the glass on his leg. "Tell me what I see."

"They are all clustered together. They will split and move in two different arms, like the claws of an attacking beast," Falconer explained.

All the longboat's crew were watching him. Bivens asked, "You have faced such an attack before?"

"Three times. It's a maneuver designed for men on horseback and camel, or so I was told. But it works well enough upon the open sea. Especially when the wind is calm enough to give smaller boats with oarsmen an advantage."

The coxswain asked, "Shall we start rowing back, sir?"

"Hold hard there," Bivens ordered. Then to Falconer, "What of their armament?"

"Most will have nothing more than four-pound chasers," Falconer replied, naming the smallest shipboard cannon, normally used only as bow guns and stern guns. "Their hulls are full of dry rot and worms. Their bottoms

214

have never been beached and scrubbed. A heavier gun would blow them apart."

The coxswain complained, "Begging your pardon, Lieutenant. But me and the lads, we'd hate to sit here and let our shipmates handle such as these without us."

"Hold fast." But this time Bivens lowered his telescope and spoke warmly. "If there is any risk of attack, I'll give the order for us to return."

"Risk? Sir, have a gander at—"

A cannon fired from a ship behind them. One shot that compressed the air where they rolled upon the waves.

"That's the signal," Falconer said.

Bivens worried, "Harkness left it too long, it seems to me."

"Harkness did correctly," Falconer replied. "He had to get them close. And La Rue needed to reveal his ships as being on the attack."

As though in confirmation of Falconer's words, the Arab vessels released a furious volley. The smaller guns sounded an octave higher than the merchant ship's cannon. A cloud of smoke rose and dispersed in the wind.

Bivens returned his attention to the sea and demanded fretfully, "Where's the response?"

"Response from who, sir?" the coxswain demanded.

At that moment, thunder exploded from a clear blue sky.

The English vessel had used the same ruse as their longboat, sailing straight out of the sun and thus masking its appearance from the attackers bearing down on the merchant ship. Captain Clovis had also positioned himself so that his ship could use every ounce of speed the morning wind would grant him.

The English vessel passed within two lengths of their longboat, dwarfing them in the process. The portals on all three gun decks were open. The dark barrels protruded like vicious teeth. Every ounce of sail was open and filled. The bow cleaved as deep as a wooden ax. The rigging was filled with sailors, and the aft deck swarmed with the ship's contingent of marines.

Captain Clovis appeared on the lee side of the quarter-deck. He shouted down to Falconer's longboat, "Top of the morning, sir!"

"You are an answer to fervent prayers, sir!" Falconer called up.

Clovis had a laugh far too large for his diminutive body. Nor did he require a speaker horn for his voice to cover that distance. "I have been called many things, sir. But this is a new one for me!"

A voice from the crow's nest cried, "The nasties are coming about, sir!"

"Five points to starboard," Clovis roared. Then to Falconer, "Hold where you are, gents! I must give chase and try to capture those I can before they make harbor!"

Chapter 25

Despite the fact that all the Arab vessels scrambled safely back to port, Clovis was in fine fettle when he returned to where the longboat drifted upon high seas. Once Falconer's vessel was lashed to the side of the battleship and they had come aboard, Clovis ignored Soap's discomfort at being seated among the ship's officers, treating them all as welcome guests. Over a meal of roast goat and dates, Clovis described how a single Arab vessel, the largest, had broken out of the prince's standard and objected most strenuously at the British frigate's attack.

The admiral's vizier had shouted angrily that all the other boats had merely been an honorary escort. Clovis and his lieutenants laughed over how they had responded in kind, that the British warship was simply escorting the merchant vessel. They had left the vizier in negotiations with Harkness and Reginald Langston. The final exchange of signal flags between Clovis and Harkness had contained three messages. First, that neither hostage was on board the Arab vessel. Second, that Harkness and Reginald congratulated Falconer on being correct in his forecast. And third, all the ship's company wished them godspeed.

After dinner, Clovis sailed them back to a point just over the horizon from the ruined desert city, now the caravanserai. Falconer and his men were to be rowed ashore, and the coxswain was to rendezvous the longboat with Clovis, again beyond the horizon. Clovis would then tow the longboat back to Harkness, who remained stationed near the Tunis port.

Falconer was accompanied by Soap and Bernard Lemi, plus two men from the British vessel. Clovis's men were a villainous pair, as massive as temple pillars and battle scarred. Each went by a single name only. The dun-colored Arab with one milky eye was Wadi. The dark African with tribal scars on his cheeks and forehead was Nebo. Both, Clovis related, had escaped from slavery.

Clovis had told Falconer of both men when they initially met and discussed Falconer's plan. A favorite British naval watering hole off the west African coast was found in the Cape Verde Islands, where slaves worked on vast Portuguese plantations. Like a number of naval officers who had witnessed the effects of slavery firsthand, Captain Clovis loathed the evil trade in human flesh. Whenever visiting Cape Verde, Clovis anchored in a small, uninhabited inlet on the main island's southern coast. Nine times he had been rewarded, rescuing escaping slaves who swam out to his vessel. All had been sworn into service; it was a tradition in the British navy that any man, regardless of race, who served out a full term was granted citizenship. Seven now served with navy allies skippering other vessels.

As soon as Wadi and Nebo had heard of Falconer's plan, they had pleaded for the chance to come along.

The small group made landfall in the breach between sunset and moonrise. The sea was inky black, and the waves crashed in palest silver. Falconer gripped the side gunnels as they approached the ghostly shore, but the oarsmen knew their business and expertly handled the longboat through the currents. They rode a rush of foam and then the keel scraped against the sand. Instantly Falconer leapt over the side, his trouser legs hiked above his knees and boots slung over his shoulder with his pack. The four other men followed his lead and hustled onto shore.

They clambered to a rise forty paces inland. From there they watched as the longboat slipped back into the dark waters. Bivens offered them a final wave, and was gone.

Clovis had proven to be a wily skipper, for in his hold had been stored a small Arab tent and several djellabas. That he possessed these robes used by the local desert tribesmen obviously meant he previously had sent teams ashore on information-gathering missions.

They walked a league inland and made camp for the night. Falconer, unaccustomed to the desert tent's design, watched with Soap and Bernard Lemi as the two former slaves made fast the guide ropes. The tent was pegged in a cross-tier fashion, and then the two men hauled upon the front ropes and the tent rose as gracefully as a sail. They lashed the two final ropes into place, and by the time the moon rose to bleach the surrounding desert silver, all was done.

Falconer found himself so utterly exhausted he made no protest as the two Africans asked to proceed into the caravanserai alone. He simply asked how much gold they required.

Both of Clovis's men squinted hard at Falconer. "Gold?" the African said.

"It is what we carry. English sovereigns."

Nebo and Wadi exchanged looks before one said, "Three guineas, and we will have silver when we return."

Falconer handed them four. Soap cast him a glance of consternation, clearly concerned that these strangers might never return.

Falconer sank down upon the tent's flooring, feeling

the pebbles beneath his blanket. Concern over Matt and the coming venture and Amelia Henning's words had disturbed his sleep every night since leaving Marseilles. He listened a moment to Soap and Bernard speaking softly outside the tent, released a single breath, and was gone.

Hours later, he awoke from a dream that a bullet was slowly grinding its way into his rib.

Falconer shifted and groaned. He had not moved since falling asleep, and a stone beneath his chest had bruised him deeply. He sat up and rubbed his eyes. Desert sunlight lanced through a sliver of space between the tent flaps. Soap slept to one side, Wadi snored softly on the other. Falconer grabbed his boots and crawled from the tent.

The desert light temporarily blinded him. He rubbed his eyes and rose slowly to his feet. The smell of wood-smoke drifted in the still air. He turned his back to the sun. On the western side, in the tent's long morning shadow, a fire burned. The African known as Nebo rose from his crouch and offered Falconer a metal cup shaped like a tulip bloom. From it came the heady scent of sweet mint tea.

"Thank you." Falconer sipped and sighed at the pungent flavor and the rush of memories. With his free hand he accepted the round desert flatbread. The unleavened bread lasted far longer than western-style loaves, and was more easily packed. The fact that it was relatively tasteless was overcome by swallows of the sweet tea.

Then he heard a grunt. Falconer shifted about and found himself facing four camels and two mules. The nearest camel chewed its cud in a sideways manner and eyed him calmly.

Falconer eased himself down beside Bernard, and said to the African, "You did well."

Nebo used a charred cloth to lift the long-stemmed teapot from the fire. "More?"

"Please." Falconer watched as he reached across the fire and refilled Falconer's cup. "Was there any trouble?"

"We know these people and their tongue." Nebo's accent was very thick and his grammar curious, but he was easily understood. "We pay in gold. There no trouble."

Bernard Lemi gestured to the east, where the caravanserai's crumbling towers cut silhouettes from the sunrise. "Will they accept us as genuine?"

Falconer nodded thanks to an offer of yet more tea. "We are not the only foreigners who come looking for slaves."

"You have traveled here before?"

"Not this area." Falconer took a slow and deliberate sip. "Somaliland."

"That is where?"

"Indian Ocean. By Yemen."

"These waters I do not know." Nebo refilled Bernard's cup and asked the banker, "You have been here?"

"Never in the desert." Bernard blew on the hot tea. "I'm sorry, but I know nothing of this world."

Nebo nodded once in acceptance of the man's admission. "Drink much tea. The desert drinks from you."

Falconer spotted two leather bags used as tethers for the pack mules. One of the beasts shifted over to a meager clump of grass. The bag clinked, and Falconer winced at the sound.

Nebo saw Falconer's grimace and responded, "Slavers must carry slave chains."

Falconer did not want the man to think he criticized the man's purchase, so he merely repeated, "You did well."

Nebo refilled his own cup and slurped his tea in the desert fashion, sucking off the top layer. Then, "We go to rescue two children, it is so?"

"One child, a girl of nine, and one man who is about twenty-seven."

"These captives, they are family?"

"We are not related."

Nebo sipped thoughtfully. Falconer recognized the African courtesy of not asking further direct questions. If a man chose to respond to what was not asked, it was his decision. No insult was made because the question was never voiced. But this man was an ally who was also risking his life. So Falconer said, "I carry the great shame of having once been a slaver."

"Ah." It was not a word so much as a deep sigh.

"Now I am committed to helping those in chains wherever and whenever I can."

"This is good, your oath." Another careful sip. "You made this promise why?"

That was a more difficult one. "My freedom was freely given. I seek now only to serve."

The forehead crinkled in confusion. "You in need of freedom?"

"Yes, I was a slave to sin, to evil. Now I seek to serve my Savior. The one who freed me."

"I do not know this word. Savior."

"You serve on a British vessel and you have never heard of Jesus Christ?"

"Ah. The name. Yes." The tribal scars deepened into caverns as he smiled. "The lieutenant, he cries the name very loud when angry."

"That is not how I choose to speak my Lord's name."

"No." Another thoughtful sip. "I think I would like to know more of this mystery. What do you call it?"

"Salvation."

The African shrugged. "The power that changes slaver into man who rescues slaves. This is great power indeed.

You will speak to me of this, yes?"

"I would count it an honor."

Nebo grunted. It was another sound drawn from Falconer's past, a proud man who rarely uses an actual word for thanks. "How are you called?"

The African already knew his name. The exchange was meant to mark them now as true allies. "I am called Falconer. And you are Nebo."

Another smile came and went in the strengthening day. "Already I be glad I make this voyage."

They mounted the camels and set off in the late morning. At first the desert was kind to them, as far as a waterless waste of heat and sand could be kind. A fresh wind blew off the ocean, strong enough to cool their coastal road.

But less than an hour later the wind turned southerly and strengthened, and the desert's other face was revealed.

The dust struck them with brutal force. Wadi showed them how to wrap a burnoose about their heads, such that the leading edge formed a shield for their eyes.

Their plan had been to allow most of the local merchants to depart before them. Moving more swiftly than the lumbering caravans, they intended to sidle up from behind and meld into the road traffic's rhythm, arriving in Tunis in one great mass. Instead, the rising wind blanketed the ruined town such that only one of the four towers was visible at all. The houses and corrals and most of the outer wall were lost to the swirling golden cloud. Falconer could hear shouting voices and bleating animals, but saw no one.

Nebo sidled his camel up beside Falconer. "The merchants wait out storm."

"Should we?"

Nebo used his quirt, a supple stick as long as his arm

and wrapped in beaded leather, to point up to where Wadi led the way. "He will say if storm harm camels."

"Your friend does not speak much."

"He was born slave. As boy, he must sing. Day after day. Now he hates all words. I am his friend because I speak for him."

The wind grew steadily and lashed at them. The pack mules brayed a constant protest against the stinging dust. The camels snorted and plodded in a sameness Falconer felt in his very bones. He had never been good with horses and had ridden a camel only once before. His lower back and thighs felt on fire.

Bernard Lemi sidled to Falconer's right. He uncorked his waterskin and swilled his mouth so that he could ask, "How much further?"

In truth, Falconer had no idea. But Bernard needed reassuring. "Not long."

"This storm is worse than I had ever imagined."

Nebo closed the distance behind them, while Soap moved in on Falconer's left. Falconer knew there was greater risk to them being so tightly clustered. Although not much. The dust was so thick he could not see the camel's footpads.

Nebo said, "This is not such bad wind."

Bernard twisted in his saddle, but in the wrong direction, for the dust struck his unprotected eyes. He twisted back and used the burnoose's edge to clear his vision. "You must be telling tales!"

Falconer said, "Further into the desert, storms rise that can strip a man's bones in half a day."

Wadi glanced back, as though in confirmation, but said nothing.

Soap's voice was dry and cracked. "I smell a storm brewing out to sea."

Falconer grunted. "I doubt it will strike here."

Soap knew their plan well enough to fret, "What if it does? Rain will put paid to all our plans, it will."

Nebo shook his head. "The rain passes out to sea. Not for years does this land see rain."

Bernard broke in, "Why can't we stop?"

Much as Falconer wanted the very same thing, he replied, "Because this storm is our ally."

"Impossible!"

"Look at those hills." Falconer pointed to his right. A brief clearing of the dust storm revealed steep cliffs that rose and fell in ocher waves. Eons of wind had blasted peculiar caves and narrow defiles. "This is a breeding ground for bandits."

This time, Falconer was certain Wadi's glance was agreement. He went on, "Desert tribes prey on smaller parties like ours. But we are hidden from them. The wind and dust are our best shield."

Bernard slumped on his beast. "My body is one enormous ache."

Falconer heard Soap mutter agreement. "We will halt as soon as it is safe."

Falconer awoke to a hand upon his shoulder. Wadi stood over him, waiting until Falconer was fully alert. The Arab then slid into his own bedroll and within three breaths was snoring quietly.

Falconer emerged from the tent to a breathless night. The storm had disappeared while he slept. He moved to the rear of the shallow cave, where a low fire burned. He poured himself a cup of tea and feasted upon the dried bread and salted meat left out for those standing watch. He drank almost an entire pot of tea before his thirst was slaked. He refilled the pot from a waterskin, cast in more tea leaves from a leather pouch, and set the pot on a stone by the fire to brew. Then he walked around the sleeping men and entered the night.

Their shelter was a spoon-shaped enclosure hollowed by storms beyond time. It stood at the cliff's far eastern edge and faced out to a flat expanse that went on forever. Numerous piles of cold ashes attested to other travelers who had used the cave for shelter. Falconer moved to a rock shaped like a miniature throne, where one of the earlier watch keepers had left a blanket. The rising moon transformed the desert into a black and silver sea. He studied the vista and finished his tea.

There was a certain flavor to desert nights, unlike anything Falconer had experienced elsewhere. The slumbering men had no effect upon Falconer's isolation. The night blanketed him with an aloneness so complete he could space out his thoughts as he did his breath. He recalled his farewell from Matt and ached anew for the young lad. His mouth shaped the silent word *son*. Falconer recalled other days when his heart had yearned for such a gift and his world had been a vacuum for what he thought would never come. Now the lad was bonded to him by love and shared grief. And their shared quest. Falconer recalled the day in the woodlands between Salem and the coast. What a remarkable lad Matt was. *What a blessing* was all he could think to express what he felt.

He lifted his gaze and stared at the heavens. The stars were a wash of light, eternal signs of the Creator's borderless sea. Falconer spoke aloud the first solitary prayer he had uttered since setting his beloved Ada into the ground. Just twelve words. But he knew God was fully aware of the condition of his soul, knew that he was a man of stumbling prayers in the best of times. *Thank you for my son. Keep him safe. Hold him close. Amen.*

When he lowered his gaze, it seemed to him that Ada had entered the night. He vividly sensed her presence. Not wracked by her final illness, but as she was before. As she was *now*.

Falconer also sensed a great change within himself and knew it was vital. Yet he did not wish to give it either thought or emotion, because he feared that Ada's closeness might vanish. But her invisible presence generated a remarkable understanding, as though she spoke to him in heaven's voice, silent and close and illuminating. Deep in his chest he felt his heart unfold, and knew that the moment held a greeting and departure both. Dear, sweet, beloved woman. The gift he had not thought would ever be his. Every day a treasure. If only there could have been more. If only . . .

And then it happened.

He did not see a vision. But the image was clear just the same. So vivid, in fact, that to Falconer's mind the revelation would have been no stronger had it risen before him in physical form.

It seemed that something like Jacob's ladder appeared before him. Just as it had to the son of Isaac in the desert of Haran, where he had laid his head upon a pillow of stone. Upon the ladder, angels descended to earth and rose to the heavens. Over and over in a smooth and constant stream.

Ada was with him still. Though his attention was focused as tight as a storm-drawn hawser, Falconer knew she was there because of his heart's fullness. And through this loving presence Falconer saw the ladder, this bridge to heaven, in a new way. He watched with his mind's eye as angels proceeded from God's throne to the desert floor and back. A constant stream of heavenly presence and light. Falconer saw the ladder as his own life. He saw how God was with him in every stage. In the moments of divine exultation, when heaven was almost close enough to touch, and God's glory filled his being. And He was there in the desert times. The times of basest despair. The dry bones of human existence, the days of empty wasteland and biting storms, the moments when his heart was a stone lodged in his chest. *God was*.

The image faded. Ada remained an instant longer, gracing him with a last sigh of eternal love.

Falconer's eyes blinked and refocused. He realized he stared into the first faint tendrils of a new dawn.

He pushed himself from the rock and walked further into the desert, so that his sobs, not of grief but of joy, would remain unheard.

Chapter 26

They resumed their journey the hour following sunrise. The air held the nighttime stillness, with not a breath of wind. It seemed to Falconer that he had scarcely settled into the saddle before the previous day's discomforts returned. Clearly Bernard Lemi and Soap felt the same, for each sway of their beasts brought winces. But neither man complained.

By midmorning, Falconer had the measure of his men, or so he hoped. Soap was a game foot soldier, loyal as they came. Nebo had decided to trust Falconer, which meant the African would obey him. And that was enough for Wadi. The three more seasoned men clearly questioned Bernard Lemi's mettle, and wondered silently why Falconer had allowed the banker to come along. Falconer questioned it as well, though not overmuch. He had a warrior's trust in his gut. And his gut told him there was more to Bernard than met the eye.

They knew they were arriving at their destination long before the city came into view. A tall yellow cloud of smoke, soot, and desert dust hung over the east, like a bilious mountain suspended upon nothing save heat. Then came the smells, a distinctly desert mix of charcoal and animals and meat and cumin and men. The camels snorted and the mules brayed. Wadi had to draw hard on his reins to keep his beast from galloping forward, drawn by the scent of water.

Falconer motioned to Soap. "Give Nebo a handful of gold."

Soap squinted against more than the glare, but did not speak. He reined in his camel, swinging it so that he drew alongside the African. He opened his money belt and passed over a cluster of glinting sovereigns. The clinking music drew Wadi's head around. Both former slaves stared at the money, then at Falconer. A British seaman was promised a guinea a year, and not always paid. Nebo held more than both men together could hope to earn in a life-time.

Falconer said to them both, "You two are to speak for us and pay for everything as you see fit."

Nebo studied him a moment longer, then slipped the handful into his cloth belt and tied it shut. "It will be as you say."

Wadi, however, was slower to return his attention to the road. He lifted the hand from which his quirt dangled. He touched the tips of his fingers to his heart, his lips, and his forehead—the desert salutation of respect.

The desert gave way grudgingly. The road swept south-ward and entered a valley with gently sloping hills. There was water here, for the hillsides were planted with date palms and ancient olive groves. Sheep and goats cropped the meager grass beneath the trees. The farmhouses were all the same, low and square and flat-roofed. Children watched from doorways, silently observing the constant flow of traffic upon the ancient road. Falconer noted that their group attracted no more attention than any of the other travelers.

They passed through one small hamlet, then more

farms, then a larger village. They finally paused when the ancient walls came into view. Falconer pushed back his burnoose to look at the space where the old gates must have once stood, with the road framed by two mounds of rubble as high as the surrounding hills. The mounds had been flattened and brick guard stations built atop them. But the flagpoles were empty, and Falconer saw only one bored sentry loitering inside the shaded doorway.

Falconer pulled their group over to the side of the road and instructed Bernard and Soap to stow away their Arab robes as he was doing. Tunis was used to foreigners of all kinds.

The road's traffic condensed inside the city walls. The five men allowed themselves to be slowed and pushed more closely together. Falconer tried to stay alert to danger, but he could not keep himself from gaping. They passed a side road given over to weavers. The road was roofed with drying racks and strung with a rainbow collection of dyed yarn. The road curved north and broadened into a teeming market. The stalls were jammed cheek by jowl. At one, three lads as young as Matt pounded designs into copper plates. At the next, a small girl pulled upon a string looped to a turnstile, while an older man chiseled a block of wood into a table leg. The girl's attention remained fastened upon the road, while her hands continued in constant motion. A woman approached them with two chickens dangling from each hand. Her face was tattooed in the intricate tribal fashion, and her voice was as shrill as a chattering bird.

Wadi slowed his camel further and nudged Falconer with his quirt. The one-eyed Arab made a tiny gesture with his chin. Falconer followed the man's focus and saw a pair of Europeans seated at an outdoor tavern. "We stop there," Falconer said.

Soap had seen them as well. "Is it safe?"

"Nothing is safe inside this city," Falconer replied, his voice low. "So long as we remain, we stand upon the knife's edge. Remember that, all of you."

When their direction was clear, the innkeeper emerged from the tent's shade and barked a command. Instantly a pair of lads shot forward to take hold of their reins. The innkeeper greeted them with the traditional salaam as they descended from their animals. He personally seated them, vanished, and swiftly returned with a copper basin and towel, which he offered first to Falconer. The towel was almost as filthy as the innkeeper's robe. Falconer dipped his hands into the basin in the ceremonial fashion, then swept his fingers through his hair and retied the leather thong. He could feel a dozen sets of eyes upon him.

Anywhere else, the tavern's shape would have seemed most curious. Here, it was so common as to be unremarkable. The rear area was desert brick and Falconer knew it would be separated into kitchen, storeroom, and a single great room for guests during storms. Today's weather was clear, however, so the guests sat at tables beneath a rectangular awning. The tentlike cover reached to the road's edge, such that camels and customers passed within inches of the closest table. From old habit, Falconer selected a table far back, lost to shadows and where he could sit with his back to a solid wall. The two other westerners occupied a table at the restaurant's far side and pretended to ignore the newcomers.

The five took tea and bread and hummus and olives and skewers of meat which Falconer hoped was lamb. The innkeeper came and went, setting down more small dishes and asking elaborate questions to which Nebo responded in tight monosyllables. Wadi ate standing. When he was full, the Arab moved to the awning's outer edge. He studied the brilliant day in utter stillness for a time, then vanished.

Nebo glanced at Falconer and gave a tiny shrug. If he had no idea where his mate had gone, he clearly was not concerned.

Soap sniffed the air. "I still smell a storm. Right over the horizon, it is." As though able to smell beyond the city and the dust.

Falconer felt an idea begin to take form. "Perhaps. But all we will see here is wind."

Nebo slipped the burnoose down around his neck. His head was a misshapen bullet, smooth and hard and pocked with old scars. His eyes watched Falconer unblinkingly as he said, "You trust me with your gold."

"That and much more."

The African grunted his acknowledgment and waited while the innkeeper set down a plate of chopped mint and coriander in olive oil. "To know of such wealth puts your life in my hands." He straightened in his chair and said formally, "I thank you for this gift of trust, Falconer."

"I thank you for your good right arm, Nebo."

"It is good to have allies in dark places." He returned his attention to the meal. "Does this God of yours teach trust?"

"Among many other things. Trust is easier when you seek to value eternity."

"You are a hunter, yes? A man of many battles. I think you hunted a very long time to find this God of yours."

Falconer smiled for the first time since landfall. "It took me years to understand that my God was hunting for me."

Nebo ate in the Arab fashion, using only the first three fingers of his right hand. He took a bit of bread, scooped up grilled meat and coriander, and ate in silence. It was the desert manner, to show respect through such pauses. There was no rush to speech, no question immediately piled upon the next. Several bites later, he continued, "This power of yours."

"My faith."

"I wish to know what this word means."

Bernard demanded, "Is now truly the time for such talk?"

Soap dipped his bread into the hummus. For a small man of advancing years, he showed a remarkable ability to store food away. "The hour before a storm and the hour before battle. The two longest hours on earth. Makes a man know just how alone he can be. Good time to be asking such questions and answering them, methinks."

Nebo examined the sailor. "You share this power?"

"I have been a believer for almost twenty years. And I tell you the truth. The day of my turning is the day my life changed."

Nebo mulled this over, then asked the banker, "And you?"

Bernard stared at the scarred tabletop and was long in answering. "I seek as well."

"It is good to know question, and to have trust in man who knows answers." Nebo looked at Falconer. "Speak to me of this."

Falconer chose his words carefully. "You feel a hunger, one all the food in the world cannot fill. It is so?"

"Yes." To everyone's surprise, it was not the African who murmured the word. It was Bernard. "Oh yes."

Nebo glanced at the banker, then returned his burning gaze to Falconer, who said, "Knowing the glory of Jesus for one's self is to satisfy this hunger forever."

"How do I know this thing?"

The market and the road and the noise all faded into

the distance. "I can tell you of His gift. When you feel you are ready, we can pray together, and you give Him your life. Everything."

Nebo's voice was soft, yet cut through the surrounding din. "More words I do not understand."

Falconer pondered on how best to explain. Finally he said, "When you travel desert ways, you will sometimes search out rock buried in the sand."

Nebo nodded. "It is so."

"You jam your knife blade down in the sand until it touches the rock. Then you place your temple upon the knife handle."

Nebo rocked his upper body back and forth. "It is as you say."

"You do this because you have trained yourself to listen beyond the edge of hearing."

Nebo's words were soft drumbeats. "Sounds pass through the blade and into my brain. Sounds the ears do not hear. Suddenly the empty reaches are empty no longer."

"When I pray," Falconer said, "I search for the eternal voice that is beyond the reach of man."

Nebo was still mulling those words when Wadi returned. The Arab remained in the daylight and gestured to Falconer with one finger. Come.

Falconer rose from the table. He said to the others, "Stay where you are."

Chapter 27

Falconer followed Wadi down a series of teeming market lanes. Everywhere they went, his presence drew stares. Falconer was now dressed in what had once been his standard slavers' garb. He wore a buccaneer's black trousers, fitted loose enough to hide any manner of items in the deep pockets. Added to them were black smugglers' boots, so called because the tops were rolled down, masking pouches in which money and knives and even a small pistol could be hidden away. Though Falconer's sword belt held a long curved dagger and two pistols, he would hold to his vow and not take another man's life—not even if it meant the loss of his own. His shirt was black also, and unlaced at the neck.

But his menace came neither from his clothing nor the arms he bore. He towered a full head and shoulders above most of those they passed. His hands were the size of mallets. His shoulders were twice the breadth of the Arab who led him onward. His features were hewn from stone and storm and rage and battle. The scar on his face was not his worst, only the most visible. No wonder the locals stared.

As they entered a broad plaza, Falconer reflected upon the shame he carried from all that had shaped him into the man he had been. Yet this character of his was also why

Nebo spoke with him. Warrior to warrior. About the God stronger than even his loss.

Wadi drew Falconer's attention back to the present by halting and stepping into a shadowed alcove. Falconer had seen such recesses before. Ancient tradition held that a wealthy local merchant would buy such a niche, but not for a market stall. Instead, a small fountain would be set in place and water offered free to all who passed. In this case, however, the fountain was dry and the mosaics in the rear wall, which once had spelled out words in Arabic, were chipped and frayed. A pair of beggars with outstretched hands whined once, then upon catching sight of Falconer, withdrew their hands and went silent.

Wadi was armed as a desert soldier, with a cutlass and brace of pistols slung from his cloth belt and a longer curved scimitar hung from his back. Its two-handed pommel was bound in snakeskin and rose menacingly above his right shoulder. He jerked his chin at what lay directly across the square.

When Falconer saw what had drawn Wadi's attention, he felt a sudden clenching in his gut. The sensation was not so much fear as knowing that by stepping into the sunlight he was crossing a line from safety into battle. Falconer offered a prayer, terse and concise.

Then he stepped forward, into the light and danger.

Wadi followed a pace behind, in keeping with a bodyguard and servant. The corral had a symbolic boundary of crumbling stone. But there was no chance that any of its human captives would escape, for they were well fettered. The road's dust so cloaked them it was hard for an untrained eye to name them as either male or female. But none of those who stood at the periphery were untrained. Falconer was not the only buyer dressed in western attire. Two uniformed officers, possibly German, discussed a slave held up by a beast of a guard who gripped the neck chain and kept the youth on his toes. A dandy in immaculate riding boots held a perfumed handkerchief to his nose as he discussed the array of human wares with an Arab in a multicolored robe.

Falconer knew the routine with heart-wrenching familiarity. These were newly arrived charges. The market would be up ahead, probably the place Amelia Henning had described. Slave markets were often by the harbor, as most buyers and sellers would arrive in small lateen-sailed ships disguised as coastal fishing vessels. But these poor wretches had made the overland journey. They were corralled here no doubt because this was close to the slaver's personal compound. They were to be fed and bathed and perhaps oiled before they were moved on to the market. The merchants gathered here sought to pierce the road's dust and the slaves' exhaustion to find an early deal.

But this was not why Wadi had brought Falconer over.

Two of the owner's personal servants moved about the cluster of perhaps eighty captives. They permitted the slaves to drink only once they had been washed. Dippers of water were poured over their heads and then they were rubbed down with rough burlap. But three men Falconer observed refused such treatment. They were lashed by their neck to a central pole, a standard yet brutal punishment for slaves. The servants approached them nervously. When they came within range, the nearest man stretched as far as the neck brace permitted and kicked the bucket from the servant's hand. The two servants squawked and flapped their hands, clearly telling the three men they would receive nothing to drink. The man tried to kick them again. The bargain hunters laughed at the sport.

Falconer turned to Wadi and asked, "Will you speak for me?"

The Arab's voice sounded rusty with disuse. "If I must."

"You could fetch Nebo."

Wadi shook his head. "Let us do this thing."

Falconer nodded his thanks. "Approach the trader."

Wadi approached the man in the multicolored robe and plucked at his sleeve. The slaver bowed himself away from the dandy, then added his own invective to the trio lashed to the central pole as he walked by them. Falconer's fierce glare bothered him not one bit. Slavers were not known for their great store of human kindness. Clearly the man saw in Falconer's burning rage just another member of his own clan. He salaamed a greeting and spoke to Falconer in French.

Falconer's voice was deepened to a growl by his rage. "I am American."

The trader switched effortlessly to the other language. "Forgive me, effendi. We see so few of you these days."

Falconer recognized the subtle threat. American slavers had never worked along the North African coast. And recently the American Congress had outlawed the importation of more slaves, as an appeasement to the nation's growing opposition to the entire slave issue. Falconer made no attempt to mask his fury as he replied, "I work for others these days. My oaths of duty are no longer to my homeland."

"Of course, effendi. I completely understand. Your curious American codes have made outlaws of many."

Falconer took a deep breath. "I am interested in the three you have bound to the pillar."

"They are a troublesome lot," the trader warned. "You have seen that for yourself."

Falconer released a trace of the internal cauldron. "I have broken men before."

The trader bowed low. "You are welcome to inspect my wares."

As Falconer stepped over the low wall, he snapped at Wadi as any slaver would his personal servant, "Bring water."

Wadi's bow went far to easing the trader's natural suspicions. "Effendi."

In an attempt to buy space and secrecy, Falconer said to the trader, "Make sure my man is given a bucket and show him the nearest well."

Falconer stepped over the men and women and children separating him from the trio lashed to the central post. They were all so coated by dust their skin color was impossible to tell. But the men had full beards, which was extremely rare among Arabs and almost never seen on Africans. Closer still, Falconer saw the two men facing his direction both had light-colored eyes.

They drew their legs in tight, readying for another strike. Falconer took this as a very good sign. They were emaciated and wore nothing but rags. Their feet were bare, their ankles festering from the leg chains. Yet they still had fight in them.

Falconer crouched down, a half pace out of reach. He took out his dagger and rammed it into the earth between them. It was a common warning between slaver and newly acquired charge who did not speak any known tongue. He felt the trader's gaze upon him from across the corral. Which was enough to keep his voice battle rough. "Do you speak English?"

The two men who faced him licked their lips and said nothing. But the third man, lashed so that he faced away from Falconer, tried in vain to swivel about.

That was all the response Falconer could want. "Listen to me carefully." He now dropped his voice and spoke quickly. "I am a former slaver, brought to my knees and to new ways by my Lord and Savior, Jesus Christ. I ask that you trust me. We have a few seconds only. Who are you?"

One of the men tried to speak but could not. His eyes turned to watch as Wadi approached with a bucket. Falconer lifted the knife from the sand, as though readying for opposition. This time, however, the man allowed the ladle to be lifted to his mouth. He sucked greedily, then rasped, "Sailors."

"One more question only. If I free you, will you give me your allegiance?"

The man sucked more water, then managed, "You give your word you're not a slaver?"

The man's accent suggested a hint of French, which could mean Canadian. Which meant a whaler. "By my eternal soul, I give you my word," Falconer assured him.

"We're your men."

Falconer rose and slipped the dagger back into his belt. "Tell my man all you can."

He walked back over to the waiting trader. Each footstep was a burden, a battle. He dared not glance at those he passed. Their misery and his own helplessness left him clamped so tight in grief and rage he could scarcely form the words. He stopped before the trader. "They are a risk. But I am thinking they might bring a profit for the one who can force them to submit."

The trader bowed lower still, so that when he straightened, his greed and his relief over getting rid of these impossible charges was well hidden. "Naturally such as these would draw great interest in the harbor market."

Falconer gripped his dagger's haft with one hand, the pistol with the other. Anything to control his fury. "Name your price."

Chapter 28

Falconer left Wadi with the three men, his scowl so grim it parted the teeming market crowd and silenced the tavern tent. The innkeeper bowed Falconer back into his seat without leaving his own position by the rear kitchen fire. Even Falconer's men were made anxious by his obvious anger—all save Nebo. Falconer seated himself at the table and watched as the African poured him tea. Though his throat was parched, he could not make his hands reach for the cup.

"You were taken to the market?" Nebo asked.

Falconer gave a terse nod.

"Market?" Bernard asked.

"For men," Nebo said, his eyes fastened on Falconer.

Soap sighed a release of tension and leaned back in his chair.

Nebo said, "It is hard thing to face, this market for living flesh. Especially for you, I think. A man who once worked this trade."

"I feel as though my very soul has been branded."

"Here is what I think." Nebo planted two muscular arms upon the table and leaned forward until Falconer could not avoid his gaze. "I think your God very pleased with you."

The words enabled Falconer to take his first steady breath since leaving the corral. He met the African's stare, his only response.

Nebo leaned back, satisfied. "Tell us what we must do next, Falconer."

Before Falconer finished with his directives to Soap, Wadi returned. Falconer demanded, "I thought you were guarding the men."

"You tell merchant you pay him in gold. He guards them with his life."

Nebo grinned at the sound of his friend's voice. "See now," he rumbled in his own deep tones. "Rain falls in desert."

Wadi fastened his good eye meaningfully upon his friend, then returned his attention to Falconer. "They whalers, out of some place—the name I cannot say."

Newfoundland, perhaps. Falconer felt another piece of his plan fall into place, though he did not know at the moment precisely how it would work. "You did well."

Falconer's further instructions sent Nebo and Soap scurrying in different directions. Falconer sent Bernard off last, for his duties required the longest explanation. None of his small company dared question the odd set of orders, especially not when they were given in the terse bites of a man scarcely able to contain his emotions.

Wadi remained with him, the customary guard that any slaver would rely on to protect his back and his money belt. That done, Falconer turned toward the innkeeper, who clearly tried not to cower at his approach.

A voice said from across the tables, "I know you, don't I?"

Falconer glanced at the man. "I doubt that."

"So did I, at first." The man rose from his table. Instantly Wadi moved in, hand on dagger. At that, the second man at the stranger's table rose and cocked his pistol.

The innkeeper stood quickly, framed in the kitchen doorway, and cried, "No, effendis, please, I beg you, this is peaceful establishment!"

"You wouldn't remember me. We never met proper-like." Ignoring both the innkeeper and the tense men, the stranger raised empty hands as he approached Falconer. His grin, showing teeth misshapen and yellow, was framed by a scraggly beard falling across his collar. His eyes were as cold as dirty snow. "You marching in here with that motley crew, I wondered for a bit. There seemed something different about you. Then you came back alone, and right there I remembered. Zanzibar, it was. Someone pointed you out to me. Captain John Falconer. I'm right, ain't I?"

At Falconer's single nod, he slapped his thigh. "Knew it, I did. Klein's the name. Out of Mombasa of late, though I lived all over. Where's your ship, Captain?"

"Lost it."

The spark of interest faded from the gaze. "Pity, that. On account of how I'm at loose ends just now. Me and my mate here. Drink?"

Falconer wanted to walk away. But his plan required a smooth road, and he needed no new watching eyes reporting suspicious acts. "I've got to keep a clear head. There's work ahead this day. But I'll sit with you a minute."

"You're here to buy, are you? Slaves."

Falconer slipped his hands beneath the table to hide their clenching. "If I can find the wares I'm after."

Klein paid Falconer's tight response no mind. He wore a tattered suit that might once have been navy in color but now was shaded mostly by the desert. He filled glasses for himself and his mate. Falconer caught the old familiar whiff of arrack, the desert liquor. Klein asked, "Who's paying for your wares?"

"I don't see how that's any of your business."

The dirty teeth emerged and vanished. Klein's smile did not reach his eyes. "No harm in asking, is there?" He downed his glass in one gulp, then emitted a sigh that smelled of alcohol. "You need an extra pair of hands?"

"I'm buying a half dozen slaves, no more. Obliged, but we can handle that."

"There's bandits aplenty on the roads west. Even more if you're headed toward Alexandria."

Falconer deflected the probing question. "If you've heard of me, then you know how I am in a fight."

The implied threat was tossed away with another empty grin. "Well, if you change your mind, we're your men. Been beached here far too long."

"I'll remember that." Falconer rose from the table.

Klein tossed back his drink. "Shame you arrived when you did."

Falconer halted in the process of turning away. "Why is that?"

"On account of the monthly market being done six days back." Klein examined his empty glass. "You bought yourself the dregs, you did. And paid top dollar. See what a man like me could do for you?"

"I'm grateful for the offer. But I hold to different ways." Though the words jammed hard in his craw, he forced himself to add, "But I'll pay for your advice. Let me buy you your dinner."

Though visibly frightened of Falconer's menace, the innkeeper had spent years taking gold from hard men. His English was extremely poor, so Wadi was forced to translate. The innkeeper twice stumbled in his haste to obey Wadi's bidding.

By the time Soap and Nebo returned with the three chained men, Falconer had negotiated what he wanted with the innkeeper and taken possession of a small corral behind the tavern. Their camels and donkeys were tethered by the gate, leaving an open stretch at the rear where the wooden fence joined to the ancient city wall. They were clearly not the first to bed down close to their newly acquired charges, for tent rings hung from stout posts imbedded deep in the earth. Falconer watched as Nebo staked the three newly purchased men to the post furthest from the gate. Soap left and returned with a meal bucket, rags, water, and a canister of salve.

While the men ate, Falconer helped Nebo raise their tent, using it to mask his movements related to his new acquisitions. The three men hunkered tight together and watched him with red-rimmed suspicion. Falconer called softly, "Soap."

The seaman murmured, "All clear."

Falconer dropped to one knee and swiftly unscrewed the ankle bracelets. He then dropped the keys by the men. He kicked a dust covering over the keys to hide them from prying eyes. Falconer rose and stepped back to lean against the wall. Back in view of any who took the alley down behind the tavern. He crossed his arms and scowled at the men. Just another slaver inspecting his new charges. "I must ask you to keep the chains on for now," he said, his lips barely moving.

Their leader watched as Nebo knelt and began spreading the yellow grease over their wounds. He directed his question at Falconer. "You're Christian?"

"I am now. Before that, a slaver." Falconer let that sink in a moment, then asked, "You're American?"

"Canucks, the three of us. Name's Randall Sands. This here's Bert. The young one there is my brother, Rufus."

Whatever number of years Rufus might have carried must have been multiplied a hundredfold by his recent experiences. "You were taken off the Canaries, I hear."

"That we were. With nineteen months' oil in our hold, floundering in rough waters and easy prey. We're all that's left of fifty-eight good men."

His brother began trembling so hard his chains rattled. "We're . . . we're free?"

Falconer murmured, "First we have to get you out of here. And we can't do that until we free two captives from the fortress."

"They're held in the dungeons?"

"Aye."

"You must have a good plan, then."

"I hope so."

The man called Sands glanced at his two mates, then asked Falconer, "What do you want us to do?"

The manner of their appearance drew stares but not suspicion. Falconer did not walk so much as take possession of the land where his boots trod, stalking the earth as only a commander would. Wadi strode a pace behind him, the faithful guard, his hand resting upon the hilt of his scimitar.

Bernard Lemi did not walk but rode his day's purchase. More than a mere horse, it was a prancing desert beast. It was also a declaration. Riding such a steed with a man like Falconer at his side meant this seemingly weak and untested dandy possessed either wealth or power or both. Nebo strode on Bernard's left, his hand upon the stirrup.

No wonder the desert people stopped and stared.

Bernard held embroidered reins with bright golden tassels. He wore new gloves of Moroccan leather. His dusty jacket had been replaced by the sort of cloak a prince might wear, velvety in feel and desert yellow in color. The tasseled edge fell across the horse's flanks. "You're certain this is necessary?" he said from the corner of his mouth.

Falconer rested one hand upon his pistol and met every pair of eyes with a scowl. No one looked his way for long. "I told you what the slaver said. The market is done for now, and we overpaid. Our actions will be watched with great attention from now on."

Tunis, or Carthage, as most of its inhabitants preferred to call it, was not a pretty place. Yet the central plaza possessed an aura of ancient vigor. The square was over a mile wide and surrounded the double harbor. The outer harbor was small by current standards, built as it was two thousand years earlier and meant for galleons. The inner harbor was more cramped still, less than a hundred paces wide. The port's outermost wall was a mound of crumbling stone that rose thirty feet above the water. A single tower, the lone surviving remnant of an old harbor fort, rose at the wall's end. The inner harbor was bordered by a wall only slightly taller than a man. Falconer had seen other such ancient harbors, and he knew the inner harbor was normally used on only two occasions. The first was against a storm great enough to push waves over the outer harbor wall.

The other was a time such as now, when danger lurked out to sea.

Across the harbor, the square's eastern rim was bordered by a long line of fancy inns. The lane fronting these taverns was broad and smooth-stoned and shaded by reed mats. Pedestrians in fine robes filled the promenade, followed by servants waving fans in the still afternoon air.

Falconer's band entered the square from the west, which contained an array of the city's wealthiest shops.

The promenade on this side of the harbor was even broader, the reed shade mats laced with colored yarns, such that the stones underfoot were rainbow streaked.

The fortress occupied the market's southeastern corner. The outer gates were wide enough to permit six riders abreast. One stubby tower rose within a wall that was more rubble than proper brick and stone, as Amelia Henning had described. Here and there along the outer wall Falconer spied guards with pikes and ancient blunderbusses. More soldiers paraded in pairs around the central square.

Falconer did his best not to stare to his right, where the fortress wall had been stripped of enough stone to form a waist-high wall around a broad corral. At the corral's heart rose a stone dais, upon which were three pillars. Chains dangled from the pillars. More chains were strung around the dais. Still more hung from the fortress wall, a long line of woe that extended around the corner and down the connecting alley. The fact that the main slave market was empty did not matter. To Falconer's mind, the stones themselves wailed from their burden of ancient and recent sorrow.

A single belch of thunder sounded to their left. The horse whinnied nervously. Bernard patted its neck and glanced over, as did everyone they could see. Only Falconer did not look about. He did not need to. Five leagues distant, a merchant vessel tacked back and forth across the otherwise empty sea. The fort fired a second cannon, announcing the departure of a single lateen-sailed vessel, one flying an ornate royal pennant.

Bernard said, "We draw suspicion especially now, is what you are saying."

"Our appearance at this moment is vital. They will now conclude that we follow the lead of a dandy who lets gold fall through his fingers like water. This explains much," Falconer confirmed. "What did you hear in your discussions with the merchant?"

"The legate has demanded fifty thousand sovereigns."

"That's ten times the original ransom."

"When the first ransom was set, there was not a wealthy merchant sailing in his own ship within sight of Tunis port," Bernard replied. He reined in the horse. "We have arrived."

Nebo took hold of the horse's reins while Bernard climbed down. The door before which they stopped was instantly opened. A white-bearded man and two servants in gold-embroidered vests hurried out. The man salaamed Bernard in the genteel fashion of a wealthy merchant greeting his equal, ignoring Falconer entirely. Precisely what Falconer intended.

Bernard refused the man's invitation to enter. He spoke in French, the second language of the coastal merchants after Arabic. Bernard peeled off his gloves. He pointed to the empty market arena. The merchant was most apologetic. Bernard peevishly slapped his gloves against his palm, obviously irritated he had missed the slave market. The merchant spoke again. Bernard sniffed his disdain. The merchant snapped his fingers. Instantly one of his servants bounded across the square toward the line of fine inns. Again the merchant invited Bernard to enter. Bernard declined, and permitted the merchant to take his hand in farewell. He turned away, flipping the robe behind him in the manner of a true French dandy. The merchant salaamed to Bernard's back, his eyes cold with scorn.

Bernard remounted his nervous horse, gripped the reins, and muttered, "I feel such a total fool."

"You handled that perfectly," Falconer told him. "The merchant has gauged you as just another spoiled son of a rich banker. Did you explain that your father has sent you down on a fact-finding mission, with me as your father's aide?"

"I implied it was punishment for foul deeds," Bernard replied softly. "Alas, I have all too much practice at the speech and the manner."

From the horse's other side, Nebo observed, "The merchant wishes to pluck you like his very own goose. He will protect you with his life."

"And explain your presence to officials in the fortress, if anyone asks," Falconer added.

"He has sent his servant to obtain rooms for me in the city's finest inn." Bernard pointed to the opposite promenade. "Over there."

"Let us take the long way," Falconer said.

They were being watched, Falconer was certain. In such lands all strangers were spied upon. Falconer forced himself neither to flinch nor turn away as they passed the stone-lined arena. The stench rising from the empty sunlit stones was both fierce and all too familiar. The market now housed a small contingency of armed men on one side, their animals on the other. The soldiers sprawled about a campfire and paused their game of dice long enough to observe the quartet's passage.

Bernard asked, "Why are the boats crammed together so?"

The outer harbor contained only six vessels. The interior harbor, however, was so tightly packed Falconer could have walked from one side of the port to the other using the boats as a bridge.

"They fear the ship's guns," Falconer explained.

"What distance does a hundred paces make?"

Nebo said, "The inner harbor places them within the shadow of the fortress walls. They think your ship would not risk hitting La Rue's castle with its cannon."

The square's tightest point was where the fortress wall jutted out, making a stone boundary between the slave market and the eastern promenade. Thirty paces on they passed the fortress's main gates. Falconer made what he hoped would appear to be a casual inspection.

His gut quaked at this first examination. The gates had been rebuilt to form a killing ground.

These new gates were set back from the main wall. The recess was eighty paces across and paved in mosaic tile worn almost colorless. The fortress wall formed three sides of an open square. From the ramparts warriors could pour a devastating amount of fire onto any would-be attacker. The gates themselves were forty feet high and the same in breadth. Three guards stood to either side of the open doorway. More guards stood along the upper wall. A crowd of petitioners waited patiently in front of the guard station.

The small group turned away and started down the promenade. A wind blew steadily off the sea, erasing the market's last lingering traces. Bernard asked, "Why are there not more soldiers?"

"Do you not have eyes?" Nebo said. "Armed men are everywhere."

But Falconer understood the question. "This is a pirate stronghold. His men are not trained for wearing uniforms and standing on sentry duty. They fight for gold."

The merchant's servant came rushing toward them, calling loudly and gesticulating toward an inn midway up the promenade. Falconer and Nebo stepped back, permitting the servant to take their station by Bernard's horse.

When five paces separated them from the pair, Nebo asked, "Will it work, this plan of yours?"

Falconer did not respond until they had halted before the inn. He then made a slow circular inspection of his surroundings, burning the square into his memory. The inns, the castle, the market, the merchants.

The port.

Falconer turned to the African and said, "You know what to do."

Nebo salaamed, his muscles gleaming in the sun. "It will be as you say."

They were committed.

Chapter 29

The afternoon was spent in secret urgency. There was nothing odd about servants using the infamous Carthage market to stock up on supplies for a desert crossing. Tripoli was, after all, a full six days' march. And that was where they were headed, or so Nebo complained to all who cared to ask. Driven eastward to the Egyptian port by a spoiled dandy whose father sought to harden his youngest child. No worry given to the poor charges whose sweat would ease the boy's way. For boy he was, Nebo grumbled time and again. A child whose loss would be missed by only one man.

So the three men went from stall to stall. The silent Arab and the tall African and the wizened English sailor who spoke neither Arabic nor French. Buying desert provisions here, dates and twice-baked bread and congealed coconut oil and ground chickpeas mixed with lemon and olive oil. At the next stall they bought two small casks of whale oil, the cleanest burning oil for lamps, while the African groused over good money wasted on orders which made no sense, for who would bother with a reading lamp in the desert night? Which of course would draw every bandit for miles. Which then meant stocking up on powder for their guns. And waterskins, of necessity, enough for an army. Plus a quarter league of good hemp rope, to keep man and beast together in the storms that would no doubt plague them the entire trek. The market holders laughed and groaned sympathetically at the African's antics, and salaamed the fools from one stall to the next. For the dandy's men paid for everything in good English gold.

Bernard and Falconer were on a mission of their own, the dandy riding his horse the entire way around the town's center, pausing here and there to buy nonsensical items, with Falconer in attendance on foot. Falconer did not complain aloud. But his scowl was enough to silence both beggars and all but the hardiest of merchants. The dandy purchased a shawl with silver baubles for a woman back in France. A flask of myrrh, which cost more than a mule. All of which was to be sent to the tavern in the city's poorer section, back where his servants resided. It took the dandy more than three hours to circle the fortress, by which time the entire city knew of the spoiled young man who let gold drip through his fingers. No matter that the slaver who guarded the dandy complained in nasty tones about the father and the trouble they would have crossing the desert with these items. His master spent and spent and spent. Of course he was welcome. His appearance at each alley brought cries of delight from the merchants, who flipped open chests and plucked out their most valued treasures. The merchants whose wares were chosen tried to hide their mirth at his foolishness behind their hands, and often failed.

Falconer had forgotten just how fast a desert sunset came and went. One moment the golden orb floated in a vessel of cloudless blue. The desert dust, lifted by the day's heat, briefly became a mystical veil. Then the light simply vanished. The sun dropped below the horizon with the speed of a snuffed candle. Darkness conquered. Stars emerged. The temperature dropped. That was another lesson he had forgotten—how cold the desert furnace swiftly became without its source of heat.

He ate a solitary meal in the tavern's front room. When the beached slaver Klein entered with his menacing mate, Falconer ordered the innkeeper to feed them again. No drink. Klein accepted the gift with a grin and pretended no offense at Falconer's decline of company. Falconer toyed over his final cup of mint tea, idly watching the constant stream of traffic. Finally his worry could be held back no longer. He rose from the table, ignored the innkeeper's salaam, and hurried around back.

Soap was in the same position as he had been left, leaning easy against the stall's gate. To anyone who passed the alley, he was merely another guard lolling through wasted hours. But there was only one way in or out of this rear hold. Which meant Soap's keen eye was enough to protect the others from prying eyes.

Given what they were doing, this was essential.

Wadi was off playing guard to Bernard, who fretted that his role kept him far from the action. The others, Nebo and the three former whalers, worked with quiet frantic haste.

Falconer leaned against the wall by Soap. He gave the yard and the walls and the alley and the tavern a careful inspection. The kitchen's rear door was rimmed by a wall intended to keep out beggars. This wall had a second door, but Soap had jammed the lever with a stick, such that they would be warned by anyone wishing to come or go. In any case, the tent's side wall shielded the four men from any who did not actually walk over. Satisfied with their security, Falconer asked, "What does your nose tell you?"

"Same as it did the last time you asked," Soap replied.

"There's a big storm brewing."

Falconer sniffed hard, but for once his senses refused to obey. All he could smell was dust.

"Surprised you even have to ask," Soap went on.

"I'm too worried over what's about to happen," Falconer confessed.

"Which is why I'm not worried at all. Confident as ever I've been."

Falconer felt the knot in his gut ease somewhat. "We need that blow."

"Just beyond the horizon, it is. You wait and see."

Wind and no rain. Everything depended upon that combination. "Be ready to move."

"Been ready," Soap rejoined. "Been ready since the hour before sunset. Go see to your charges and leave off with the fretting, that's my advice."

Falconer slipped around the tent to where four men crouched in the dust. By the light of the yard's only torch, he watched the men at work. Nebo and Sands and the two other whalers were surrounded by their gear and a growing pile of finished product. Sands' younger brother held a skin as the man named Bert filled it from the cask of whale oil. Nebo was adding gunpowder to the mix. Between them and Sands were several rags glistening with oil and flecked with yet more powder.

"Have you eaten?" Falconer asked.

"Aye, Skipper. Haven't been this full since I don't know when." Sands did not pause in his motions. Nor did he smile. But Falconer could sense a new lightness to the man.

"How much longer?"

"Few minutes more should see us done here."

Falconer cast a glance behind him, then crouched down beside them. He hefted one of the packed waterskins. "Tell me again what I need to do."

"Not much to it." Sands pointed at the rags crammed into the skin's mouth. "Jam that end into your tinderbox and run."

"What if the wind comes up?"

"Long as your tinderbox holds a flame, the plan should work fine. There's more powder in them rags than oil, and they're soaked with oil right through." Sands used a dagger to jam the rag into another waterskin, tightening it down to where the skin would not leak. "Your only worry is about getting away before this thing lights up the night."

Falconer checked everything one final time, then said, "It is my habit to pray before setting off."

Nebo gave a solemn nod. "I be glad to hear words between you and your God."

As Falconer crouched down beside the men, Soap stepped back to where he could both be a member of the group and keep an eye on the alley. Falconer said, "In the book of Ephesians, we are told to put on the armor of God. That we may withstand the evil day, we must wear the breastplate of righteousness and the helmet of salvation, shod our feet with the gospel of peace, and carry before us the shield of faith and the sword of the Spirit. We must do these things so that we can speak boldly and be an ambassador of eternal truth."

Falconer felt five sets of eyes upon him as he settled his back against the rough stone wall. "When the apostle Paul wrote these words, he went on to describe himself as a man who shared their plight. To me, this is a deep confession. Paul does not speak as one who has left behind human woes. Paul is both free and not free. Just as I am. I am a believer and thus a new man. And I still am crippled by the woes of this world. God has often seemed very far from me."

One of the men supposedly chained to the central pillar coughed. Or it might have been a choking sob. Falconer did not look up to see. He went on, speaking to the dust at his feet. "On some days, the prayers of my mouth have not resonated in my heart. But does this mean I fail? Have I lost my hold on God? I find my answer here, in the words of a teacher who is also chained. Does he wear physical chains? Is he ill? Whatever the external issue, I think Paul is also weighed down by his internal failings. He says, Brothers, I speak to you not as one who has once been where you are. No. I am there with you *now*."

Falconer found the courage to lift his gaze. "No matter what may befall me this night, still I know. Not think. Not hope. I *know*. That come the day I leave this earth, I will enter my eternal home. The glorious door has been opened for me, as sinful a man as ever has lived, by Christ. Who died for me. That I might live. Forever. In God's glorious presence."

He let the words hang in the dry and dusty air. The torch crackled from the iron stand overhead. The market noises drifted back from the alley. But here in this space, the world seemed far away.

Falconer asked softly, "Who will pray with me this night?"

The six of them knelt together. In the dust of a corral that had harbored misery beyond time, they joined together. A former slave, a slaver, a seaman, and three still bound by earthly chains. Falconer prayed words he scarcely heard. He knew he spoke. He knew at least two of the men wept, perhaps more. But a sensation filled him, one so strong the sounds could not penetrate.

God was with him still.

When he was done, a silence held them all. Falconer remained there upon his knees, reluctant to release the moment and return to the dust of life.

Soap rose to his feet. He took a pair of steps from the group. A moment passed. Then he said quietly, "Ho, the wind."

Falconer rose to stand behind the older seaman. Not satisfied, he walked down the alley. Beside the tavern's entrance, the wind was much stronger. Lanterns illuminated the first whirlwind, as tight as a man-sized fist.

Falconer went back to where Nebo was lashing the final skins to the pack mule. Falconer tested the knots himself. Satisfied, he said, "We move."

Chapter 30

A storm, Soap had predicted. And the seaman was right. The wind carried a plaintive desert cry.

Date palms by the market wells swayed crazily. Wind whipped around corners and down the deserted lanes. All the torches fronting the main roads were blown out, and the stalls and inns were quickly shuttered.

Now in a desert robe again, Falconer shielded his face with part of his turban against the biting dust like everyone else they saw. He had covered the waterskins on the back of the horse with Bernard's shawl. But the storm made such precautions unnecessary. He and Nebo were merely two more robed figures struggling against the wind, leading a horse and a loudly protesting mule.

Both men held the turbans to their heads with one hand, while the other gripped the reins. The horse pulled fretfully at its traces, although not overmuch. It was, after all, a desert animal. The mule, however, twice nearly pulled Nebo off his feet in its frantic attempt to flee. Finally Falconer shouted, "Wait!"

He tied the horse to a wall stanchion, pulled Bernard's fancy shawl off the waterskins, and retied it over the donkey's face. The animal disliked it but at least it stopped trying to drag Nebo backward down the lane.

When a turn in the lane blocked the wind somewhat, Falconer called, "What if the tinderbox is snuffed out? How will we light the torches?"

Nebo's booming laugh was out of place with the night. "First you worry storm does not come, now it is too great?"

Falconer muttered an admonition, "O ye of little faith."

"What say you?"

"That you are right and I am wrong."

The darkness opened into the main square. The wind felt gentler here, without the alleys' funneling effect. The torches remained unlit, however. A few unshuttered windows beckoned windswept passersby into cozy inns. A few people rushed past, too concerned with fleeing the storm to pay Falconer and Nebo any mind. The fortress parapets, and any guards stationed there, were lost to the gloom.

Nebo hissed, "Do you see our friends?"

Falconer's eyes continued their search around the square. Overhead, the reed mats rattled angrily against the wind. Then he spied two men gripping turbans and moving slowly. "There."

Bernard was dressed as Falconer had instructed, the yellow robe whipping behind him like a flag. "Take that off," Falconer said in greeting. "There's no one here to question why you're out."

Bernard plucked the cape from his neck and lofted it skyward. The wind whipped it away. "Then we're still going ahead?"

"Why should we not?" Nebo replied for them both.

"I was just . . . I suppose I am being afraid and cowardly."

Falconer and Nebo exchanged a glance. "There not

anything cowardly about warrior knowing fear," Nebo told him.

To their surprise, Wadi agreed. "I glad you with us this night."

"The storm is a gift," Falconer said. "We must use it while we still can."

Falconer watched the young banker's shoulders straighten. Bernard took the horse's reins from Falconer's hands. "Then let us do this thing."

The wharf was utterly deserted. Falconer walked the uneven rock barrier separating the outer harbor from the inner and reflected that the sound of water was clearest in a dry land. Far to his left, waves broke over the top of the port's outer wall, sending foam and spray cascading over them. To his right, the boats crammed into the inner harbor creaked against one another in constant protest. Falconer saw no one.

He moved at a crouch, searching the boats intently.

Nebo hissed, "What do you seek?"

Explaining his vow of not taking another's life would take too much time. Falconer held up his hand for patience. The boats were empty of sailors.

Then he spied something, and suddenly the search was not wasted. He leapt into the boat. "Give me your tinderbox."

The boat stank strongly of fish. Falconer stepped over the pile of nets to a storm lantern lashed tightly to the stern. He slipped his dagger from his belt and sawed through the cable. Storm lanterns, a recent invention, had a series of adjustable vents lining the top of all four sides. A simple flame required air, but wind would extinguish the flame. A storm lantern was designed with a handle to fit around the wrist or be lashed to a cleat so only one face would be presented to the storm. Only the vents protected from the wind would be opened. Falconer crouched low in the vessel, struck a flame in the tinderbox, and transferred it to the lantern.

Nebo's eyes widened when he realized what Falconer held. Falconer said, "Guards will see the light. We must hurry."

As they approached, Wadi's teeth gleamed in the lantern light. It was the first time Falconer had ever seen the man smile. Falconer told them, "Give us ten minutes to get into position. You know where to meet us, yes?"

In reply, Nebo took the lantern. "May Lord I am now learning about be with us this night."

To either side of the fortress doors, bronze braziers as large as washtubs burned tar-soaked logs. The guards lurked just inside the gates, seeking protection from the storm's assault. Falconer and Bernard passed unhindered and walked the empty lane flanking the castle's eastern wall.

A hundred paces inside, Falconer stopped. "Here."

Bernard released the coil of rope from the saddle and lashed one end to the horn. The desert saddle was high front and back, the horn carved from the same wood that framed the saddle.

Falconer looped the coil around one shoulder. "If you are challenged, flee."

Bernard climbed into the saddle. "I will not let you down."

"Listen to what I am saying, Bernard."

"Go," the banker said with a shake of his head. He patted the horse's neck to calm its skittish movement. "Hurry."

In their earlier tour around the castle, Falconer had

selected this entry point for two reasons. If Amelia Henning's recollections were correct, they now stood on the side closest to the dungeon entrance. The fortress wall had been poorly repaired here, and the crumbling façade offered Falconer a series of handholds. He tightened the turban about his head so only a tiny slit remained open for his eyes, and began to climb.

His face was tight against the stone, and every puff of wind flung grit into the small opening. He felt a shiver of sweaty dread trace down the length of his spine. The stones were so old many crumbled beneath his fingers. He tested each hold in turn, hurrying as much as he possibly could, fearing at any instant a cry of alarm from unseen foes.

Fear. He had spent most of his adult life living in danger's maw. In his former life he had been known as a cold man, hard and cruel and incapable of mercy. A stranger to fear. Yet now his heart thundered so swiftly he guarded each step, making time to carefully measure his terror. Time enough to see Matt's shining face planted there upon the yellow stone. Time to think once more of Amelia Henning and the impact her words, her presence, had on him.

He reached the top and crouched, scouting the empty rampart. His breath seemed as loud as the storm, as though both he and the desert world panted together. He felt his legs quiver, both from the climb and from fright. He searched the yard below, but saw only blackness.

He willed himself to uncoil the rope and toss it over the side. But his muscles refused to unlock.

John Falconer. Born to a woman who worked in a roadside tavern. His father left when he was four. At seven years of age apprenticed to a chimney sweep and ratter who beat Falconer hard and fed him worse. At twelve he lied about his age and ran away to sea. He fought his way

through the years and up the ranks. Until finally he won
his captaincy when a storm swept the skipper of a slaver
overboard. Brought to the Cross by the horror of a wasted
life. Brought to here. Clinging to the rampart of a fortress
from beyond time. Staring into an inner keep as dark as the
pit. Stung by another storm.

Then a new voice rose within his own internal tumult,
the storm that no one saw but him. A declaration that did
not need volume to speak above the gale.

John Falconer, the voice whispered over the tempest's
howl. A man loved by an orphan child such that the lad is
able to look beyond his own pain and trust him to lead
them both upon a vital quest. Befriended by men who
trusted him for more than physical strength. Men who
were lifted up even in this dark city of slaves and woe by
the knowledge that Falconer no longer lived for himself.
No longer fought for selfish gain. No longer walked alone.
These same men sought the direction he could reveal to
them, spoken in words that communicated to their hearts,
spoken by a man who was once as they were. And had
found the strength to turn away, to change.

Falconer felt himself lifted from the fear and despair.
He was filled with the most astonishing sensation. Someone was praying for him. An ally on this earth approached
the throne of heaven on his behalf.

What, then, should he fear?

Falconer hoisted the rope off his shoulder, but before
he could drop it down the wall, a subtle alteration took
hold of the night. The storm still howled over the parapet.
But the night was dark no longer.

A volcanic glow rose from the direction of the sea and
the harbors. At the same time, a shriek louder than the
storm rose from the castle's front gates.

Again Falconer dropped flat against the parapet stones.

Below him, the inner keep suddenly boiled with noise and movement. His cheek pressed to the stones, he looked over the edge as a hundred voices echoed the alarm. A hundred blades. A thousand. Unseen until that moment. He realized that soldiers had been driven inside the castle walls to escape the storm.

There to greet him had he dropped down a moment earlier.

The fact that fear had saved him left him trembling once more. He crouched on the cold stones and watched the light grow to where it colored the horizon like a giant lantern. The soldiers pushed and jostled and shouted as they rushed for the gates, driven to a fierce panic by the news that the inner harbor was on fire. All the city's fishing vessels, all the attack galleons, all ablaze.

Chapter 31

Falconer waited while the noise faded. He looked through the gloom around the keep, then dropped the rope over the side. If there were still soldiers about, they paid no mind to a shadow slipping silently down the wall.

Save for the glow beyond the main gates, the inner keep was utterly dark. Falconer knotted the rope to the back of his belt, turned his back to the burning in the distance, and waited for his vision to adjust. The storm still howled overhead. The wall might have blocked much of the wind, but a constant rain of dust and grit fell into the keep, so thick no doubt both their torches and the soldiers' campfires had been stifled.

Falconer peered into the dark, fearing Amelia Henning had remembered wrong, wondering what he would do if he could not find what he sought. Then it appeared before him, a hulking shadow that resembled a grave mound more than a hut. Falconer crept forward, his heart pounding so loud he could hear it over the storm.

The dusty murk was so thick he would have walked straight into the two guards had they not chosen that moment to speak.

Falconer was too close to hesitate. As soon as the forms separated themselves from the hut's shadow, he rushed forward, gripped two handfuls of greasy hair, and brought the heads together hard.

The dungeon guards collapsed at his feet.

Falconer quickly searched one guard's supine form, then the other. Neither had keys. He felt his way around to the front of the hut. As he feared, the door was locked from within.

He dragged the unconscious guards to the rear of the small structure, thus keeping them from the view of any in the main keep. He tossed their weapons toward the unseen wall, then used their cloth belts to bind their wrists and ankles.

Falconer returned to the front of the hut and the locked door. He untied the rope from his belt and lashed it around the bars that formed a viewing port in the dungeon's door. Hand over hand, Falconer drew in the rope's slack. There was so much extra rope his fears had time to rise into certainty that Bernard had untied his end and vanished.

Then the rope grew taut. Falconer tightened it further still and felt a jerk in response. He sighed with shaky relief, took a firmer grip, and hauled back hard.

There was a moment's hesitation, but only a moment. Then the rope sang through his hands.

Bernard had not merely ignored the flood of warriors racing toward the fire started by Wadi and Nebo. He had remained at the ready.

At Falconer's tug, Bernard had spurred his horse. The desert steed had obviously been storing up its own share of nervous force, for in the space of a single heartbeat the rope went from coiled at Falconer's feet to tighter than a noose.

The door exploded from its ancient stone frame.

Falconer did not hesitate one instant. He flew down

the stairs so fast he scarcely touched them at all. Speed was his strongest ally now. Speed and surprise.

The storm entered even here, drumming within the windowless stone chamber and causing the torches to flicker nervously. His boots crashed upon the landing. Two tunnels branched out before him. He searched one, then the other, and spotted movement.

He roared as he ran. The jailer was a rotund man with a belt about his bare midriff. His mouth gaped about a scraggly beard at the sight of this bellowing apparition. Falconer struck one blow to the jailer's right temple, and the man went down hard.

"*Byron!*"

Falconer made a mess of unlashing the keys from the jailer's belt.

"*Catherine! Kitty!*"

The keys would not come free.

"*Byron!*"

A faint call resounded from somewhere further along the tunnel. Falconer heaved so hard upon the keys he lifted the jailer from the stones. The leather strings fastening the ring to the belt finally gave. The jailer thumped back to the floor with a groan.

"*Byron! Kitty!*" Falconer raced down the endless stone tunnel, its ceiling so dismally low he had to move at a crouch.

This time the sound was much clearer. "Say again! I can't—"

"Here!"

He was guided by a frantic pounding upon one door. Falconer fumbled through the keys, selecting one after the other until one finally fit. The lock creaked back.

A young man's terror-stricken face, half covered by a

matted black beard, blinked in the light. He croaked a single word. "Who . . . ?"

"A friend of your mother's." Falconer reached in and gripped the young man's arm. "Come quickly."

The young man scrambled in petrified confusion out the door.

Falconer shouted the girl's name. Again. "Have you seen a young girl?" he asked the man.

But Byron was too terrified to make sense of Falconer's query. "My . . . my mother?"

"Listen to me." He shook Byron as gently as his own nerves allowed. "We don't have much time. A young girl. Blond. Her name is Kitty."

"I . . . No."

"Come on, then." Falconer debated whether he should have moved further down the tunnel. He glanced behind them. The cavelike passage snaked back to be enveloped by its own gloom. Falconer opted to head back toward the opening. *Kitty!*

The stairs appeared ahead of them. The young man allowed himself to be led forward, until he realized that Falconer intended to head down the other dungeon passageway. "No!"

"Come on, man. There's another—"

"No!" Panic granted him such strength he almost managed to weasel free of Falconer's grip. "I want to get *out* of here!"

Falconer had no time to be gentle. He took hold of Byron's neck, wheeled about, and pressed him into the stone wall. "You must be still and listen to me."

"No! I want—"

Falconer lifted him free of the wall and slammed him back. A motion of less than six inches. But it carried enough force to shock Byron into immobility. "It's your foolhardiness that brought us here in the first place. You *will* obey me. Now *be still.*"

The strength of Falconer's grip, or what the young man saw in Falconer's face, caused him to whimper and go limp.

"That's better. Now listen carefully. I am here to find *two* of you. Do you hear me? Two. We leave when I've located a young girl. Blond haired. Nine years old. She is named Catherine but she goes by Kitty." When Byron's eyes tracked upward toward the dusty night, Falconer thumped him again upon the wall, but gently. "Pay attention. Do you know her?"

"I-I might have heard the jailer say something."

"Did he say where?"

"I . . . No . . ." His eyes could not help but track upward again, but this time he pointed down the other corridor. "Perhaps down that way."

"Good lad. Let's hurry now." Falconer peeled Byron from the wall and returned his grip to the man's arm. "Believe me, I want to get out of here as much as you. So do us both a service and add your voice to mine."

The young man was so shattered by his ordeal he could produce no volume at all. But Falconer had said it mostly to focus him upon the task at hand. He shouted for the both of them and led them down the smoke-stained fetid tunnel.

After ten paces, he halted and pressed a hand upon Byron's chest. "Quiet."

A whimper came from another six paces or so down the tunnel. "Kitty!"

The whimper was louder now. Not really a word. But definitely a child's voice.

"Kitty, lass, we are friends of your mother's. If it's you, please, please, raise your voice."

She did not give it much strength. Just the same, Falconer clearly heard the word *Here*.

Falconer ran to the next door. "Is it you inside there?"

"Y-yes."

He rattled the keys, trying one after the other. His hands fumbled and grew sweaty as he went through them all.

"Why are you taking so long?" Byron fretted.

"Because none of them work." Falconer thought furiously as he tried yet another, certain now all had been fitted at least twice. "La Rue must have decided the jailer wasn't to be trusted. The admiral has kept this key for himself."

"Who?"

"Never mind." Falconer turned to the man. "There was a pike propped on the wall next to the jailer. Run fetch it."

Byron's trembling grew worse. "B-back?" He sagged against the wall.

"Hurry now." Falconer slipped his dagger from his belt. "You can't get free without me, and I'm not leaving without her."

Byron pushed himself away from the wall and staggered away. Falconer attacked the frame around the lock. He feared he chipped as much of his blade as he did the stone. "Kitty, lass, or would you prefer I called you Catherine?"

Her voice was a faint whisper, but more audible now. She had lowered herself so that she spoke directly through the hole at floor level, through which food would have been passed. "Kitty."

Falconer struck and struck and struck. He tried to keep his voice calm, but the panic and the effort made it difficult. "Your mother sent me after you. You remember your mother's name, don't you, lass?" he panted out between blows.

"A-Amelia." She broke over shaping the word. "Mama sent you?"

"Aye, that she did." Where was Byron? Falconer's chipping had revealed a lighter colored and harder stone beneath the first layer. Another chip, and the dagger blade broke off an inch from the haft. He resisted the urge to shout and rage at the obstinate lock. *"Byron!"*

"Here."

"Good job, excellent." Falconer gripped the pike, his hands fitting comfortably around the wooden haft. "All right. Go back and stand at the base of the stairs. If you hear anyone coming, you give us a shout."

"W-why aren't there any guards?"

"My friends caused a bit of a diversion. Go on, now. Kitty!"

"Yes?"

"Stand well back of the door, lass." Falconer stepped back himself. The pike was tipped with a steel arrow eight inches long and shaped like a nine-pointed star. He took aim not at the stone, which he feared would break this blade as well. Instead, he aimed for the lock itself. He braced himself against the opposite wall and pushed off as hard as he could.

The blow resounded through the tunnel like the booming of a great drum. Falconer retreated and rammed it again. A third time. Over and over, the booms pounding and echoing through the stone corridor. He was roaring now, giving the attack every bit of energy he could summon, hoping and praying there was no one around to hear the din he was making.

The lock exploded from the wood, punching a hole through the door. Puffing hard, Falconer dropped the pike with a clatter, gripped the hole with both hands, and tore the door open. "Lass?"

A filthy little waif with matted blond hair crouched beside the rear wall.

Falconer swiped at his face and forced his voice down to as gentle a rumble as he could manage. "There's nothing to fear from me, Kitty."

She whimpered and crouched more tightly still.

"Remember what I told you? Your mother sent me. Amelia Henning. She's waiting for you, sweet little darling." Falconer reached out one hand. "Now you just come and let me get you free of this hole."

Chapter 32

Falconer lifted her quickly into his arms, and they scrambled up the winding stone stairs and into the starless night. The storm thrummed in the air above the parapets, with dust falling in a constant fitful stream. Neither of Falconer's charges seemed to notice at all. Byron sobbed great tearless breaths of air. He gripped Falconer's arm with both hands and stumbled on faltering legs. The girl clung limpetlike to his neck and whimpered continually.

Falconer found the rope by finding the door. He unlashed the rope, an action made awkward because Kitty refused to release him. He handed the rope to Byron. "Follow this to the wall. Climb."

Byron started forward, asking yet another of his one-word questions as he moved. "Climb?"

"Our way to safety lies up and over the wall. It's not far to the top. But you'll have to do it yourself."

Byron arrived at the wall and looked up with an expression lost to the gloom. Falconer understood. "I can't manage you and the lass both."

From somewhere beyond the gloom, a voice shouted words in Arabic. Byron stiffened in panic. Falconer urged, "Hurry, now."

Byron's panic granted him the required strength.

Falconer watched him scrabble up the wall. There were more voices now. Falconer did not know if they were raising an alarm or if it was soldiers returning from the fire. Perhaps keener eyes, than his own had managed to pierce the dark and spot their escape. He gripped the rope and hissed, "Hold me tight as you can."

Kitty clutched him with all the strength she could muster, arms and legs both.

Falconer gripped the rope and began to climb. He found the going easier than he had dared hope, for the half-ruined stones offered ample stepping points. Even so, when he reached the ramparts he was puffing hard and his limbs had gone rubbery. "Byron?"

"Here."

"Find us a hook or bar or . . . Wait, I have one." Falconer had to kneel this time, and even so his weariness and the girl's weight almost pulled him prone. He lashed the rope's end to an iron hook imbedded in the stone. Rust flaked off in his grip. He tested it with his full weight, then handed it to Byron. "Let yourself over and down."

"I . . . I . . ."

"A friend awaits us. His name is Bernard. Hurry."

How Falconer made it down that wall, with the girl clinging to him and his legs as weak as water, he had no idea. Nonetheless he did, and at the base there was Bernard. The young man hefted Byron onto the donkey, then tried to pull Kitty away. But the girl began wailing and Bernard relented. He guided Falconer over to the horse and used his back as a support while Falconer heaved himself into the saddle. Bernard slipped the reins into one of Falconer's hands and a waterskin into the other. Falconer settled Kitty so that most of her weight was taken by the horse. She loosened her grip enough to glance about, and then to drink. Then her eyes closed and her head disappeared onto Falconer's shoulder. He could not tell if she was asleep, only that her whimpers grew fewer and softer.

They held to a straight, easterly course. The streets remained mostly empty. A few people rushed past, all headed toward the dimming glow behind them. Falconer felt enormously exposed. He knew those who passed would not help but notice them. A young man led two beasts. One, a donkey, held a bearded man dressed in rags and prison grime. The other, a horse, held an equally filthy young girl who looked to be a Westerner with hair that might be blond beneath its matting of dirt, who clung desperately to a tall stranger dressed in black. No, their only hope lay in leaving the city well behind.

The storm began to abate. The tightly wrapped awnings of shuttered businesses stopped drumming out their angry beat. As the wind's noise died, Falconer could hear a rising swell of voices behind them. The entire city seemed drawn to the havoc around the port.

Falconer recognized their turn by the stench. It was precisely as Nebo had described, a smell so vile not even a desert storm could mask it. Falconer drank from the waterskin, then spoke for the first time since their journey began. "Here. We turn here."

Bernard wordlessly turned the beasts south.

They entered the quarter occupied by the city's butchers and skinners and tanners. It was the same in every desert city Falconer had ever known. These people had not just their own quarter but their own wells, market, temples, and taverns. Anyone who noticed the group's passage would be loath to report anything to soldiers, most of whom would pay gold not to enter. Or so Falconer hoped.

Neither of Falconer's charges gave any sign they even noticed the stench. Or the direction. Which was very good, for Falconer could not risk explaining what they had planned.

The tanners' quarter ended by a broad, shallow lake. To the south and east rose hills, a jagged silhouette against the gradually clearing sky. Beyond the hills, Falconer knew, rose the newer part of Tunis. To the south and west was a flat, empty wasteland that stretched on for hundreds of miles.

The southern city wall had long been robbed of stones to be used for houses and corrals. Only one watchtower remained of the former parapet, and it rose from the desert like a ragged thumb. Without instructions from Falconer, Bernard left the road and headed toward the moonlit mound.

Figures separated themselves from the tower's silhouette and started toward them. Falconer recognized the bowlegged shape of Soap, who led a donkey that held one of the former slaves. Next came the tall, lean form of Wadi, who led two more mules piled high with provisions. Another of the whalers walked. Nebo led two more mules carrying the last freed man.

The walking man came in close enough for Falconer to recognize the whaler called Randall Sands. He peered at Falconer's charges a moment, then asked, "This them?"

"Aye." Falconer's voice sounded low and ragged as the last trailing wind.

"So you broke into the dungeon and freed them both." Sands' teeth flashed through his beard. "Glad you're on our side, mate."

Nebo pulled his mules around. "Dawn comes soon."

"We go," Falconer agreed.

They passed the tower and headed away from both the city and the road. South by west. Away from people and water and food and the sea.

Into the wasteland.

Chapter 33

The desert held a multitude of moods, all of them distinctly their own. The wind rose again soon after dawn, blasting the travelers with the tail of the storm's final assault. Falconer quickly helped those new to the desert to fit burnooses and accepted Wadi's assurance that this storm would not last. They forced the animals to kneel in the sand, then shielded themselves behind the beasts as best they could. No one complained. Falconer leaned his head against the mule and slept through the heat and the wind, easy in mind and body for the first time since scaling the fortress wall. Even the wind was his friend now, even the biting grime.

When the wind vanished and there was only the heat, they rose to continue their flight. Falconer and Nebo glanced behind, then shared a weary smile at how their trail was now obliterated.

They rested once at noon and again at midafternoon. Falconer walked now, for the horse's flanks were lathered in sweat. He had to be very firm with the little girl, refusing her cries to be held. She did not protest in words, nor was he certain she actually understood his explanation that he was too exhausted to hold her. But she remained on the horse only so long as he walked beside her, close enough for her to reach out every now and then to touch his shoulder.

The sun was a blazing orb directly in front of them. They were no longer walking south, but west now, and a sliver toward north. The heat was all consuming, and they seemed to have moved into a blazing lake of fire. Still they continued on.

Night came in desert suddenness. Falconer saw no more than the next step and trusted others to guide his feet. The reasons for their forward speed were no longer clear. Instead, a jangle of images came and went in his fevered brain. He was back upon the fortress wall. Then he was down in the dungeon tunnels. He was trapped inside a cell of his own. The sky overhead was filled with a river of sparks. The fire raged to his left, his right. Still they walked.

The moon rose, though Falconer did not lift his head to study it. The desert beneath his feet became a shade of pewter and felt cool through his boots. They turned and headed north. Falconer knew because the moon's silver shadow shifted.

"Wait here."

The words were spoken by Wadi. Falconer was too drained to comment over the silent man having spoken twice in the same day. Or perhaps it was not the same day at all. Falconer dropped to the desert floor. He felt as much as saw the girl slip into his lap. Someone handed him a waterskin. Falconer drank, then fitted the nozzle to the girl's mouth. He realized her lips were chapped and broken. He wanted to tell her to use salve upon them before they blistered. But he was asleep before the words were formed.

He had scarcely drawn a single breath of slumber before someone was nudging him. He wanted to protest, to beg them to leave him be. But his mind obeyed against his body's silent protest. He lifted Kitty from his lap into the saddle. She whimpered. He agreed.

Only then did he realize that he could see her. And not by silvery moonlight.

Dawn had come.

A sliver of his mind awoke him enough to understand why Soap and Wadi and Nebo were urging them forward. He saw them force a weakly protesting Byron onto the mule's saddle blanket. He wanted to tell the man that they had to be hidden before daylight arrived. They were in bandit country. They must find a place out of sight. But he discovered he could not speak. Though his mouth worked, the words did not come. So Falconer did the only thing he could think of. Which was to wind the horse's reins around his left wrist and begin walking.

Aimed straight north now, they headed toward hills that rose like ocher teeth. The desert was rock strewn and slanted. The horse stumbled on the rocky slope, but caught itself and did not fall. The stallion whickered a soft protest, no doubt as weary as the men. Falconer tried to remember the last time he had known a decent night's sleep. Was it two nights ago? Three? It did not matter. He had the strength for one thing only, making the next step. And the one after that.

They climbed more steeply now. Wadi moved up beside him. Pointed ahead and to the left. Falconer nodded, though he could not truly say he saw what Wadi indicated. His task remained the next step.

The sun now was strong. When had it risen? How long had they walked in full daylight? Falconer could not say.

Then the horse neighed, a single sound, and pulled upon the reins so that Falconer realized the beast was moving ahead of him. Which could only mean one of two things. Either the horse smelled water. Or . . . Falconer could not think of the other reason.

Then they entered a place of shade. The gloom fell upon Falconer like a wash of comfort and ease. The rock beneath his feet was gone, replaced by sand, whose coolness rose around him and entered his bones. He breathed a great sigh and lifted his gaze. The cave was a hollow running back fifteen full paces. The walls were laced with the strands of ocher and orange and black of a wind-carved grotto. Falconer stood in a stupor of fatigue and watched Wadi pull the lass from the horse. He accepted a waterskin from a man he did not see. He drank. He cast himself down upon the sand.

He breathed once. And was gone.

When Falconer awoke, the night was a desert collage. The moon painted the empty reaches with a smooth, silvery brush. The hills were pearl monuments with faces of impenetrable shadow. The wind came and went in regular breaths, as if the earth itself slumbered quietly. Falconer moved to crouch by the saddlebags, and ate and drank his fill. As he started to rise, he noticed that Byron's eyes were partly open. He regarded Falconer in the manner of one trained to be wary.

Falconer slipped over and knelt beside him. The man groped his way up slightly, so that he reclined against the cave's back. Falconer asked, "Have you eaten?"

"My belly feels tight as a drum."

"That is very good. We will need to push hard when we leave. Store up as much now as you possibly can. Especially water."

Byron mumbled something, the words almost emerging, then slipping away unformed.

"Say your piece. I am your father's friend and ally. Perhaps someday you might choose to see me the same way." When Byron still did not speak, Falconer went on, "Well, then. When you're ready. There is something I wish to say to you. Now is as good a time as any. Back in the dungeon I said . . . well, I said something."

Byron's words were a soft moan. "That all this is my fault."

"Aye. And I want to apologize for speaking as I did."

"But it's true."

Though Falconer wanted to deny it, to try and ease the evident pain, he could not weave a falsehood into this moment. "Byron, we all make mistakes. I have made errors that make your own vanish like shadows at midnight. No, don't protest. What I tell you is harsh and cutting truth. But this I know, and this I want to leave with you now. Our Lord can do miracles. If you allow, God will take these misdeeds and the wounds they have caused you and others, and weave them into a cloak of hope and purpose."

Byron wiped his eyes. "That is impossible."

"No. I'm sorry to be so blunt, but you are wrong. I could give you examples from my own life. But I don't need to. It has already happened. To you. In the here and now." Falconer pointed at Kitty. "Had you not been imprisoned, we would never have known of this young one's abduction. I tremble at the thought of what might have happened to her had we not been drawn in to look for you."

Falconer watched Byron's gaze move over and digest the thought of having aided in her release. "No matter what you carry, no matter how foul the burden, God will heal your wounds and turn your dross to gold. I stand as living testimony of this miraculous power."

Falconer rose to his feet. "Come join us, if you have a will."

When Byron remained seated against the cave wall, Falconer turned and started for where the others sprawled by the entrance. He had the sense that these men had been speaking of him.

Nebo asked, "The young lass still sleeps?"

"Aye."

"The man, he woke once. He came out and looked at the desert for a time. He ate and he drank. Then he went back and slept."

Soap offered, "He's nothing but skin and rags and bones."

Falconer and the others turned at soft footfalls in the cave sand. Byron approached hesitantly. Soap made room on his rocky perch and said, "Come rest yourself, son."

When Byron was seated and had been passed the waterskin, Sands the whaler said, "They kept us in a cell for a time. Three months, best I could reckon it. When they let us out, I couldn't get over a world without walls."

"Or chains," his younger brother said, and rubbed at the sore on his left ankle.

Falconer hefted the waterskin at Wadi's feet and drank. Bernard turned to Nebo and said, "Now's your chance. You may as well speak to him as you did to us. I too seek answers to the questions you formed."

Nebo shifted on the bench beside Falconer. "Your manner with the two prisoners. It was . . ."

Falconer set the skin down on the earth between their feet. He settled his back against the wall. And waited.

"Curious," Nebo finally decided. "The warrior—he plans and fights and leads. Then he gentles two frightened ones he never seen before. They know him not. Yet sound of his voice quiets fears, ease them to rest."

Falconer waited until he was certain Nebo was done. "A man can only give to others what he has gained for himself."

Nebo drummed deep in his chest, a distinctly African sound of agreement.

"Most of my life, I lived only with hate and fear. And pain so deep I could not name it," Falconer added.

"And you fight," Nebo said.

"I fought and won. Yet my victories were hollow. The prize only brought more of the same."

"So you seek your God."

"Jesus Christ is His name."

"He speak to you, this Jesus?"

"Not in words. He did not need to."

"Yet when you speak of Him, I hear call of one friend naming another."

Falconer thumped his chest. "The love you find in me is His. The peace. The victory without anger. The ability to find hope even when I am immersed in the sorrow of loss. The prize beyond value. All His."

Nebo straightened fully in his seat. A warrior coming to full alert. "I would know this God."

From Soap's other side, Wadi spoke softly. "And I."

"And the Lord Jesus," Falconer replied, "would know you both."

Nebo asked, "What is the prize required of me?"

"There is none, if by prize you mean dowry or sacrifice."

Wadi leaned forward to examine Falconer.

"It is required that you declare your realization that your ways have not brought you where you wish to go. That your choices have led to wrong paths and worse actions. That you ask Him to be the center of your heart and life."

"This act." Nebo stared into the soft gray of a very young daybreak. "It seem too small."

"That is because, brother, the true act has already been made."

Chapter 34

They waited through the day with the patience of men who had known other battles. They ate and drank everything they carried, storing fodder like desert beasts. Every time the two saved from the fortress dungeons awoke, they too were urged to eat and drink. Byron and Kitty did not join with them, but neither did they hold themselves apart. The men made them welcome in the calm, silent way of the desert.

The men talked without barriers between them. With the moonrise they would be leaving the cave's safety and travel north. Between them and the sea was a region none of them knew and enemies they could not foresee. Beyond that lay the sea and no guarantee the ship would be there to meet them. The forces of Tunis would blame the ship for the attack and destruction of their port. And if any ships could be found to transport the Tunisian warriors, they would strike in return. All the risks remained unspoken, but they lay heavy upon the men. And this burden drew them tightly together as friends for life.

The whalers spoke of their cold-water home and of loved ones who had by now given them up for lost. Nebo spoke of a village burned by slavers and a home he still visited in his dreams. Wadi alone did not speak. Instead he listened, and twice the fierce warrior was seen using his burnoose to rub his face. Falconer spoke of his quest to free slaves, of the gold mine and of how it had helped finance the secret project, the Underground Railroad for slaves in America.

They prayed.

As the heat rose with the sun, they retreated into the cave. Before Wadi entered the cool stone recess, however, he used a branch to brush the sand upon the ledge, replacing any evidence of their presence with the random designs of wind and time. Nebo shook his head over his friend's caution but said nothing.

By midafternoon, back in the cave where the animals were tethered, Sands, the whaler captain, was describing what it was like to hunt the world's largest beasts. He stood to describe the power it took to hurl a harpoon. Rufus, his young brother, stood guard by the cave mouth. He turned and whistled once, a quick warble.

The cave instantly went silent. They watched as Rufus slipped deeper to the side into the wall's shadow. With one finger he pointed to Falconer and motioned him forward.

Falconer and Wadi and Nebo moved forward at a crouch.

"There," the young whaler murmured.

Falconer heard Wadi hiss an indrawn breath. Stretched out along the desert floor was a long train of camels and horses.

Soap moved up behind them. "Caravan?"

Falconer shook his head. "Two outriders ahead, two behind."

"Bedu," Nebo agreed. "Hunting."

Wadi lifted one arm. He moved a finger along the descent to their left. Then the finger paused. Directing them to a stone, a cluster of desert sage.

Falconer saw it then. A flicker of motion.

Instantly he gestured to the others. Together they slipped back, all but Wadi, who took up the same branch he had used upon the ledge and began sweeping the cave floor. Back and forth, his motions almost unhurried despite the danger.

They gathered up their provisions and packs and bedrolls, Byron and Kitty watching in tense panic. Falconer could do nothing about that now. He pushed them deep into the alcove, behind the mules. He settled a waterskin between them, then hurried forward. Nebo and Soap and Sands had all taken hold of the animals' reins. The men stroked their muzzles and gentled their flanks. Wadi continued his slow sweeping motions. Falconer resisted the urge to hiss at the man, to hurry him along. Wadi knew the danger better than he.

The Arab joined Falconer in the mouth of the alcove. To Falconer's mind the shadows around them did not seem nearly enough cover. A horse shifted its weight and whickered softly. He heard Soap murmur to it and pat a flank.

Wadi hissed. A quick sound, barely more than a sigh of wind.

A desert figure stepped into view at the mouth of the cave. The man's robes drifted about his feet. He carried a rifle in one hand. He peered into the shadows. He knelt and studied the dust. He rose to his feet. Falconer felt the air trap in his lungs. The man did not move.

Hours passed. Eons. Or so it felt to Falconer.

The man moved on.

They remained motionless. Even the horses seemed to be holding their breath. Nothing moved outside except the heat, rising in constant waves.

Wadi crouched and crept forward, holding fast to the western wall, where the gloom was most dense. He arrived at the cave entrance and dropped to his belly. He crawled forward.

His hand rose in a flicker of motion.

Falconer crept forward to join him.

The desert floor was empty. The hunter on foot was nowhere to be seen.

Wadi muttered, "They circle back, attack from above, or they go on."

Falconer whispered, "Do we go or stay?"

He shrugged eloquently. "We leave, they could see us. We stay, a chance we safe."

"A chance."

The Arab shot him a quick grin. "Good to make peace with God of all heaven."

Falconer realized what the man intended. "I will go," he said firmly.

Wadi's smile grew broader as he shook his head. "You trained to melt into desert floor?" He did not wait for a reply. "If I not return in hour, run."

Wadi was back before the sun had shifted ten degrees. Falconer had no idea how long that was in minutes, for the day was stretched taut. One moment the cave mouth was empty. Then Wadi was dropping down from the roof overhang. Before Falconer could raise a challenge, Wadi said, "I here."

Falconer offered him a waterskin and waited to ask, "What did you find?"

"They move ever further west." He drank again. "But there are other parties. Some bedu, some soldiers. They scour the desert like ravenous wolves."

Falconer pondered this long and hard. Finally he rose and moved back to the rear alcove. "You can come forward. But stay quiet and well back from the entrance."

Soap emerged first. "There are more?"

"Aye."

"What will—"

"Rest and ready yourselves," Falconer replied. "We leave at moonrise."

Falconer watched from the cave opening, resting but not sleeping. Nor were any of the others, as far as he could tell. The hours crawled by. They were alert and moving about the cave long before the first shard of moon appeared beyond the hills. When all was made ready, Falconer stepped to the rearmost portion of the animals' alcove. Byron and Kitty had remained there since the hunters had appeared. Falconer could see only their forms, so tight against the stone they clung. He saw a faint gleam reflecting off Kitty's gaze and knew her eyes were again enormous with fear.

Falconer knelt in the sand before them. "There are two things you must remember through all that comes. The first is this. Kitty, your mother awaits you on the journey's other end. Byron, your stepfather stands beside her. Or kneels, for I am certain the both of them are praying as fervently as they know how. They await you both with outstretched arms. The second is this. I will guard your safety with my life. Do you believe me?"

Byron whispered, "Yes."

"Kitty?"

"I'm so afraid."

"I know, lass. But safety lies beyond these hills. It is our job to be strong for the both of you." He rose to his feet and held out his hands. "Come."

Chapter 35

Even the animals seemed subdued as they crept from the cave. With scarcely a breeze, the night held a breathless quality, as though the moon-washed rocks, the brush and sand, shared their apprehension.

Wadi took the lead, being careful not to move so far ahead as to lose sight of Falconer. Falconer acted as a connecting point between Wadi and the others. Soap, the whalers, Byron, and Kitty all rode. Nebo and Bernard brought up the rear. The going was hard but their pace steady. Falconer had to trust Wadi's instincts, as he saw no real trail. The crescent moon rose to become a sky-borne lantern.

Falconer knew they had reached the summit when the twin monoliths came into view. When Falconer had first spotted them from the ship's quarterdeck, he had thought they were natural outcroppings. As he approached them now, however, he saw they were both round and man-made, with huge bases as wide as six men holding arms.

Wadi signaled from the ridge's far end. Falconer whispered, "We rest."

As he approached the pillars, moonlight played upon the surface, causing the figures of the soldiers carved upon them to march in ghostly unison. Falconer traced his hand over the timeworn surface. They now were only monuments to some forgotten triumph, set upon hills whose name only bandits remembered. The empire was dust now, as were its warriors who had once thought themselves invincible.

Wadi found him there by the eastern pillar. He accepted the waterskin, drank deeply, then said, "We leave mounts."

"The noise?"

Wadi nodded and drank again, then handed back the skin. "And trail. It steep. Narrow."

Falconer walked over to where Sands rested upon the other pillar's base. "Can you and your men walk from here?"

"To freedom?" Teeth flashed in the moonlight. "Barefoot the entire way."

The descent was treacherous, particularly as Falconer again carried Kitty. Twice Wadi lost the trail entirely. Both times Falconer and the others waited in the best cover they could find, which was not much. The hillside was so steep his group was strung out single file. Falconer prayed no watcher lurked below to pierce the gloom or hear the falling pebbles.

Midway down they came upon a flat space that so resembled a terrace Falconer wondered if it had been hewn by man. Then he spied a fragment of wall where the hill swept in tightly, and he realized it had once been a fortress—maybe a watch station for whoever built the hillside monuments. The view explained the setting, for a waning moon behind them glistened upon the open sea. There was just enough light to make out the empty road below, a silver ribbon that stretched out in either direction.

He spied Nebo kicking at something in the dust and walked over. As he approached, he caught the scent of ashes. He watched as Nebo bent down and rubbed the charcoal between his fingers. Falconer asked, "How long?"

"Two days, or three."

Falconer searched and asked the empty night, "Which direction do you think?"

Nebo rose and dusted off his hands. "Perhaps they move on to the caravanserai."

"Perhaps."

Neither expressed the other prospect, that the soldiers or brigands had found a watching place closer to the road.

Falconer's group could have rested there for hours. But the moon was setting, and the waning light made the going even more difficult. No one protested as Wadi led off.

Falconer moved up alongside Byron, who limped and chose each step carefully. But he made no complaint and held to the pace set by the others. Falconer patted the young man's shoulder and offered the only words of hope he could think of. "Your parents would both be proud of you this night."

Byron looked up from the trail. His eyes glinted in the moonlight. "But you said it yourself. I caused this."

"They have already forgiven you, Byron. The question now is, what will you do with their forgiveness?"

Byron's gaze returned to the next step. And the one after. Finally he said, "I want to be more than I am."

"It is a most worthy aim."

"Will—" Byron hesitated, then finished—"will you speak more with me about prayer?"

"Aye, that I shall. As will they." He patted the shoulder once more. "Very proud indeed."

As Falconer moved forward to resume his place behind Wadi, Kitty said, "I can walk some."

Falconer was tempted, but not for long. "Better you

save your strength, lass, in case we all need to run later."

"Are they chasing us?"

Falconer did not need to ask of whom she spoke. The child's shiver said it all. "Remember what I said, lass. I will do everything in my power to keep you safe."

The descent continued long enough to have Falconer feeling the weakness seep back into his muscles and bones. What the weakened bodies of Byron and the whalers were enduring, he did not want to imagine. Even though he could hear their rasping breath, they did not slow their pace, for the moon was almost gone, and it grew increasingly hard to see their way ahead. Even so, he knew they could not take much more. Just as he was ready to whistle and call Wadi back for yet another rest, the trail eased. Falconer did not allow himself to believe it at first. But the trail leveled off and then joined with the loose sand that signaled the base.

Wadi signaled and Nebo whistled, both men at the exact same moment. Falconer did not need to search for the reason.

Wadi pointed to their right, at a crevice that opened beside the trail. The shadows by now were so impenetrable Falconer could not tell if the crevice was five feet deep or a mile. Wadi scrambled down into it and disappeared. Two heartbeats later, he emerged and waved them forward. Falconer whistled his own urgent signal, still uncertain what the two guards had seen or heard.

The crevice was about fifteen feet deep and long enough that they could all remain hidden. Which was most providential. Because no sooner had they arrived at the base than Falconer heard the soft pad of footfalls, the soft chink of metal upon metal.

The moon was completely below the horizon, though the stars remained. Not enough light for their little group to find its way along an uncharted hillside, but more than enough for men to walk a familiar road. Soldiers or brigands, Falconer could not tell. He lay in the dust next to Wadi with Soap to his other side. Kitty's face remained buried in the point where Falconer's chin met his neck. They remained frozen and silent as men and camels and horses passed fifty paces away. In the fear-laced night, they seemed close enough to touch. Falconer counted thirty mounts. Muskets and scimitars sprouted from shoulders and saddles, a forest of danger and doom. Falconer thought he might have recognized their abandoned mounts among the others.

The minutes required for the caravan to pass seemed the longest of Falconer's life. The final outrider passed so close Falconer could see the tassels dangling from the musket's stock. From deeper in the crevice there came not a sound. No one breathed. The darkness covered them in a blanket so impenetrable the crevice itself went unnoticed, or so Falconer assumed, for the soldier did not even glance their way.

Soon after the force passed, the sky whispered of dawn's arrival. The sea was close enough for faint brushstrokes of fog to slowly replace the stars.

Only with the dawn came yet another problem.

Faint tendrils of the mist drifted in from the sea. Not enough to blanket the road. But the shoreline, five hundred paces beyond the road, became indistinct. The sea was lost to them entirely.

Daylight arrived with remarkable swiftness. But the mist stubbornly refused to disperse. Likely the ship—if it was near—was facing the same veil on the opposite side. Falconer rested upon the crevice's embankment, his eyes just above the level of the stones. The now-empty road was thirty paces straight ahead of him. The stretch from the road toward the shore was flat and empty. Neither shade nor refuge.

Soap occupied the position to his left. Softly Falconer asked the seaman, "Any chance of another storm? It could cover us while we cross to the water. Though whether or not the ship can see the monuments . . ." His voice drifted to a stop.

"Your nose is as good as mine."

"Not in this desert, it isn't."

Soap breathed in deeply. "Rising mercury, is my guess. Clear as a crystal bell. More's the pity."

Bernard spoke from Falconer's other side. "We can't stay here much longer. The shadows will be lost in a half hour or less. We're still too far from the coast."

Soap responded for them all. "The ship won't be able to identify the pillars. Which means they can't find the place to land the longboat."

"Captain Harkness will not let us down," Bernard declared stoutly.

Falconer glanced over. The young banker was unrecognizable. A burnoose dangled loosely, about his head and shoulders. The lower half of his face was lost behind a surprisingly thick beard. His eyes were red rimmed and bloodshot, lips cracked, hands as filthy as his clothes, which were far more dust-yellow than their original black. His dandified boots were ruined. One sole remained in place only because he had lashed a rope about the whole shoe.

"I never thanked you," Falconer said.

Bernard blinked at him uncertainly. "Thank me? Whatever for?"

"For remaining at your station outside the fortress wall," Falconer replied. "For not giving in to fear. For doing exactly as we had planned. For your strength and skill in a time of direst need."

To Bernard's other side, Nebo murmured, "I be wrong in my thoughts of you."

Soap muttered, "As was I."

Bernard's head swiveled back and forth. "I suggest we perhaps discuss the matter at hand. We are far from the sea and the sun is erasing our cover!"

Falconer clambered to his feet. The road stretched out flat and empty in both directions. The fog was almost gone over the land and the shoreline but clung stubbornly to the sea. A hundred yards beyond the sea, the water was swallowed in a blanket of gray.

There was no sign of any boat. Nor of decent cover beyond where he stood.

Nebo asked softly, "What say you?"

Falconer glanced down. The crevice was utterly revealed, and all the people who crouched inside. "We go."

Nebo scrambled up to stand alongside him. He frowned at the flat and utterly exposed shoreline. "Go to where?"

"Harkness promised he would find us," Falconer said, offering Soap a hand. Then he crouched down so Kitty could climb on his back. "He did not say he would come if there was no storm, nor fog, nor enemy. We must trust him to have spoken the truth of what he would do."

They trooped through the gathering heat. The light exposed just how weak Falconer's charges had been made by the nighttime march. The whalers limped and struggled, their faces set with the grim determination of men focused upon either freedom or the grave. Byron leaned heavily upon Nebo. Bernard hung back with Wadi, who scouted the road and walked backward.

The sea remained stubbornly cloaked.

When he caught the first fragrance of salt and drying seaweed, Falconer felt a sudden rush of relief. He set Kitty down upon the point where dried salt marked the high tide. He said to the others, "Hunt the shore. Gather everything you can manage to carry. Sticks, seaweed, anything. We must build a barrier between us and the road."

The mound took shape slowly as they gathered everything they could find. Falconer walked back to where Wadi knelt. He checked the empty road, then turned and studied what the others were building. Sands and his brother dragged a white log. Nebo and Soap bore armfuls of dried seaweed. Falconer hoped aloud, "It just might work."

Wadi did not need to glance back. "Just as likely, it draw attention of a hunter who passes."

Falconer sighed his agreement. Close to the shoreline, the sea was as calm and flat as pounded pewter. The mist was an enemy, devouring the ocean. Falconer said in resignation, "We will give it another hour, then retreat to caves and wait for the morning."

Wadi said softly, "They search all caves on this side."

"The weak among us cannot climb back over the top to the hills on the other side," Falconer replied, though he knew Wadi had spoken the truth. "We will hide the best we can."

Wadi shifted his grip upon the musket. "We split into two. Warriors down, to draw fire. Others higher up."

Falconer mulled it over briefly. "If they find one group, they will very quickly find the others. We stay together."

Wadi did not insist. Instead, he rose slowly to his feet. "What is it?"

Wadi handed Falconer his musket without turning from the road. He shielded his eyes with both hands.

Falconer felt the sun gather and press hard upon his shoulders. "Soldiers?"

"Someone."

He saw nothing but the heat dancing upon the yellow road. But he did not doubt his friend's ability to pierce the distance. "Should we run for the caves?"

"Too late." Wadi spun about and grabbed his musket and started for the shore. "Gather all."

Wadi in one direction, Falconer in the other, both men running in a half crouch. The whalers saw him coming and froze. "To the shelter," Falconer called. "Hurry!"

Everyone now was limping. It made the moment worse, for there was so little reserve for any escape. That is, if they managed to remain unseen.

The barrier was shaped like a crescent moon, built from seaweed and driftwood and sand. They had to crouch and tuck in tight to fit behind it. Falconer shielded Kitty with his body. He felt her slight form tremble and wanted to offer her assurances, but he could not bring himself to lie.

He risked a final glance. They were indeed warriors. Too many to count. "Down," he breathed. "Still as stones."

Yet despite their best efforts, a great shout rose from the road. And gunfire.

Then the gunfire was answered—from the sea.

Falconer flipped onto his back and lifted his head slightly.

A longboat appeared from the mist. Ten men pulled strongly upon the oars. Lieutenant Bivens gripped the tiller. He pointed ahead, to where they crouched, and shouted words lost to the rising clamor of the approaching danger.

"To the sea!" Falconer roared. He lifted Kitty bodily and handed her to Nebo. "Hurry!"

Chapter 36

The desert silence was blasted away as horses galloped and whinnied, men shouted, and muskets coughed. The hills to the south collected all the sounds and echoed with a dull rumble that sounded like thunder. Or battle.

"Row like your lives depended upon it!" Bivens' roar carried over the other noises. *"Row!"*

Falconer crouched low and alone behind the makeshift barrier while the others were pushing ever further into the water toward the longboat. The placid sea was too shallow to offer quick protection, however. Thirty paces from shore, the water was scarcely knee deep.

Turning back to look over the barrier, Falconer realized his first concern were the two outriders galloping well ahead of the main company. The riders were crouched low to their mounts, urging them on with snarled oaths. One raced along the shoreline. The other had crossed from the road's opposite side and was aiming straight for the barrier. Whether either had seen him, Falconer did not know.

Another swift glance over his shoulder was enough to guarantee that Falconer's worst fear was at hand. No matter how hard Bivens pushed his men, they would not arrive in time.

Falconer turned back to the attackers. The warriors

were now split in two companies. Twenty or so galloped on desert horses. Behind them rode as many again on camels. The hump-backed animals loped at desert-eating pace, yet the horses drew steadily ahead. The two outriders would sweep in and harass the little band until the full company attacked. There was only one chance to save his group.

Falconer turned seaward once more and roared a single word. *"Nebo!"*

The big African glanced back and instantly understood. He did not hand Wadi the girl so much as toss her across the sea. Then he separated himself from the others, racing back now to confront the outrider approaching on the side.

Wadi in turn handed the girl to Soap and leapt after his friend.

Falconer faced the second outrider. The element of surprise had been lost by his shout. The horseman's scimitar glittered in the hard light as the man aimed his horse straight at the barrier.

Below the top edge of the barrier, Falconer hefted a driftwood branch, about as thick as his arm and half again as long. At the last moment, he stood, his sturdy club at the ready. As hoped, the horseman made a critical mistake, going for Falconer's weapon and not the man. The warrior swung his blade in a glittering arc. The scimitar chopped off nearly half of Falconer's branch. But the horse was then forced to jump the barrier. Landing his horse safely meant the desert warrior could not make a backhand jab for Falconer.

While the horse was in midair, Falconer gripped the warrior's stirrup and flipped him, saddle and all. The saddle strap snapped like a gunshot and the rider fell with a cry.

The horse was thrown off balance as well, and landed

upon the man, who shrieked in pain. Falconer leaned back as the horse stumbled to its feet, and then he reached in and cuffed the warrior unconscious. He kicked the musket well out of reach before grabbing the man's sword.

He stepped over the barrier. Directly in front of the oncoming soldiers.

"Falconer!"

The voice which called his name was so shrill he could not tell which man had shouted, or if perhaps it was even the young girl. He took a two-handed grip upon the sword's haft and lifted it to the level of his chest. A warrior ready to parry and give battle.

He would not intentionally take another man's life. But he would defend his charges even to the death.

"Falconer!"

The band of horsemen were a hundred paces away and closing fast. Falconer could see the lather flecking their muzzles, see the warriors' snarling rage, see the killing lust in their eyes.

Into your hands, Lord, he prayed, staring straight at the oncoming doom. *Into your hands.*

He took what he supposed was his last steady breath and found three faces before his mind's eye.

Ada, dear sweet Ada.

Matt, with his shining face and wisdom beyond his years.

And then, to his utter astonishment, he saw Amelia Henning.

As though in response to his shock, the air overhead was ripped apart.

The sound was of a giant swath of fabric being torn in two. Then the earth exploded.

Falconer was showered in dirt and pebbles and noise.

Another cannonball arched overhead and blasted the

earth between him and the road. Through the swirling smoke, Falconer saw the horsemen thrown into complete disarray. A half dozen horses milled about riderless. The others were turning tail and racing for safety.

Falconer did exactly the same.

There before him, rising out of the thinning mist, lay the merchant vessel. Two other longboats were lashed to its bow. Men strained upon the oars, pulling it closer to shore. The ship's cannon portholes were open and smoking. As Falconer splashed into the sea, the ship's guns blasted another barrage of smoke and fire.

Arms reached over the longboat's side, urging him on. A dozen and more faces stretched taut as they shouted words his ringing ears could not hear. Nor did he need to. Falconer pushed hard until the water rose to his waist and the boat was finally in reach, and hands were there to grip and pull him over the side. He lay there upon the gunnels, gasping for breath, as the longboat swiftly turned and began pushing hard for the vessel.

And safety.

Falconer was in the process of seeing Matt off to bed when the soft knock came upon their cabin door. "Enter."

Amelia Henning appeared in the doorway. "Forgive the intrusion, sir."

"You are always welcome, ma'am," Falconer replied, and meant it. "Is it Kitty?"

"She calls for you."

"May I come too, Father?" Matt asked.

Falconer did not have the heart to tell the lad to remain abed. Since their safe return, Matt had clung to Falconer almost as much as the little girl had. "Slip into your trousers and boots, then."

The boy wore his nightdress as a shirt, the long tail bunching up inside his trousers. He kept hold of Falconer's hand as they followed Amelia back down the upper-deck hallway. As they passed the third passenger cabin, the door opened. Byron's face emerged into the candlelight. Falconer asked kindly, "Can you not sleep either?"

The young man's haunted expression said it all.

Falconer glanced a query at Amelia Henning, who nodded her agreement. He said to Byron, "We were going to go sit with Kitty for a time. Would you care to join us?"

From inside the cabin, Bernard called out, "May I come as well?"

Amelia Henning responded before Falconer could object. "Of course."

The five of them seemed to reduce the small cabin's air. The little girl was seated in her bunk with her back against pillows, the pillows piled against the wall. Falconer settled Matt at the foot of Kitty's bed, opened the porthole slightly, then sat down between the two children. He did not need to ask how the girl was. One glance was enough to know the shadows were still deeply embedded. He reached for the little girl's hand, but instead the child climbed into his lap and nestled upon his chest. "What a dear sweet lass you are," he murmured, stroking her hair and looking at her mother.

Amelia's small nod as she settled into the chair next to the bed was permission enough. Now she reached over and patted the girl's trembling back. She lifted her gaze to Falconer, silently imploring his help once again.

Their first dinner back on board had been a quietly contented affair. Though they had returned safely, the imprint of all they had endured remained close. The sea had stayed calm and the day windless, so the longboats had rowed the merchants well away from land. Harkness had ordered their dinner be served upon the quarterdeck to take advantage of the cool sea air and to keep watch over the night. The three whalers had been invited to join them, and Byron was seated next to his father. Captain Clovis was there as well, his vessel lying a cable's length northward. Nebo and Wadi had joined them also, but only because both captains had ordered them to be seated with the officers.

Amelia Henning came with her daughter and introduced them all to the beautiful little child, now bathed and brushed with hair almost the same shade as Matt's. The two had not seated themselves at the table, however, for Kitty wished to remain nestled against her mother, and Amelia did not consider that fitting behavior for the captain's table. Though Harkness had implored Mrs. Henning to join the others, she had preferred to sit apart with her daughter, who had stared out over the open waters with weary wonderment.

Falconer was not surprised to find the girl was now unable to sleep.

He noticed that Matt was snuggling close as well, and Falconer shifted the girl over slightly, then extended one arm to envelop his son.

He felt the week's exertions to the very depth of his being. He thought a moment of the hairsbreadth between this earth and his passage to the great beyond, and his arm tightened around Matt.

"Before my son and I set off on this journey," Falconer said softly to his small audience, "we made ourselves a pact. We would treat this journey as a quest. We already had a mission. We were to aid Reginald Langston in freeing his son. But one morning there upon the road, Matt said something that suggested we needed to identify a quest for ourselves as well."

Falconer glanced at his son. "Do you wish to tell these friends what that quest was?"

Matt's voice too was soft, but crystal clear. "We were going to find a new future for ourselves. A future with hope and happiness."

Falconer's hand came up to touch the boy's face. "Do you mind, Matt, if we talk about this in front of the others? Because we can wait for another time if you wish."

"I don't mind, Father John."

"Have you found an answer to your quest?" Falconer phrased the question as carefully as he knew how.

"Yes. But I'm still a little afraid."

"What of?" When Matt did not respond, Falconer answered for him. "That you might dishonor your mother's blessed memory?"

When he felt the boy's nod against his arm, Falconer said, "I have feared that very same thing, lad. I need to tell you, though, that out there in the desert, I discovered a remarkable thing. That God was expanding my heart. I had already found room within to love my Savior, and your mother, and you. And now my heart was growing larger still, so that I could love others. New friends that Ada never knew while she was here with us. People and places and new experiences that would enrich us both."

Falconer felt a presence enter the candlelit chamber. One that could not be seen with his earthly eyes. One that did not require acknowledging, but one that was present just the same. "That was a miracle I could only have experienced because I set off on this quest. I did so because I wanted *you* to be whole again, my son. I could not say if my own time of restoration was over. I simply wanted *you* to have a future and new joys. And what did I discover, but that God was great and good enough to heal me as well. I learned something else too. That Ada was with me still. In my heart. Where my love for her would never end. She would remain with me until the end of time."

Matt stirred in his embrace, and said softly, "I discovered something else, Father John."

"What is that, son?"

"When you left on the boat that day, I was very afraid. I thought I could stay brave. But as I watched you row away, I worried that I would . . ."

"Lose me like you had lost your mother and your father," Falconer quietly supplied.

"And then I felt Mrs. Henning put her arm around me," Matt went on. "She said that she would give me comfort and strength, and pray with me."

Falconer turned to face the woman. Her upturned features were illuminated by the candle's glow, and by a deeper light. One that emanated from her features and her gaze, melting away the shadows of loss. "Did she, now."

"Yes, Father John. And I felt my fear go away. Then I knew—I knew just what you said. That friends can help us in the bad times. New friends. Now I see how the fear I was feeling was why we became friends. I don't want to be sad again. And I don't like being afraid. But I know that if bad times do come, I'm not alone."

In the silence that ensued, Amelia Henning whispered, "My child is fast asleep."

The figures packed into that small space remained absolutely silent for a long moment, then one after another just as silently slipped out the door.

Chapter 37

Falconer emerged on deck to discover a swiftly rising breeze. Captain Clovis moved across the deck, doffed his hat, and bowed an officer's farewell. "Captain Harkness has described how it was your idea to include us, sir. I offer you my sincere thanks for the opportunity to take part in this grand effort."

"We could not have succeeded without you. I never would have thought a cannon's thunder could be as welcome to my ears." The two men chuckled, then sobered.

"That's as may be," Captain Clovis responded, "but you indeed are the hero of this saga." The officer offered his hand. "It has been an honor, sir."

"Likewise. Might I have a word with your two good men?"

"But of course. I must ask you to make haste, as we must take advantage of the favorable wind."

Falconer moved to where Nebo and Wadi stood by the lee railing. At his earlier request, Soap had passed them both a handful of gold. But in the desert manner, such payment would not be mentioned now. He offered his hand. "I am in your debt."

Nebo took hold with a fighter's grip. "The debt be my

315

own. We speak as friends. You share mystery of your life. Your God."

Falconer took a firmer hold of his new friend's hand. "*Our* God."

Wadi said nothing as they shook hands, but he nodded his agreement.

Falconer stood a long time at the rail, watching the sails become smaller and finally disappear into the night.

Their own sails were set, and miles soon separated the merchant ship from the north African coastline. The rising moon joined together with a brilliant wash of stars. Though within sight of the night watch, Falconer and Amelia Henning found an intimate space upon the foredeck. She declined his offer of a seat upon a water barrel and instead joined him at the railing. "Your son has continued to amaze me with his wisdom. I found him such a healing balm, such a joy to be around."

"He called you friend."

"I count that friendship as a lifelong bond," she replied. "And a reward beyond measure."

He stared at her rather frankly now. "I have never been one to speak easily of my thoughts, because in truth inward scrutiny does not come naturally to me. Yet I feel inclined to confess my deepest reflections to you, Mrs. Henning."

"Please, call me Amelia," she invited softly. "And speak your heart."

Falconer related to her the realizations of the desert night. Then he took a deeper breath and told of how her face had appeared in the moment of crisis and quickly approaching danger. He hurried on before she could say anything to that. "The answer to my quest was born in the furnace of danger and conflict. For this is the world I know best. I offered my strength to a friend in need, because it was all I had to offer. Peril is the language I was raised upon. I have discovered that knowing God does not make me either safe from this or free of the world's woes. Yet I have found peace even here. And God's great hand is there to guide me. Through storms and through pain, through loss and through sorrow. He has remained with me, and I am most undeserving but most blessed by it."

Her gaze was soft in the moonlight. Her features shone with a quiet calm, one completed by the tone of her voice as she said, "You are a poet, John Falconer."

"I am a fighter, one redeemed by a God whose compassion is so great I feel choked with the honor of being included in His fold."

"A poet," she repeated softly. "One who honors me with his confession."

"I must return to Salem. Matt has inherited an inn. I need to provide the lad with a chance to see whether he wishes to remain with his Moravian clan. If so, I will reside there with him. If he wishes otherwise, Reginald Langston has beseeched me to come work with him."

His next breath was the hardest by far. "I ask that you travel with us, Amelia. You and Kitty. I know that you are still in a time of grieving, of uncertainty. I ask for nothing save the chance for us to remain together until we know God's will for us. If nothing else, I can promise you this. You have a friend for life."

She studied his face for what seemed like hours. Then she placed her hand upon his and said, "I accept your kind offer, and sense the Spirit's direction within your words."

Falconer's strong form was so overtaken by tremors he had difficulty shaping his response. "I did not count joy among my blessings until this very moment."

Looking for More Good Books to Read?

You can find out what is new and exciting with previews, descriptions, and reviews by signing up for Bethany House newsletters at

www.bethanynewsletters.com

We will send you updates for as many authors or categories as you desire so you get only the information you really want.

Sign up today!

From Beloved Authors
T. Davis Bunn & Janette Oke

In 1753 the lines of separation were firmly drawn between the French and the British over Acadia, a new province on a new continent. Even though the villages might be merely a stone's throw apart, most settlers could go an entire lifetime without speaking to someone from the other side.

During this time when lives were shadowed by nations in conflict, Catherine Price and Louise Belleveau meet at a chance encounter in a meadow and begin a friendship that will propel them on a journey from which they can never turn back. From this unexpected friendship, Oke and Bunn spin a tale of devotion, loss, and renewal, of bonds stronger than blood and of faith stronger than tragedy.

SONG OF ACADIA:

The Meeting Place, The Sacred Shore, The Birthright, The Distant Beacon, The Beloved Land